The Power of Magic

The largest of the Shadows had returned, a vast black shape with burning eyes rising slowly straight up the shaft with long, powerful beats of his broad wings. Other Shadows, half a dozen or more, were swarming up the sides of the shaft, clinging to the rough stone as they climbed, their heads turned upward and their red eyes full of fury and deadly intent. Even as he watched, the largest of the Shadows began to drift toward him, and he knew immediately that it meant to make an end to him. . . .

Einar used the only weapon he had, and when the Shadow opened its mouth he tossed the Core of Magic right inside. . . . The Shadow arched its powerful neck and screamed, and its entire form began to flash as if translucent to a blue-grey light within. Stricken, it lost its hold on the stone and slowly fell backwards into the depths of the pit.

DRAGON'S DOMAIN

THORARINN GUNNARSSON

ACE BOOKS, NEW YORK

This book is an Ace original edition,
and has never been previously published.

DRAGON'S DOMAIN

An Ace Book / published by arrangement with
the author

PRINTING HISTORY
Ace edition / July 1993

All rights reserved.
Copyright © 1993 by Thorarinn Gunnarsson.
Cover art by Den Beauvais.
This book may not be reproduced in whole
or in part, by mimeograph or any other means,
without permission. For information address:
The Berkley Publishing Group, 200 Madison Avenue,
New York, New York 10016.

ISBN: 0-441-16665-2

Ace Books are published by The Berkley Publishing Group,
200 Madison Avenue, New York, New York 10016.
The name "ACE" and the "A" logo
are trademarks belonging to Charter Communications, Inc.

PRINTED IN THE UNITED STATES OF AMERICA

10 9 8 7 6 5 4 3 2 1

Dedicated to the Memory of Jim Henson
"We are dreaming of you"

DRAGON'S DOMAIN

☙ PROLOGUE

IN A TIME before the kingdoms of Egypt grew up out of the desert sands, nurtured by the waters of the Nile, or before the first warlords of ancient China built their bright palaces and marched their soldiers into battle. In a time when mortal men were still only forgotten creatures of the dark forests and the windswept plains, and did not yet know the taming of horses or the growing of grain. In a time even before the coming of men, there was another and far older age of this very old world.

It was a time of magic.

The Age of Faerie was long, and much of its history is forever lost. The First Age began in the dark depths of time, when magic was still new, fresh and vigorous. And because of the presence of magic, the world of that time was a very different place from what it has since become. Nurtured by magic and by the warm, wet climate, strange and remarkable creatures came into being, growing and adapting into a vast variety of complex forms. The greatest of these were the ancestors of the dragons, the Dragon Lords, beings that were vast and powerful, hunters of the night, their armored forms riding the wind on strong, broad wings. In time these fathers of dragons first brought the greater magic into the world, the faerie magic, and they became so powerful in their own magic that they were no longer mortal. They became so strong in both magic and wisdom that they survived the great cataclysm that nearly destroyed the world itself, which swept all other creatures of the First Age of Magic into the dust.

Then began the Second Age of Magic, that men came to call the Golden Age of Magic, which the mortal folk knew but never saw. It was a new, more subtle and mature Age of Magic. In this time the dragons became refined in their form, not so large and vicious as they had been, but wiser, more civilized and more powerful and shrewd in their magic. Now they became as the first men in the world remembered them at the height of their dominion: curious, wise and generous, and above all else loving every moment of their endless lives.

In this time the faerie magic filled all the world, and for the first time it brought about spontaneous new creatures of magic, the many and widely varied Folk of Faerie. Some were vaguely in the form of men, as if magic made diverse essays in the type that nature would eventually bring forth in mortal form. Some say that these were indeed the most distant ancestors of men, brought forward well ahead of their time by the magic of that age. Many other races of Faerie were derived from animal forms, or else from a strange synthesis of forms. Whole kingdoms arose whose realms existed in the shadows of the ancient forests, and empires that endured thousands and millions of years existed beneath the waves of the sea and deep in the stone of the mountains.

And always there were the dragons, whose long history had spanned a hundred million years, oldest and wisest. They were different, unique among all the races of Faerie. Their origins disappeared into the depths of time and they shared a special bond with both magic and nature, for they belonged both to the wilds of the world and to the magic.

But then a new age began, the Third Age of Magic, which was also the First Age of Men. In that time the magic first began to fade as the world slowly became more mortal, and both the great beasts of the wild and the folk of Faerie began to decline. Even the dragons began to have few young, although that was not a matter of great concern to an immortal race, and in all other ways they seemed much the same as always. The dragons had always been, from out of the very depths of time, and it seemed that they always would be.

The Third Age of Magic was drawing to its inevitable end, and many of the races of Faerie had already disappeared into the dust of forgotten years, when the great decline came even upon the dragons themselves. Where once they had been vast and colorful, now they were becoming smaller and more compact than they had been, their armor heavier and now dark in color, grey or deep green, or even black. In some ways they were becoming as they had been in the First Age of Magic, swift hunters of the wind, cunning and solitary.

But more deadly to their kind, the dragons were no longer at all the same in thought and spirit. Where once they had been generous and jovial, now they were becoming quiet and reclusive, jealously hoarding their magic and their wisdom against the Dark Age that was soon to come. And deadliest of all, the dragons began to grow weary with their long lives and to despair of the loss of their former greatness, and many began to long for the peace of the long Sleep Between the Stars.

Perhaps it was, as the dragons themselves feared and believed, that the decline of magic and of themselves awakened within them a desperate instinct for preservation. For unlike mortals or the lesser folk of Faerie, the dragons could never die in truth, but would transform themselves into a form that was no longer entirely real, certainly not alive and yet not quite dead. In such a form they would lie dormant, to wait out the mortal ages that were to come against the hope that a new Age of Magic would return. Although the other Faerie Folk that had died away would never return, at least the dragons could endure a hostile age in their long Sleep, to be reborn.

But this might come to pass only if men declined, and magic again returned to the world. On this point even the dragons themselves did not know the future with any certainty. Some said that the magic of this world was used up and would never come again. Still others believed that they would not have been granted the refuge of the Sleep Between the Stars if there was no hope at all, and they cast their spirits to the night winds without regret. But most were afraid and they hardly knew what to do, for they were less wise and noble than they had been. The lingering years of the Third Age of Magic passed and the dragons grew less and less, as one by one they faded into weariness and despair and committed their spirits to the stars.

❦ SPRING

The Season of Beginnings

☙ ONE

EVEN IN THE height of their desperation, when it seemed that their ancient race could endure no more adversity, a new and far deadlier peril came upon the surviving dragons. For there came into being a new race of magical beings, born of a magic that was decadent, distorted into a form that was vile and evil. In size and shape they were in all ways like the true dragons, except that they were as black as the depths of a cave, misty and indistinct to the mortal eye, and for this reason the dragons called them the Shadows. They were in truth creatures of the dark magic without real physical form, although they were solid to the touch and could suffer hurt and death. They were like evil images of the dragons, and even the dragons themselves did not know why they had ever come to exist. They were ever the enemies of the true dragons, harassing them and seeking their destruction.

Even so, the dragons died reluctantly, fighting the inevitability of their fate, for it was never a part of their nature to surrender. Driven by the attacks of the Shadows upon themselves and their delicate eggs, they retreated from out of the far east, beginning their long migrations into the west as they sought a land where the old magic still lingered and men had not yet come. Some passed even beyond the Great Sea into the lands of the distant west, and even there their last hopes were cheated. Others lingered where they would, singularly or with their dwindling tribes, in the quiet and remote places of the world.

In this way the Third Age of Magic was drawing to a sad end, and all of the other races of Faerie had long since passed into obscurity and death. It was for the dragons a time of loneliness and exile, and a bitter confrontation with the ragged end of their hopes. And yet, it was even in this dark time that something happened to the dragons that had not happened in many hundreds of long, weary years. For it happened that there was laid not one but two dragon eggs, each in separate tribes half a world apart. And that seemed to the dragons to be a sign of hope.

One tribe of dragons had been late in leaving the lands far to the east, and they lingered high in the rocky, snowy mountains of the Himalayas, south and west of their ancient home in China. There they remained through the long years, until in all the world there was only their own small tribe and another in the mountains by the sea far to the north.

By this time, there were only a dozen dragons left in all the world.

The leader of the tribe of the southern mountains was named Halahvey, and he had been one of the oldest dragons in the world even before the time of their decline. Oldest and wisest of his kind, he waited now only to see the final fate of the dragons, adamantly refusing to surrender to the Final Sleep until he knew. Of this small tribe there was also a younger female known as Kalfeer, who alone of their group had belonged originally to the same tribe and clan as Halahvey and had come with him out of the distant west, where they had dwelt for uncounted years before the coming of men.

When Kalfeer knew beyond any doubt that she would bear a child, she began to think of the Shadows. Although that vile race had not bothered her tribe in a very long time, she recalled that they would sense this new life and that they might seek to steal or destroy her egg when it was laid. She spoke of her fears to old Halahvey, and he helped her to convince the rest of the tribe that they should journey into the far west so that all the dragons left in the world should be in one place, to better protect their young.

The journey was long and difficult, for the tribe was late in starting. Kalfeer was near the time for laying her egg, so that she could not travel far in a single flight. Dragons bear their young unlike any other creatures of this world, for the females carry their single child within themselves, growing very slowly for a whole year, before it is encased in a protective shell. The egg is very soft and leathery at first, like thick, damp parchment, before it hardens in the air to a consistency of thin, springy wood, warmed from within by its own magic. Two weeks later, perhaps three, and it is ready to hatch.

The tribe had traveled far, but had still some days' flight yet to go when Kalfeer knew that she must find herself a protected den in a mountain cave, where she could build a warm nest and lay her egg. They had by that time reached the high Alps, still many long miles south and east of the northern mountains where the other tribe of dragons had dwelled for centuries on the edge of the western sea. They found a deep, protected cave high in the steep, rocky slopes of one mountain, large enough for them all, and Kalfeer laid her egg in a nest lined with the soft down of eagles and the wool of mountain sheep that the other dragons had brought to her.

It was late on a clear, cold night when danger came. Kalfeer sensed it first. Responding to a vague feeling of waiting danger, she rose from her sleep beside the nest and paced slowly and carefully to the entrance of the cavern, past the shapes of resting dragons. The interior of the cave was lit by the fitful flickers of the two small fires kept for their light and warmth, filling the dark edges of the chamber with doubled shadows. She lifted her head and looked out into the night as she stepped outside. The entrance to their cavern was in the form of a long, narrow ledge of stone, making an extended stage for their landing, descending in a series of deep steps to either side. The stars were bright, but there was no moon and only a light wind stirred through the stones of the heights.

The dragon on watch at the end of the ledge turned his long, powerful neck to look at her, his bright eyes glittering in the dark, and she was pleased to see that it was Halahvey. He was the oldest and wisest of their kind and his magic was still both strong and subtle, although barely an echo of what it had been in the days of his youth in the far east. He was also the acknowledged sire of her unhatched child, although they were not bound mates.

"The Shadows stir," she said simply but with certainty.

Halahvey nodded. "We knew that they would surely come. We are now more vulnerable to them than we have been in centuries. They are devoted to our destruction, so they could hardly ignore the chance to end our first new life in so very long, before it had even begun."

"We must discourage an attack," Kalfeer said. "The egg could well hatch any time now."

The other dragons had stirred, instantly awake and alert in the manner of their kind, standing in the main chamber of the cavern behind her. Halahvey rose and approached her with the slow, graceful tread of a cat. As with all immortals, there was no hint of his incredible age in his proud, elegant form.

"They may have come only to scout us out," he said. "They may intend only to hold us besieged to this cave, knowing that we cannot flee. We will watch outside, and be ready for them. You at least must remain inside with the egg at all times, to be ready as a final defense."

Kalfeer laid back her tall, slender ears, a vague gesture of her frustration and concern. Her maternal instincts were those of a true dragon, strong to the point of being predatory. She turned aside and paced back inside the cave, as the other dragons made way before her. Then they went outside to join Halahvey in his watch, as devoted in their way to this new life as she was herself. Kalfeer returned to her bed, coiling her long body about the nest of her egg. She lay motionless through the long hours of the night, although she did not sleep but lay with her eyes open, her gaze locked on the one entrance to the cave.

The first and only warning of attack came suddenly, with a single roar of challenge and the solid impact of heavy armored forms, the very abruptness and savageness of that attack calculated to break the defenses. Two dark shapes hurtled through the narrow entrance of the cavern, crouching before her in a tense stance, ready to spring. They stood with their necks thrust well down, their heads bent almost to the floor of the cave, with their legs braced wide and their wings furled tightly to their backs. They were blacker than a moonless night, as black as the smothering darkness of the deepest cavern which only a dragon's magical eyes can pierce, but their eyes glowed like red flame.

Kalfeer calculated her chances in the barest instant frozen out of time. She was outnumbered two to one, so she could afford no mistakes. As she had expected, the larger of the two, fully as large as herself, sprang directly at her while the smaller, the one with his eye on her nest, darted in toward her egg. She thrust herself forward at the final moment, dropping to her belly as the larger of the pair, missing his target, passed above her. Then she thrust her head up to catch his neck in her powerful jaws. Bracing her legs wide, she jerked the Shadow about sharply to throw him solidly onto his back, a blow heavy enough to stun. In that same swift move she whipped her tail around blindly, its heavy ridged plates snapping the second of the two attackers on the side of his head. The impact was enough to knock him back across the cavern against the stone of the outer wall beside the door, and he crumpled into a limp pile.

Kalfeer still had all she could manage with the larger of the pair. The massive form beneath her began to struggle fiercely, using his slightly greater size and weight to break her hold. The Shadows might have been creatures entirely of magic, but they were real and solid enough in this world and her sharp teeth could never penetrate his armor. He arched his spine suddenly and tossed her over his back, and both of them rolled across the floor into the darker interior of the cave, farther away from the egg that Kalfeer would have wished to be.

Desperate to protect her young, Kalfeer pulled away and leaped back across the width of the cave. Crouching low, she drew back her head, her deep chest expanding as she drew a quick breath, and she directed a blast of flame at her opponent. The Shadow barely had time to respond, bringing up his head to fend off her flames with his own icy breath. The two opposing forces met almost directly between them, each at first seeming to cancel out the other. But their flame was the one advantage of the dragons over the cold breath of the Shadows. Kalfeer's fire ate away at her enemy's icy defense until he was forced to duck his head and leap aside at the final moment, just before her flame scored the cavern wall behind him.

Kalfeer prepared to spring after him, pressing the attack, but the massive draconic form of Halahvey hurtled through the entrance of the cave, striking the larger Shadow. Locked in battle, the two rolled across one of the small fires that were kept within the cave for light and warmth, into the depths of the interior. She could spare them no more thought. The smaller of the two Shadows had recovered, and he was loping through the entrance of the cave on his hind legs, carrying her egg.

Neither dragons nor Shadows were made for runnin upright, which left them slow and awkward. But if h could have made it outside and taken to the air, then h would have been very hard to catch. Kalfeer had reco nized the tactics of the Shadows from the first, sending large attacker to keep her occupied while their smalles swiftest flyer stole the egg. She overtook him in only three long bounds, bringing him down heavily on the ledge just outside the entrance of the cave. The egg popped out of his grasp, tumbling down the stair-step of stones beside the ledge, rolling into the darkness beneath the leaves of a small pine.

With sharp cries of fright and desperation, the small Shadow broke from Kalfeer's grasp and thrust himself into the air, fleeing with long, swift strokes of his black wings. His fearful escape came as a sign of retreat to the other Shadows, who broke off their attack on the dragons to follow. The last to flee shot out of the entrance of the cave and away into the night, followed a moment later by Halahvey. The old dragon paused at the end of the ledge, watching the retreat of the Shadows. Then he turned to find Kalfeer.

He did not see her at first, but he saw that the other dragons were drawing about the right side of the ledge. Halahvey crept close to the edge of the stone, looking down into the shadows.

Kalfeer crouched a short distance below, reaching into the deep shadows of a crevice in the rocks, half hidden by a small pine. Moving very slowly and gently, she lifted out the egg and set it in a bed of dry pine needles before her, bending her long neck to peer at it closely. Her large, piercing eyes glittered in the dim light.

"Is it well?" Halahvey asked anxiously, when it seemed that the other dragons were afraid to speak.

"It is cracked," she answered. "But it also begins to move. I believe that it is about to hatch."

She lifted the egg then, handing it up to him, and he took it carefully in his own large hands. At once he could feel its first feeble movements. Dragon eggs were very tough, and even a new born dragon was indeed quite durable, but this one had endured much. The entire tribe gathered close about them both, watching and waiting. Kalfeer lifted herself up the tumbled wall of stone, then took the egg that Halahvey offered and carried it to the center of the ledge. She laid it gently in a natural depression in the stone, where it was not likely to roll itself back over the side of the ledge with its increasing struggles.

The hatching came quite suddenly. The egg began to rock vigorously, and the cracks caused by its fall widened. The dragons quietly drew even closer, watching motionless and silent with bright eyes beneath the brilliant stars. The egg split suddenly along one large crack, and a small, damp form fell out. So it lay for a moment, its long neck stretched out limply across the cold stone while most of its small body still lay hidden within the broken shell. Then, after a brief rest and its first breaths of air and life, the tiny dragon renewed its struggles, dragging itself feebly from the egg. Once again it collapsed, its slender limbs and wings sprawled across the stone.

Kalfeer bent her head and nuzzled the dragonet gently, a gesture that was curiously tender for a creature so proud and predatory in appearance as a dragon. It lay with its large eyes closed, its head tilted to one side as it took its first deep, noisy breaths, the soft armor of its chest expanding deeply. Then she looked up to see that the other dragons of her tribe were still watching intently, as if enthralled by some enchantment of fascination. She sat well up on her haunches, her head lifted proudly as she faced them.

"This is life!" she told them. "This is hope. Perhaps not for us, as we are still doomed to our Long Sleep in the end. But at least our race may yet survive. For I take this as a sign that our young are returning to us, and that they have adapted to this new world."

"Perhaps," Halahvey agreed cautiously. "But this is the dawn of a world of mortal men. Will there be room for dragons in a world of men?"

"Room shall be made," Kalfeer declared. "Our new young will survive and thrive. We have been masters of this ancient world for a hundred million years. Mortal men are as children to us, dull of wit, heedless and uncouth. Soon we will again be strong enough to demand our own places in this world where they will not come, or they will face our wrath."

"Mankind has never provoked our wrath," Halahvey reminded them all. "They may be willful and foolish, but that is mostly just the innocence of their young race, and the want of deep wisdom that is the failing of those doomed to a short life. In the past they have always recognized that we are older and wiser, and they have always heeded our word scrupulously. I hope that it may be so in time yet to come."

"But the Shadows have taught men to fear us," said one of the others.

"The Shadows are as few as ourselves," Kalfeer reminded them. "When we have regained our strength, then we will send the last of them into their own Long Sleep and set this old world straight. Men are no threat to us for the simple fact that they are mortal and we are not."

"Yet men prosper," Halahvey added. "And they will continue to prosper, growing in their own strength quicker than ourselves, I am sure."

"And that is why those few of us who have survived from the previous order of dragons must endure for as long as we are able," Kalfeer said. "We must be here to protect our young, and to teach them our ancient learning and wisdom."

The little dragon stirred then, struggling to sit up. It sat for a long moment, staring up at them with eyes that were as deep as the stars and as blue as the clear sky of a cold winter afternoon. Then they could see for themselves that the words of Kalfeer were true. Even though this young dragon was as small and delicately formed as any young, its armor light and soft with just the barest trace of ridge or horns, yet it was like an image of what they had been in better days, before their decline. It was large for being newly born. Nor was it dark and dull like themselves, but deep brown on its back, wings and tail, lightening almost to gold on face and chest.

The little dragon blinked at them, its expression one of fascination and some confusion, as if it could not understand this attention. Then it yawned hugely, showing a long, tapered snout full of the splinters of sharp teeth. Gaining in strength almost with each moment, the dragonet stood and stretched each limb one after the other, then fanned its small wings. Although only minutes out of the shell, it seemed ready to go forth to meet life.

"It is male, and his name shall be Kalavek," Kalfeer declared.

One of the other dragons had gone into the cave and now returned with the haunch of a mountain sheep roasted on the fire. Kalfeer dipped her head to acknowledge the offering, and the meat was placed on the cold stone before the little dragon. Kalavek stared at it, sniffing almost cautiously at the warm scent, then attacked the haunch with the eagerness of a predatory instinct.

"Feast well, my proud little Kalavek," Kalfeer said softly. "You must grow big and strong enough to fly. Soon we will depart for the far north to join our tribe with the others of our kind, and you will meet the little one who is to be your mate."

*   *   *

The dragons lingered for a time in those mountains, while little Kalavek grew strong enough to travel. Young dragons were born almost fully formed. They could walk almost at their hatching, and they could fly within two or three weeks. All the same, the dragons delayed in their journey north until the little one was ready for longer flights, and also until the winter that had been threatening at the time of his hatching had passed into a gentle spring. Kalavek had grown during that time in the way that young dragons did, more than four times as large as he had been at the time of his hatching. He could already fly very well, with a wingspan twice that of the largest eagle.

At least young dragons did not have to be taught to speak. Dragons were creatures of magic and their native magic guided their thoughts, turning the words in their minds into the spoken words to match the language of the one they were speaking to. Thus Kalavek grew quickly and he learned well, for he was curious and quick of mind even for a dragon. But because of this, his early life was one long mystery of things that he did not understand, as his awareness of the world exceeded his ability to discover its secrets. The older dragons were amused with his endless questions and explorations, for they had not had a young dragon about to test their patience for a very long time.

Although they had never spoken it aloud, the other dragons had hardly dared to believe that this hatchling could mark the beginning of a new age for their race. At first, their hope had been founded only in Kalfeer's determined belief, elevated in her own mind to the proportions of an actual prophecy. But the small dragon prospered, and the life and magic contained within his young spirit was obviously so much stronger than their own had been in many long and dark years. And so they too began to believe that Kalfeer was right, and to share in her own eagerness and devotion to a new future for their kind, even if they would themselves live only long enough to see the dawn of the new age of dragons.

For the first time in centuries, the relentless press of time and the pain and despair of their fading magic was lifted somewhat. It was good to feel a little less old and tired, and to look toward a new future that did not fade into complete darkness, like the failing light of a gloomy day.

Spring deepened, bright and temperate, and the dragons knew that the time had come to continue their journey. They made their way slowly, moving in small steps following the course determined by their scouts. They had half of western Europe yet to cross, and that was even in those days a very populous place. Dragons had been in decline for so long that men had seen little of them in many long years and had decided, in the limited wisdom of their short lives, that dragons had never existed. And the dragons preferred matters that way, ever since the races of men and dragons had become estranged following the evil deeds of the Shadows. The tribe went first to the north, passing quickly and quietly through the ancient forests of Austria and Germany, before they hopped across the islands of Denmark and disappeared into the wilds of Sweden.

Little Kalavek took the long journey in stride, often darting aside from their path to investigate something new and different, until Kalfeer hurried him back into the tribe. But most often he followed close, gliding on his small wings while he held to the tails and ridges of the older dragons.

Late one night, still early in their long journey, the dragons passed near to a place where a great castle stood atop a hill, rising like an island out of the sea of the dark forest. Kalavek bent his neck to stare, even after they had passed. He had seen little of the strange abodes of mortal men, just simple shepherd's huts in the mountains that had been his home. Certainly nothing like this, with its high towers and walls, and its many windows filled with warm light. For once something stirred that was more than just his own insatiable curiosity, but a distant longing for a life that was different from the one he knew. He wondered what it would be like to dwell in that place where it was always bright and warm, surrounded by music and the conversation of ever-changing companions.

"Will we see the Kingdoms of Faerie?" he asked, and abruptly lost his hold on his mother's tail, tumbling away.

"No, no. The Kingdoms of Faerie passed from this world a long time ago," Kalfeer said, pausing in her flight and very discreetly looking back over her shoulder. Even young dragons had their pride. "Some of the races of Faerie may linger still, in forgotten caverns, or in the shadows of ancient forests or the black depths of the sea. But most have long since gone, and their kingdoms disappeared from this world centuries ago."

"Oh," Kalavek muttered in obvious disappointment as he caught hold of her tail. "I would have liked to have seen the Kingdoms of Faerie. The world seems so dull without magic."

"Boring to death," Kalfeer agreed, although she muttered those words under her breath.

"Can we look for them?"

"You can look for them all you want, when you are older," Kalfeer told him. Dragons were loners. She had absolutely no desire to seek out the ragged remains of the faerie races, even if any did still survive. She thought that Kalavek would lose most of that desire himself in time, although she hoped that he would never lose his delight with this world.

"What was it like, in the days of the Kingdoms of Faerie?" he asked.

She glanced over her shoulder at him. "You would best ask that question of Halahvey. I remember only the later days of the Age of Faerie, and most of the races of Faerie had by that time become close and elusive."

"Before the coming of men?"

She smiled. "Men have been in this world longer than I have, but only just. I have seen the passing of more than eight hundred thousand years. Halahvey has seen twelve million."

She paused, knowing that Kalavek could not have had the slightest sense of such time, not when he had yet to see his first year. Yet she hoped that he would remember her words, to comprehend in his own time in the event that she was no longer there to recall those words for him. Dragons remembered everything, and they forgot nothing with the passing of years. That had made the darkening of their world all the harder to bear, remembering the ages of their prosperity as if those times were only just past, and remembering mates and young and companions long departed as if they had flown the bright skies of this world only yesterday.

"I never saw the Kingdoms of Faerie at their height, in the days before even the hint of the approaching darkness had shadowed their lives," she continued after a long moment, checking her course to follow the dragons in the vanguard of their flight. "But I came into this life early enough in their decline to see the lingering image of what the Faerie Kingdoms had been, at a time when the faerie folk where still vainly acting out the lives that they had once enjoyed in the innocence of their age, before they ever foresaw or could even contemplate an end to their bliss or a change in the world they knew and trusted.

"Those where grand times. When I was young, I explored the deep places of the forest with the elves. I flew above the centaurs as they raced across the grassy plains. I sported in the waves with the sea folk. In those days the dragons did not keep entirely to themselves, but we delighted in exploring the lives and thoughts of every living creature and absorbing their interpretation of the greater whole of life. We would often attend the midsummer festivals with the elves and the centaurs, and there would be music and food, and they would sing and dance away that shortest night of the year. But the midwinter festival was our own, the longest night and also the dragon's new year. Then dragons would come from across whole continents, gathering in the high, private places of the mountains. Then we would just sit, each alone on one great stone, with our heads raised to the bright stars, and there would be dragons scattered motionless here and there for as far as the eye could see. All through the long night we would weave our thoughts

together, until we filled the world with a vast chorus to the
cold stars that only the mind could hear. Such music has
not been heard in this world for a long time."

Kalavek had been holding to her ridges with both hands,
suspended on his motionless wings, as he shared her images
in his mind. That only reminded him of all the wonders that
he would never see, and how the world had become such
a dull and gloomy place, just in time to torment his young
life. He looked up. "Why did the world have to change?"

"No dragon knows the answer to that, except to say that
change is the first rule of life. It might take millions of
years, or it might happen all in an instant. To us, it seems
that the world has grown cold and cruel and lifeless, but
we were made for a very different world and we have not
adapted as fast as it has. I am sure that the world is no less
wonderful or exciting than it ever was. Things have just
changed from what they were, and we just have to learn
how to be a part of it."

"They all died," Kalavek muttered, uncomforted by her
assurances.

"They did not simply die," Kalfeer corrected him. "For
the most part, they just drew in to themselves. The goblins
hid themselves deep in their underground kingdoms and
locked the few doors to the outer world behind them. The
centaurs and the unicorns and certain other folk that had
long been allied to them in spirit retreated into the far west,
looking for lands where the magic still lingered. Only the
elves with their hollow pride and shallow wisdom refused
to accept the change in the world, and they withered and
blew away like leaves in the autumn wind."

"And the dragons?"

She nodded sadly. "The dragons were the very last to
feel the coming change in themselves that heralded their
own decline. Empires and kingdoms of Faerie had vanished into the dust of years, and the age of man was a
hand. And that deceived us into thinking that we we
immune. The dragons had come first, long before the /
of Faerie, and in essence we are not a true part of the fae.
magic but belong to something far older. That fooled us

into believing that this changing age was no danger to us.

"Soon after the time of our decline began, our elders reminded us of the lands beyond the western sea, where men had never come. Many of the folk of Faerie had retreated into the west beyond the seas, but the dragons have always stood alone and we were not a part of their first great migration. Then the first tribes of dragons went into the west as well, coming after a long time to the edge of the Great Sea. Many rode the winds across the western sea and few ever returned. Our hope was cheated, for men were there before us."

"What happened?"

"It was a land of strange magic, magic that returned all the folk of Faerie to their former grandeur, but in forms that were strange and frightful. Even the dragons, who became wise and noble as in our former days, but taking shapes that were feathered or snakelike. In time they passed from this world into a sleep of strange dreams, from which they may never return even if a time of dragons does come again. Those few who came back across the sea warned us that the way west is closed to us."

"Then why are we going west ourselves? Is it time for us to die?" Kalavek asked in a subdued voice, as he pulled himself closer along the ridges of his mother's back.

"No, not yet, my son," she assured him, and sighed a deep, rumbling sigh that he could feel through his hold on her plates. "In the west of these lands there lingers still one other tribe of dragons, dwelling in a wild, remote land beside the stormy northern sea. A land where a shadow of the magic of Faerie lingers still. Magic that we need to be strong and wise. And it is a place where there are few men to trouble us."

"Halahvey told me that men believe that they have hunted us from the world."

"Although men like to tell themselves ridiculous stories, no mortal has ever slain a dragon and never will," his mother explained.

"Then why do they say such things?"

His mother laughed. "You are inquisitive, but that is as a dragon should be. Men tell themselves such stories because they are afraid of us. They fear us for all the gifts we possess that they do not. They fear us because we are large and strong, even in the days of our decline, while they are small and weak. They fear us for our magic and wisdom. They fear us because we have the freedom of the winds, while they are slaves to the ground."

Kalavek furled his wings, holding tightly as he sat on his mother's armored shoulders. "Are you going to die?"

Kalfeer considered her answer for a moment. "Yes, I suppose I will. It is something that I must do, eventually. But not, I think, for some time yet to come. When you were born, it showed us that the dragons are finally learning to adapt to this new world. Now we have reason to linger in this world past our time, until you and all the dragons yet to be born have found your own lives, and the race of dragons is strong again."

Kalavek thought about that very carefully. There were still many things about life that he did not yet understand, and it seemed that the life of a dragon was a very complicated affair indeed. For one thing, it suddenly occurred to him that, given the way of the world in his own time, there were far more dragons about who were dead than alive.

"But how can a dragon ever die?" he asked. "I thought that dragons live forever."

"No dragon ever really dies," his mother told him, glancing over her shoulder. "There is a greater purpose in life beyond what even we are allowed to know. We may live through whole ages of this world, but there eventually comes a time when we are called and we know that we must return to the stars. Then, on a clear, bright night, we will cast ourselves upon a cold wind and never return. No dragon of this world can tell you where we go or why, except to say that we go to await a new age of the world when all dragons will be reborn. Perhaps the ancient cycle of life has completed its long, difficult turn, and a new age of dragons is at hand."

* * *

If that was so, there seemed little cause to believe it. The world still seemed like such a cold, shallow place compared to that brighter, softer and more lively world that the elders of the dragons had known during the previous Ages of Magic. Numb was perhaps a word that they would use to describe the world in this new age of men, cold and unfeeling. They knew that this was no place for them, nor would it ever be.

And yet young Kalavek prospered, and he seemed to have no complaint with the world into which he had been born. If life in the age of men held no meaning to the older dragons, it held endless fascination for him. All things he saw delighted him. He wanted to see everything and to understand every mystery of this ancient world. And mortal men, the creatures of this new world, even interested him in a quiet or perhaps cautious way, and the older dragons saw no use in men or their dreary ways at all. They were given to trust that Kalfeer had been right, that little Kalavek was a different sort of dragon from themselves, possessing a new manner of spirit and magic that would adapt him to life in the world as it had become.

Eventually their long journey brought his tribe at last into the mountains of the far north. This was a very different land from what Kalavek had ever known in his short life. These were not the young mountains of sharp stone and bitter ice that he had seen in the south, nor that which the dragons had known in the distant east. These were old mountains, shaped by ancient flows of ice, and they now seemed to sleep beneath a blanket of green trees and soft white snow. And yet, perhaps because this was one of the old places of the world, there was a sense of magic in this land, as if forgotten scraps of the realms of Faerie still lingered here in the shadows of the woods and deep in forsaken valleys.

Still, there was a definite taint of furtiveness and decay to that magic which Kalavek did not like at all. It reminded him of something, in some vague and indefinable way, and he had to think about it very hard before he realized that it reminded him of the older dragons, with their musty antiquity and weary, shabby magic. That one, brief realization changed his life. Now for the first time, he fully understood that the older dragons were dying, and what that meant. He was determined that he was not going to die, not for a very long time. The pride and majesty of the dragons should come to more, he thought, than for the last of their noble breed to simply disappear on a cold winter night.

The final night of the journey of the dragons was cold and clear, that time of early spring when winter was finally beginning to loose her last desperate grip to the first stirrings of green life. The tribe was following the coast, a land of deep, narrow fjords and high mountains clad in thick coats of green trees, some with lingering caps of snow. There was a deep silver haze like translucent fog, hanging like curtains of spiders' webs on the night air, blurring but not hiding the steep walls of the fjord. Kalavek's eyes were mostly for the Great Sea, an endless expanse of rolling waves that filled the western horizon without end. He was thinking of the dragons who had once stood upon these shores before spreading their great wings and disappearing into the West, most never to return. He wondered about that great journey and what it must have been like to have been on wing for hours and days on end.

A sudden sound like a blast of air startled him from his contemplations. Looking down, he could see what seemed to be at least three vast forms moving through the waves near the wide mouth of the fjord. As they broke the surface, he saw large backs of smooth black hide with broad patches of white, the long blades of dorsal fins rising into the night. They were larger than any dragon, even old Halahvey. But they could not fly.

"Whales," Kalfeer said, anticipating his question. "I have not seen a whale in so many hundreds of years."

"They are big," Kalavek commented.

"The largest animals in the world today," she said, turning her long neck to glance at him. "In the deep, wide sea, there are whales even larger than those."

"Were dragons ever that big?" Kalavek asked. He was holding to the end of his mother's tail, bending his neck to watch the slow, rolling procession of the whales, already disappearing behind them into the night.

"No, dragons were never so big. Even in the days of our height, we were still only twice as large as we are now." She afforded him another brief glance. "The dragons still remember that in the days of the ancestors, there were vast creatures like whales that walked the land, and great predators so big that they could jump on a dragon and snap him up in three big bites. But they all died, while we prospered."

"Why did they die?"

"The world changed. It was no longer the world that they had been made to rule, and they did not adapt."

"The dragons did not die then," Kalavek observed, obviously pondering some mystery very hard. "Why did they die and we did not?"

"We were smarter and quicker," Kalfeer told him.

"Are we not as smart now as we were then?"

The innocence and sincerity of that simple question surprised Kalfeer, and she bent her head to look at him. "This is different. In that time, the world itself changed. This time, the magic has changed. We can survive just about anything, hot or cold, wet or dry, with little concern. But we are still creatures of magic. There is little magic left in the world, and what little is left is changed from the magic that we have always known. It has been hard for us to adapt to that."

That gave Kalavek much to think about. Although he was young, he did understand one thing very well. Dragons were not animals, for animals were at the mercy of their world, unable to survive beyond the limitations that nature had placed upon them. Dragons could think and speak. They even had hands like men to make things, although they needed so little in life and kept no possession for its own sake. Most important, they still possessed a fair measure of their former magic. He thought that there must be something they should be able to do to save themselves.

And yet his mother had told him that when a dragon was called to return to the stars, then he had no choice.

The dragons in the vanguard of the tribe had turned and were flying up the center of the fjord, disappearing into the mist. Kalavek pushed himself forward with strong, swift strokes of his small wings, eager for a look ahead. Kalfeer glanced up at him briefly, amused with his boldness and curiosity. But it was Kalavek's curiosity that got the better of him. He happened to catch a small flash of light on the very edge of his vision, and he immediately dropped into a glide as he twisted his long neck around to stare into the darkness to his left. There were four or five distant lights, winking at him through the curtain of mist. The abodes of men, and so near to the domains of the only other tribe of dragons left in the world. The thought of it excited him, and he was lured by his own fascination.

"Kalavek!" his mother called to him.

Kalavek was startled to see her winged form disappearing into the night, and he struggled to match her pace.

They continued to follow the fjord deeper into the mountains, as the crooked passage of the waves below became narrower and the slopes to either side grew steeper and climbed higher toward the stars. And suddenly the night was full of dragons, more dragons than Kalavek had ever seen in all his young life. They appeared one by one out of the mist, circling and spiraling in a slow, stately aerial dance, dragons that were brown and gold, silver and green as they drifted through mists of moonlit green. Kalavek watched in such intense fascination that he did not at first notice that he and his mother were at the center of that winged dance, as if this grand procession was meant to welcome them alone.

The assembly of gliding, wheeling dragons made its slow, steady way up the fjord, passing silently through the mists of night. They came to a wall of mountains and began to rise toward the stars, until the air grew sharp with a winter cold and peaks of grey, mossy stone rose above their cloaks of trees and brush. Kalavek had to struggle to keep the pace of that demanding climb, his young wings already tired after a night's long flight. Their escort of dragons fell away one by one, settling to stand or sit upon some great crag or pinnacle of stone or some high tumble of boulders.

Kalavek was beginning to think that this was not the home caves of the northern tribe at all. Then he had to move quickly when his mother veered suddenly to the right, settling upon one very large boulder near the top of the peak. She sat well up on her haunches, and Kalavek flipped his wings to his back and settled himself securely between her front legs. As he looked out into the night, the last two dragons drifted down out of the night and settled at the very top of the peak. The first was old Halahvey, bright silver in the moonlight. The other was a darker dragon, all black and deeper greens in the night, with just the barest glimmer of reflected light on his armor. He was beyond any doubt the largest dragon that Kalavek had ever seen.

"What is happening?" Kalavek asked softly, and then he thought he understood. "Are the dragons going to sing?"

Kalfeer glanced down at him. "Yes, the dragons will sing."

Kalavek had never heard the dragons sing in all of his short life, although he had heard it described often enough to know that it was a very rare and magical experience indeed. Very rare, for the dragons had found no cause to sing in many long, dark centuries. In happier times past, they would have sung at any time they considered important or special, or to gather themselves or their magic in common cause against some need. At the very least, they would always sing for the Winter Solstice, the Time of the Dragons. But the dragons had found no need or desire to sing in a very long time, for they were now so few and the echoes of their songs in an empty world only reminded them of how alone they were.

Halahvey settled back on his haunches with his head held high and proud, and he began the first soft, piercing words of his song. Dragons did not sing with words but with their thoughts, which for them was nearly one and the same. One by one the other dragons lifted their heads to the night and

added the voices of their own minds to that song. And as
they sang, it seemed as if the world itself slowly became
a part of their song. The song grew, sometimes loud and
sometimes gentle, moving fast and then slow, as it weaved
an endless and complex pattern into the night.

For the songs of the dragons were magic itself, and they
used the power of their songs to gather the innate magic of
the world to themselves, to compose new harmonics to the
hidden music within that native magic and send it out again.
But their songs were also the definitions of themselves,
woven of the fabric of their own long history and colored
by their spirits and their deep wisdom. The dragons were
less wise than they had been, and their spirits were sad and
faded things. In the days of their glory, thousands of voices
would fill the world where now only a dozen echoed dimly
through this cold northern land. But their song remained a
thing of great power and nobility all the same.

Kalavek sat there on that cold stone near the top of the
world and listened as that ancient song weaved its way
through millions of years and millions of lives of dragons.
He cowered in the shadow of dragons of a kind who had
not flown the skies of this world for a very long time,
dragons who were great and wise and powerful in their
magic far beyond any dragon who now lived or that he
could have ever hoped to be. He looked back into a time
that was old and dim even by the standards of his race to
the first dragons, masters of a strange and exciting world,
possessing the fierce dignity of their kind but yet to learn the
deep wisdom of the true dragons. He felt the soft, quiet love
of dragons. Their cold, abiding anger. Their immeasurable
curiosity.

For in the depths of time, in the early days of the First
Age of Magic, the first dragons had learned to speak and
to shape their thoughts into new and complex ideas. They
looked upon their world and watched the quiet workings
of nature. They delved the secrets of the earth and found
the hidden complexities and great antiquity of the world.
They soared among the clouds on leathern wings and measured the ways of the winds and the storms, of the coming

of rain and of snow, of the warm summers and the icy breath of winter. They studied the curious ways of magic, exploring its subtle depths and the seeming limitlessness of its promise.

Then came the time of the Dragon Lords, when those among them who stood forth as leaders, dragons of foresight and wisdom such as they possessed in the childhood of their race, gathered all other dragons about them in unity of thought and purpose. They cut and shaped stone into the first of their great city-fortresses, citadels the size of small mountains, with great walls of stone to shut out the rains and floods and the great beasts that still walked the ancient world, yet open above in massive arches and portals large enough for the passage of their wings in flight. And so for a short time, at least as an immortal folk would measure the swiftly passing years, they were the masters of their world. It was the zenith of their glory and their ambition, if not their wisdom or their magic.

But in time it came to pass that the dragons fulfilled their greatest quest and found the greatest source of magic in all the world, a vast passage that disappeared into the depths of the world, which they called the Fountain of the World's Heart. Thus the dragons came to know that they could summon forth great amounts of native magic, to use to their purposes or to store against their future need. They came to realize also that the Fountain of the World's Heart was in some way obstructed, and that far greater magic yet could be brought out to fill the whole world. Greatly daring, several of their most powerful warriors and masters of magic descended into the depths. Their quest was long and difficult, for they faced many dangers in the nether regions and fought fierce battles. But they came in time to the end of their long search and found the source of the greatest of all magics, and they succeeded in freeing it of its bonds so that its full strength flowed unrestricted up from the depths of the nether realm and into the outer world.

But the flood of eons had been contained behind the bounds that they had released; and so much native magic, powerful but formless, was released upon the outer world

all in a single, terrible instant. In that way the age of
the Dragon Lords came to a sudden, violent end, and the
foundations of their massive city-fortresses were broken and
they fell. All the lands were shaken, so that seas rushed in
upon the shallow lands and mountains were thrust high,
and great cracks and cones of fire and molten rock poured
forth tremendous destruction, and the skies of all the world
were darkened with dust and smoke and the weather grew
suddenly cold and harsh. The very land itself was shattered
by great cracks and began to drift apart, and the seas rushed
in to fill the voids. Then all the forests and marshes of
an older world were burned or buried, and all the great
creatures that had walked the land and ranged the seas
came to a sudden end.

The world had changed, and those few dragons that had
survived were also changed. For the magic that they had
released had become a part of their very being, and they
were now immortal. Age had lost all power to slay them,
unless after thousands of centuries they grew weary of the
world and heeded at last the call to their long Sleep Between
the Stars. In form they were now sleek and powerful, their
armor light and strong, so that they could survive almost
any harm. But they were changed in mind and spirit as well,
for they had now become true children of the wind and no
longer needed nor desired to build places of their own to
dwell or things made by their own hands, except perhaps
a few small, simple things to delight or comfort them. The
realm of dragons was now a domain of mind and magic,
and all things they truly needed in life were now within
themselves, or else given freely by nature. They withdrew
and became the dwellers of the high places of stone and ice
and wind.

But the great magic that had been released brought other
changes in time, gathering and stirring like the eddies of
a stream until it brought forth new life. These were the
races of Faerie, simple, furtive creatures at first, but they
too grew steadily in strength, wisdom and learning. Great
kingdoms and cities arose beneath the trees of ancient forests, beneath high mountains and beneath the waves of the

seas. Evil creatures of magic came into being as well, trolls and goblins and cruel satyrs of the warm southern forests, and from time to time there were sudden battles and long wars in the forgotten realms of Faerie. And always there were the dragons, first and eldest, hunters of the wind and dwellers of the high places.

The dragons did not measure the passing time or count the endless years, but the years did pass all the same. Then the magic began to fade, and the races of Faerie began to dwindle away, their ancient kingdoms disappearing slowly into the dark and dreary years of their long decline and their great cities falling away into the dust of time. Eventually even the dragons came to face the inevitable, for their world was changing, and they were dying.

And as the song passed into the sadness and helpless confusion of defeat, Kalavek began to feel himself surprised and frightened by the mood of the music. Slowly he lowered his head as he awoke from the spell of the song, blinking like a whole forest full of owls. Night was passing into a dawn that seemed to glow with golds, yellows and smoky browns as the first light of day began to spread across the sky. The dragons were gathered loosely all about him, seated on the ridges and boulders of the peaks. The song of sadness and decline fell away like old leaves and the dragons lowered their heads.

Kalavek glanced up, a very startled and guilty look on his face, and saw his mother smiling down at him. Halahvey was standing to one side on the large boulder. On the other side stood the large silver dragon whom Kalavek knew must be Selikah, leader of the northern tribe. He was indeed the largest dragon that Kalavek had ever seen, and Selikah was staring at him in a very intent and thoughtful manner.

"Did we not say?" Halahvey asked.

Selikah drew back his head, and he seemed to be pleased . . . or at least satisfied in some way. "Yes, I am beginning to believe that it must be so."

Kalavek had no idea what their words might mean, and he looked quickly from one to the other. He realized that they must have flown down to this ledge of rock while he had been distracted singing, and they had been watching him while he had been unaware.

"There will be other nights for singing," Selikah added. "But I think that any more songs will have to wait until you younger dragons are somewhat more educated and experienced in your magic."

⟐ TWO

EINAR MYKLATHUN WAS a forester and although he had never traveled, still he was quite certain that the deep, wooded fjords of the western coast of Norway had to be the best place in all the world. When he had still been very young he had often thought of going up the coast to Bergen and finding work on the old Norwegian merchant ships or perhaps a fast English clipper and see the rest of the world for himself. But that, he had soon realized, would only tell him the truth that he already knew in his heart. There was certainly no better place in all the world than the fjords of Norway. Even considering how dreary the mountains and fjords could be in the rain, which happened quite a lot of the time.

And that was why Einar had not become a fisherman as his family had been fishermen for generations lost in time, as his father would have wanted him to have been and as his two brothers had become, trusting his boat, his life and his livelihood to the ill temper of the cold Norwegian Sea. So Einar himself might have been, except that one day while he was still hardly old enough to be called a young man he had seen the notice announcing that the King was looking for soldiers, sailors and foresters. Then Einar had gone to the Postmaster and had written his name on all the important papers, and after a time the King himself (or so it seemed from the way the papers were written) sent a message back that Einar was to take himself down the coast to a village where he was needed more. And when he arrived, Einar saw that the King had chosen very well for him indeed, for that little village lay at the opening of the most beautiful fjord in all of Norway, and what seemed to him a most magical place besides. It looked to him just like a piece of Old Norway like he had heard about in the old stories, a land that seemed to be just the perfect place for giants and gnomes.

Of course, Einar Myklathun only thought that it looked magical, and he certainly never really expected that he should ever have to worry about meeting trolls and dragons. Einar certainly had no reason to believe in faerie tales; the world he saw was quite interesting enough to suit him. As much as he loved his forests, he was in all things a practical man. And so he found himself apprenticed, as it were, to the previous forester, an old man with no sons and no one else to replace him. The old forester had taken young Einar into his own home and had spent the next four years leading him back and forth through all the trails of the fjord and back into the mountains until he knew every part of the lands that the King had entrusted him to protect. Then the old forester had given Einar his musket, already half a century old and yet so well cared for that it looked new and all the gun that Einar would ever need, and then he had spent his last few years happily holding forth with all the other old men at the tavern.

But for Einar, life was only just beginning, and it seemed good. He never tired of the deep, dark woods, the sharp, fresh air of the mountains or the majestic silence of the immeasurable depths of the fjord. But Einar was not all the time in the forest, and when he came into town people were pleased enough to see him. Then he might spend a quiet afternoon or a bright morning at the tavern with his friends Edvard Berg the schoolteacher, whom the King in his great wisdom had sent to this village to teach the future fishermen and fishwives of Norway the elusive pleasures of literature and art as well as the horrors of mathematics and grammar, and also Young Thorsen. Now Young Thorsen was all that he was ever called, and everyone in the whole village except for Herr Berg, who had been his own teacher, had quite forgotten his name. His father was The

Thorsen, also of no known Christian name, who was the most prominent and wealthy shopkeeper and perhaps not by coincidence the Mayor. Some were given to say in jest that Mayor Thorsen had no Christian name because he was no Christian but the direct descendant of some old Norse God of Viking Entrepreneurs, and that the men of their line discovered their sons under stones where the King's taxmen had slept.

And so it happened one spring evening that Einar was sitting in the tavern with his friends Berg the teacher and Young Thorsen, and the discussion so far had been whether this young year would be a good one. The spring so far had been about as good as springs ever came, and some argued that this was a good indication of things to come while others argued that the weather in Norway could be good for only just so long and that the rest of the year would be particularly nasty as a result. Because Einar was the forester, he was expected by some to know what the weather was going to do, and when he insisted that he had no certain way of predicting the seasons to come then the others said that he was only trying to spare them the bad news. They were especially fond of hearing bad news: they believed in preparing for the worst, so that they would be ready for it when it comes and pleasantly surprised when it does not.

After a time they had all split up into their own small groups of only two or three each, so that they could continue to discuss their own views of the portents of the weather without the distraction of opinions that differed from their own. The Schoolmaster and Young Thorsen spent a few minutes watching Einar shrewdly, although he was too busy trying to light a reluctant pipe to notice. He had only recently taken up smoking his pipe in public, after he had spent several weeks practicing at home in the dark so that no one could hear him cough.

As far as it went, Einar had first tried smoking the big, brown cigars that Thorsen the Elder had given him, but he had coughed until he almost died and had set fire to his great, bushy mustache beside. So if he noticed the looks that the other two were giving him, he assumed that they were only trying to restrain themselves from some rude comment. Thorsen the Younger was actually very good at keeping any expression from his face, as long as he was looking somewhere else. But Schoolmaster Berg's round, boyish face with its tiny brush of a mustache looked like a balloon about to pop.

"Well, Father will skin me like a fish if I am not getting back to clean up the store," Young Thorsen declared suddenly. Which was something that he would often say at the end of an hour with his friends, although it was also something that would never happen. Whether or not he was a dutiful son, he was certainly a conscientious shopkeeper. That was why he was left to close up the shop and he took great pride in that, even if it meant no more than pushing a broom about the place.

"Yes, I must be for home as well," Berg added. "People are known to take exception to a teacher who spends too much of his time in the tavern."

"Ja vel, one would think that you both had wives sniffing out your trails at this very moment," Einar said. Then his pipe went out yet again, and he took it out of his mouth and stared at it.

"And you look in the mountains for troll wives because none here would have you," Young Thorsen retorted. Which was not true; Einar was well favored for his wit and humor. "Are you on your way home soon?"

"Soon enough," Einar answered vaguely.

"Then will you be so good as to take these two packages over to Anne-Marie?" Thorsen said as he lifted from the floor a couple of small packages, wrapped in brown paper, and set them on the table. "I was supposed to deliver these, but it is so far out to your side of the village and I must be getting back to the shop."

Einar did not look too happy with that request, but he agreed just the same. As it happened, Anne-Marie Vang was the most beautiful and charming of the eligible young ladies of the village, although she also seemed destined to be a spinster. Being Norwegians all, the young men of the village would always assume that Anne-Marie had a wealth of better prospects and so they never even bothered to ask. Homely girls, shrewish ones and even the stupid ones were wined, dined and married in short order, while Anne-Marie sat at home because all the young men of the village believed that anything good was also too good to be believed.

The only real disadvantage to Anne-Marie's company was the daunting presence of her father, the venerable Herr Vang. He was never given to violence; he had no need. Even the toughest old fishmongers feared a stern glance from him more than they feared drunken sailors or North Sea storms. He was tall and lean and very frightening to look upon even at the best of times and many people said that it was a waste, or perhaps a blessing, that he had not become a preacher or a schoolmaster, but that he was a fisherman and worked his great terror mostly upon the fish.

So it was that Einar Myklathun was apprehensive when he found himself at the door of the home of Herr Vang, even though his errand was an honest one. Now he thought he understood why Young Thorsen had been so eager to find anyone who would make his delivery for him. Einar knocked, and then it seemed to him that he spent an eternity waiting for the door to open. Indeed only half a minute passed before he heard the latch turn and then Herr Vang was standing before him, wearing a face best reserved for sucking pickles.

"I have brought these up for Anne-Marie," Einar offered, holding up the packages.

"That was kind of you," Herr Vang commented, as if he was thinking about something completely different.

"I suppose that you might give these things to Anne-Marie for me," Einar said.

Herr Vang afforded him a rather hard look. "You have not done this often, have you?"

"Well, no," Einar admitted. "Should I have Anne-Marie sign a paper, or something?"

Herr Vang afforded him a very hard look. "Ja, you indeed are very new at this. Well then, I should suppose

that the next thing is for you to come in and have dinner
with us."

Einar was not at all inclined to stay for dinner, but
judging by the looks that Herr Vang was giving him, he
thought that he should stay. If this was what was involved
in making a delivery, then he wondered that shopkeepers
ever got anything done. He found himself brought inside
and given into the care of Frau Vang, who herded him
quickly into the dining room. Einar glanced back and saw
that Herr Vang was speaking with his daughter.

"He is no longer quite so young," Anne-Marie observed
quietly.

"Neither are you," her father reminded her.

Now by this time, Einar was finally beginning to have
some idea of just what was really happening, although he
could not yet figure out why it was happening to him. In
no time at all he found himself seated at the table beside
Anne-Marie, with Herr Vang at one end of the table and
Frau Vang at the other and their two sons looking at him
as if they had secrets that they were just bursting to tell,
and a dinner was laid on the board that would have done
justice to a Yule feast. They were served mutton and not
fish, which was a surprising thing in a fisherman's house
and reserved for the most rare and special occasions, and
Einar was coming to realize that something alarming and
unexpected was happening.

"You seem almost to have been expecting company,"
Einar ventured cautiously after a couple of long and uncomfortable minutes of silence.

"Ja, we did get your message," Herr Vang said.

"My message?"

"Young Thorsen and the Schoolmaster had said that you
wished to call upon Anne-Marie," Herr Vang said, giving
Einar a sharp look as he carved the mutton.

"Oh, ja, that message," Einar agreed quickly, thinking
that he might be slain right there on the table if he was not
careful.

"I do enjoy your gifts," Anne Marie said.

"My gifts?"

"Ja, the flowers," she explained. "And the box of candy all the way from Denmark."

Now at last Einar understood just how this situation had come about, and that Schoolmaster Berg and Young Thorsen had arranged for him to court Anne-Marie, whether they thought it was good for him or if only for the jest of sending him to Herr Vang's house for dinner without his being aware. Now that he knew what was going on, of course, the most difficult and uncomfortable part of the evening was safely over. All that was required of him now was that he converse pleasantly for a while and then he could go home.

That was why he was surprised at himself when, after dinner, he found himself asking Anne-Marie to take a walk with him. For as long as he remained in the house, it seemed to him that he was courting Herr Vang and not visiting with Anne-Marie, who was at least more pleasant company than her father. By this time spring had advanced enough that daylight was beginning to linger into the early evening, and it was cool but not cold, and all the trees and the grass were once again green and full. They walked slowly along the path leading out from the village up the steeper slopes above the fjord, where there were only a few quiet houses scattered under the edge of the forest. The old forester had passed away early that previous autumn, and now Einar had the last large house at the end of the way to himself.

"Ja, this is where I live," Einar said, indicating the house. "Just on the edge of the woods, such as I like."

"You do not like being around people so much?" Anne-Marie asked.

"No, not at all," he insisted. "I just like the forest and the mountains very much as well. There is time enough for both."

Anne-Marie nodded. "It still seems like such a big, dark, lonely house."

"Ja vel, I had been thinking that I might get a dog," Einar said; then he realized to his embarrassment that she might take exception to that statement.

They sat down on a bench beneath a young but vigorous oak that grew just to one side of the path to one side of Einar's house. Now Einar was only too aware that he was not very practiced in polite conversation and even less so in courting, and so he was convinced that he was not making a good showing of himself at all. He took out his pipe and looked at it for a moment, but he thought that the time was inappropriate for smoking and he was sure that he would only set fire to himself again.

"You were not expecting what happened this evening," Anne-Marie said at last. "I think that perhaps Young Thorsen and the Schoolmaster have played a trick on you."

"So they have," Einar admitted. "Thorsen gave me those two packages that he asked me to deliver for him. Then things just began to happen, and I was so afraid that your father would be angry."

"I am sorry," Anne-Marie said.

Einar thought about it for a moment. "I think perhaps that I am not."

Well, Einar got himself into real trouble with that one, and he did not find it so easy to escape after that. Indeed, it should well be said that he did not really even try, although he pretended to be gruff and annoyed with Young Thorsen and the Schoolmaster for quite some time after that. He also began to have dinner at the house of Herr Vang quite often after that, and he very quickly became so familiar at the table that Frau Vang went back to serving fish on the ordinary plates, unless of course it was a holiday. Einar never did get himself a dog for years and years, but one bright, cool morning the following spring he was surprised to find that he had married Anne-Marie and they lived many a year in his large house with the high, steep roof and the deep eaves at the edge of the woods. Now they were not as successful as most folks in that part of Norway with children, but after five years they did find themselves with a son.

There was some difficulty with finding a name for the boy, one that would be proper, and they eventually decided that they should call him Carl. For Carl, it seemed, turned out to be the forgotten name of Young Thorsen, and he had after all made it all possible. For one thing, he never asked Einar to pay him back for the flowers and candy that had been given to Anne-Marie that first day. Of course, Young Thorsen had picked the flowers himself out of Widow Sverdrups's garden while no one was looking except for the widow's old and rather saggy cow, and Widow Sverdrup had of course blamed the cow.

And so the peaceful, happy years had passed, and when spring had come at last to the deep fjords and forests of Norway then Einar Myklathun would once again make ready for his first long journeys into the depths of the fjord and into the mountains to see how the land had survived the winter. Then he cleaned and polished his old musket and put on his jacket with the big pockets and his felt hat, and he kissed Anne-Marie and told little Carl to do well in school. And he walked off down the path that led toward the back of the fjord.

The dragons of the north lived in the most wonderful group of caves there in the mountains at the end of the fjord. The only approach for those who did not fly was up a very steep cliff of tumbled, jagged stone, more than a hundred feet high. At the very top was a very wide oval landing, more than room enough for all the dragons of both tribes to sit or stand or even dance, as unlikely as it was that the mood to dance would ever possess them. There were tall pines standing all around, especially to either side, giving the landing some protection from the winds. The entrances of the caves themselves were in a series of shallow terraces in the grey stone wall which stood at the back of the landing.

These were not the rough caves that he had known all his short life, the temporary shelters that his tribe had taken during their travels, when they could even find a cave and considered themselves lucky enough to have that. These had been shaped by long occupation, cut and smoothed into a whole series of chambers and passages, with rooms enough that all the dragons could have the privacy their nature required. There were deep, soft beds padded with fresh moss and lined with the warm pelts of reindeer taken in hunting expeditions to the far north. Moveable screens of woven mats on wooden frames could be set about to block cold drafts, and they also added a measure of both decoration and privacy. Nor were these dark, gloomy caves, but warmly lit with magic lanterns made of gold and crystal, crafted in the lost cities of the gnomes long ago.

With the resilience of the young, Kalavek felt no need to rest even though he had either flown or sang the entire night. What he wanted to do now, in his first day in this new land, was to explore. He wandered through the forest, walking and not flying, which was something that dragons could do well enough but hardly preferred. But flying was also so distant and brief, when all you want to do is have a good look, and a forest can only properly be seen from the inside. Kalavek decided that he liked this forest very much, even before he had seen very much of it from up close. The mountains where he had been born had been so cold, hard and forbidding, and most of the lands that he had seen on his travels north had been generally dull and cultivated.

These mountains were not so immense that they were overwhelming. The forest itself had a very cozy and familiar feel, in ways that Kalavek could not easily define. He had certainly never seen any place quite like this before. All that he could say for certain was that this land was constantly changing in an endless variation of patterns. There were dark, intimate stretches of dense woods, and the steep, smooth walls of fjords covered in stands of hardy evergreens, and sudden bluffs and cliffs of grey stone rising out of the forest like the crests of waves. There were chattering brooks and waterfalls, and hidden pools within small, deep valleys like secluded pockets within the mountains.

Kalavek had gone only a short way when he came to a place that captivated his curiosity. He had found a tight passage through a vast pile of rounded boulders and slabs of stone, so dark and narrow that it was almost a tunnel. The way was littered deep within by a thick blanket of old leaves, blown in over the years by wind sweeping through the cut. It went in much farther than he would have thought, then around a sharp turn that he had not expected, and farther still. He was beginning to think that it must be due to come to a sudden end when he came around a final turn and found himself with his nose almost in the middle of a thick bush. But he could see light on the other side, and he pushed through between the bush and the stone.

When he came through to the other side, he found himself staring down into the most quietly beautiful, perfect place that he had ever seen. He was on a small ledge about halfway up one side of a sheer cliff, looking out over a deep dell that was more like a cup scooped from the mountainside. The thin ribbon of a waterfall spilled over the top of the cliff into an oval pool immediately below, the overflow disappearing into cracks between the boulders that formed one wall of the tiny valley. The rest of the hollow was filled by five grand evergreens, two immense old sentinels of the forest standing to either side of three others that were respectable trees in their own right, all of them shedding a thick carpet of dry brown needles.

Kalavek just stood and stared in quiet fascination and contentment, for dragons cherished things that are both innately beautiful and also remote and private. This small valley offered both. And more than that, there was a sense of magic about this place. The ancient magic was passing from the world, but it lingered still in this northern land. In this one place, it was as if this one small piece of the Second Age of Magic had gone untouched by time.

"What are you doing here!" Ayesha, the young female, demanded.

Before Kalavek could respond, some heavy weight hit him squarely from behind and sent him hurtling over the edge of the shelf. He caught at the edge as he went over, scrabbling for some hold on the hard, smooth stone to save himself and finding none. As he fell, he made a final blind grab for the bush and came up with something. He did not let go, and it went over the edge with him, protesting furiously.

Kalavek was only momentarily aware that he had hold of another dragon of nearly his own size by the end of

her tail before they both hit the water, and he had somehow come out on top during their tumble. Fortunately the
pool was almost large enough even for grown dragons,
and very deep. Ayesha was struck nearly senseless from
having Kalavek's weight come down on top of her, but even
young dragons were nearly impossible to damage. They
were also very difficult to drown, which was also very good
for Ayesha. Kalavek struggled to pull her from the pool,
clamping his sharp fangs very firmly on the armor of the
whipping end of her tail to free his hands for swimming.

Kalavek had to trust to instinct to save them both, for
he had been born in the mountains in winter only months
before and he had never had a chance to learn to swim. He
thrashed wildly, unsure if he was doing any good until he
suddenly felt firm ground beneath him. Pulling backwards
with firm jerks, he was finally able to draw Ayesha up onto
the grassy bank.

Ayesha was recovering quickly by that time. She sat up
and shook her head vigorously. "Let go of my tail!"

Kalavek dropped her tail, looking up at her in a manner
that was surprised and hurt and just a little guilty. "I was
saving you."

"What are you doing in my secret place?" Ayesha
demanded, ignoring his logic to press her attack. "Now
you've ruined it! How can it be my secret place if you
know about it?"

"I can keep your secret too," Kalavek protested. He was
having a hard time trying to avoid having his feelings hurt.
He had come looking for the only friend that he could have
in the whole world, and Ayesha seemed determined to pick
a fight.

She just glared at him for a moment. "What were you
doing, skulking around to spy on me?"

"I was looking for you," he admitted truthfully, without
pausing first to think.

Ayesha picked herself up and shook herself thoroughly,
sending a shower of water flying. Then she turned and
glared at him, more fiercely than ever. "And who said that
I needed you?"

Kalavek blinked. "I never thought that you needed me. I just wanted to meet you."

She turned away haughtily. "Well, are you satisfied now?"

"No, not really."

Ayesha was so surprised that she turned to stare at him, but Kalavek only sniffed disdainfully and turned aside his head. "I am rather disappointed, to tell the truth. I just expected more of a dragon."

Ayesha obviously had no idea of what to make of that. That was not to suggest that she was placated, only confused. At least it did encourage her to stop shouting accusations and take a more reasonable approach. She sat back on her haunches on the grassy bank, staring into the waterfall and the ghostly rainbow formed in its mist. "You obviously do not understand at all. They have all of these plans for us, whether we want any part of it or not."

Kalavek nodded. "Yes, I know that."

She glanced at him briefly, a very doubtful stare, before she turned back. "You do not understand. They expect us to be mates. They have this idea that we have to establish a whole new line of dragons, just you and me. Do you know what you have to do to make more dragons?"

"Well, yes," Kalavek said, confused by her obvious distaste. "Well, not exactly. But I know that they do it a lot, and they seem to enjoy it."

Ayesha afforded him a second glance, one that went well beyond doubtful to absolutely withering. Then she rolled her eyes and sighed. "You really are such a child. Don't you know what we would have to do to make little dragons? We would have to lay an egg! Do you have any idea what it's like to lay an egg?"

"Well, no," Kalavek admitted, gallantly declining to point out that all the help that he was enabled by nature to provide during the process of laying an egg was encouragement. "Of course, neither do you."

Ayesha lowered her head, staring at her reflection in the pool. "It gets worse. A lot worse."

"It does?"

She lifted her head high, her eyes closed tight, as if she was about to howl aloud with despair. "Before we can be mates, I have to love you."

She punctuated that declaration with a visible shudder of revulsion.

"Oh," Kalavek sighed in sympathetic agreement. Then he paused to think about that for a moment, and he lifted his head sharply. "What is wrong with that?"

Ayesha bent her head completely around to stare at him, as if she was trying very hard to decide if that was worth the trouble to explain. She must have decided that it was not, and turned back to watch the waterfall. A long, heavy moment of silence passed and, becoming curious, she looked back over her shoulder and saw that Kalavek was just sitting there on the grass, looking completely forlorn and disappointed. She professed at least to herself to care little whether he was pleased with the situation or not, but his look of utter disappointment was a blow to her own pride. Although she would not have him know it, she already found him to be better company than any of the older dragons ever had been. They were wise and patient and precious little fun, while Kalavek was at least her age and size and possessed a curiosity to match her own.

"Well, there is nothing wrong at least with being friends," she said at last, as if grudgingly. "At least as long as you do not try yourself."

"I do not know how to try myself," Kalavek said, immediately looking far more hopeful.

"There is a place that my sire Selikah has shown me, not very far from here," Ayesha explained. "There are only ruins now, grey stone carved with odd figures, but it was once a place where elves dwelled. Can you fly very far?"

"I flew all the way here from the south," he replied proudly.

They climbed up to the top of the deep dell and high into the stones above and launched themselves into the cool morning air. Although Kalavek certainly did not wish for Ayesha to know, most of his long flight north had been made hanging to the back or tail of his mother or the other dragons. But he still had greater experience in flying than her, and because of that he was by far the better in strength and speed. He also knew that if he was ever to have his peace with her, then he must not allow her to know that. So it was that he followed dutifully behind, not too close, just over the tops of trees through narrow, twisting valleys and over the tops of sudden ridges. The day was bright and clear and the sun gently warm and it seemed good to be a dragon on the wing, no matter how young and small.

They had gone hardly more than ten miles, no more than a few minutes of flight even for little dragons. Holding her wings straight and stiff, Ayesha descended along a shaky and awkward path like a leaf on the wind right through a break in the trees, landing heavily in a shadowy clearing. To Kalavek it seemed far more dark, remote and ancient than even the rest of this old land, as if the dust of time had not been disturbed here in many a long age and left to settle deep. They were in the middle of a tumble of worn blocks of grey stone, once perfectly cut and laid, their smooth surfaces uneven and their sharp edges blunted with the weight of time and weather, and even the smallest was larger than the young dragons. They were laid out in vague lines and a few were still stacked into an unsteady wall, disappearing into the gloom of the deeper forest.

"Elves built this," Ayesha said, stepping closer to the largest group of blocks. "Watch this."

She lifted her neck high and just almost touched her nose to the grey, weathered stone and a pale blue light flowed out of her, passing across the surface of the block. The whole block of stone glowed faintly for just a moment, hardly to be seen if not for the shadowy light of the clearing, and ancient scenes that had once been carved lightly into the stone and painted with bright colors, long since lost in the depths of time, were brought forth once again. Ayesha passed slowly along the line of stones, touching them one by one with her magic and illuminating lost images of a long-forgotten past. Kalavek could see slender elfin figures dancing and feasting and making music in a time when the land had been less cold and dark, warriors in armor marching with centaurs and other odd folk into battle with creatures of the dark, and a tall and regal elfin queen on her throne surrounded by patient and devoted courtiers. Faces that were wider than those of mortal men, with large, high cheekbones and immense eyes in the shapes of tear drop opals, faces like those of some small but noble and cunning hunter of the dark forest.

The antiquity of the place was immense. Thousands of centuries at least had passed since elfin hands had cut and shaped these stones, perhaps assisted by the strong arms of centaurs or the cunning hands of gnomes. The land itself had changed since that time, so that the raising and wearing of these old mountains had tumbled the walls and nearly buried what had once been a great city. Centuries more had passed since the last elf had walked among these ways, perhaps contemplating forgotten ages when these halls had been filled with warm golden light and gentle song and there had been feasting and dancing in the forest, times now reflected only in magical images on worn stones.

"Selikah says that it is unusual that this place was spared during the long ages of restless ice," Ayesha said as the images began to fade away. "He said that he even remembers when there were elves in this land, and centaurs and all sorts of folk. Then the big time of ice began and everyone left for warmer lands. Everyone except the gnomes, of course, and they just shut their doors to wait it out. But only the dragons ever came back. The others were nearly all gone by then."

"I would have liked to have seen that," Kalavek said, as if speaking to himself. Then he looked up at her. "Do the dragons of your tribe know if there are any of them left in the world?"

"The ancient kingdoms are surely gone," she replied. "There is supposed to be the ruins of a city of the gnomes somewhere very near. Other than that they will say nothing, and the dragons of my tribe have not left these mountains in centuries. Yours has been a tribe of wanderers, so your dragons are more likely to know."

"I think that they have all gone away," Kalavek said sadly. "I want to see the kingdoms of the elves and the centaurs the way they used to be, and it is too late for that."

He stopped suddenly, lifting his head as if testing the cool breeze with both nose and ears. He spun about quickly, his head still lifted high. Then he turned slowly as he looked sharply right and left and back again, peering into the shadows behind the stones and beneath the trees. Startled by his actions, Ayesha stepped up close behind him, trying to see what he seemed to be looking for.

"What is it?" she asked softly.

"Something magical," Kalavek explained in a small, quiet voice. "Something dangerous. The sense of this magic is frightening. I think that it is looking for us."

"It is coming this way," Ayesha said, for she could clearly sense it now for herself.

"We do not want it to find us," he told her with certainty, although he needed no arguments for her part. "Perhaps the old magic of this place will confuse it, if we can move away very quietly through the dark places between the stones and bushes."

Urging Ayesha ahead of him, Kalavek indicated a path through the forest away from that sense of approaching danger. There was no question of a fight, not with two small dragons hardly half a year from their hatching, unable to defend themselves with either claw, fang or magic. Their only hope was to slip away unobserved. And that seemed more and more unlikely with each passing moment, for now Kalavek could sense not one presence of dark magic but several moving unseen through the forest and converging quietly on himself and Ayesha, well aware of where they were. The two little dragons passed as quietly as they could through the shadows beneath the brush and ferns, although Kalavek tried to keep them moving as quickly as they could, hoping to escape the net of danger that was closing around them.

A black shape emerged suddenly out of the forest before them, vast and dark as the night between the stars except for two piercing red eyes, and large white teeth snapped on air where Kalavek's slender neck had been as the young dragon leaped back in alarm. He scrabbled back as quickly as he could as the Shadow lunged at him a second time, sharp fangs flashing almost in his face, before Ayesha caught him by the shoulders of his wings and tossed him aside. He picked himself up and began to run as quickly as he could, hoping that Ayesha had the sense to follow him, and after a moment he could hear her racing close behind him. He could also hear the Shadow crashing through the brush and trees.

"Stay close behind me and go where I go," he called without looking back. "The Shadow is too big to follow us through the forest."

"How far do we have to run?" Ayesha asked in turn.

"As far as we have to go," he told her. "The Shadows can outfly us, but they are not built for running."

And that was true enough. The adult dragons, and the Shadows, were built like cats, with hind legs longer and more massive than their forelegs to allow them to climb and leap. They could be swift and graceful runners, but the inherent imbalance of their stance made it too difficult for them to run at speed for very long. The little dragons had legs more equal in length and so possessed an easier running gait. They could not stand upright or climb very well, but they could run with surprising speed and with tremendous endurance. Kalavek knew this from watching the other dragons. He also used their small size to their advantage, weaving his path around trees, between stones and under branches, cutting a straighter course when the larger Shadow would be obliged to check his speed and go around.

All the same, Kalavek had no idea what good they were doing except keeping themselves out of the reach of those sharp teeth, running too hard and fast to know whether they were moving away from danger or rushing into a trap. They gained on the Shadow and yet he was always behind them like a vast black cloud, thundering across the forest floor and crashing heavily through the brush.

The forest thinned quickly and was suddenly gone, and the young dragons found themselves running through a grassy clearing at the top of a long, steep slope, tumbling away to a swift mountain river rushing through white rapids far below. Fortunately it was still only the spring, or else they would have been running blind in the high grass. And then the Shadow was after them a moment later, his furious charge unobstructed.

Kalavek knew that they were in trouble. The Shadow was gaining on them now. The edge of the forest was too far away. Even if they could reach that safety ahead of the Shadow, they were still vulnerable to attack from the sky as long as they were caught in the open. Kalavek turned sharply and plunged head-first down the steep slope, running as fast as he could, and Ayesha stayed right on his tail. The Shadow could not switch direction as quickly, but he was able to loop about and was after them in an instant. His prey was in sight and the downhill run held his greater weight in his favor, and now he stretched himself for the final chase. He was coming up close behind Ayesha, close enough that he might have taken her with a swift dart of his head, when he became overbalanced with his long hind legs and tumbled end over end. The two little dragons darted out of his way.

Kalavek turned again and ran across the slope, hoping now to gain the protection of the forest before other Shadows could come at them from the sky. He stretched himself, running for all he was worth. At least Ayesha was still close behind him; he could hear her steady panting. Then he saw, just out of one corner of his right eye, a wavering shadow moving slowly across the grass to intercept their path.

"Here they come again!" Ayesha shouted a warning.

"I know," Kalavek called back. "Just be ready to do what I do."

He continued to run, watching the shadow as closely as he could without actually turning his head. The forest was too far away and he was frightened half to death, but at least some inner part of his mind remained very calm and practical. That large patch of darkness continued to move across the ground and he wondered which of them was the intended target, knowing that he had only one chance to guess right. It suddenly began to close with increasing speed, and it seemed to be aimed at him. He waited as long as he dared, while the shadow grew steadily in size, until he could hear the wind rushing over vast black wings. Then he stopped himself so suddenly that Ayesha, caught unprepared, ran up against him from behind, but he braced his legs against her weight pressing into his back, sliding briefly through the grass. The dark form of the Shadow shot past, crying out its frustration but too late to make a grab at its intended victims. Kalavek watched that menacing form with wide eyes, then he leaped up and ran again as fast as he could.

"Follow me!" he called to Ayesha. "We might reach the edge of the woods before he can turn back."

The first Shadow was returning to the chase at last, leaping back up the steep slope in long, powerful bounds. Fortunately he was still a good, long distance behind. What worried Kalavek most at that moment was knowing that there were more than just the two, and he could not sense the presence of any of the others. He wished that he could take that as a hopeful sign, but he did not trust his luck that far. He ran, faster than any woodland deer, and in moments the two little dragons disappeared again into the woods. But now the slope was even steeper, becoming broken and rocky. The forest was quickly becoming crowded with dense trees and tumbled stones and it was going to make for difficult running, but far less so for the small, swift dragonets than the large, heavy Shadows, and there was certainly no approach for them from the sky. Kalavek was finally hopeful of putting some distance between them.

And yet the Shadow was right behind them, a piece of blackness passing swiftly through the darkness of the woods. Kalavek was desperate, having no idea of what he might do to escape their pursuers when it was all they could do just to stay ahead in this deadly race. Although the little dragons were slowly gaining distance, he still doubted that they might actually be able to escape the Shadows altogether. The speed, strength and endurance of dragons was magically enhanced, and in his fright Kalavek was determined to run all the way home if he must. He did not know the true number of the Shadows, and he certainly did not know that most of them were trying to arrange an ambush to catch the young dragons while the two behind kept them running.

Soon the ground became so steep and uneven that the dragons could only run sideways across the slope. Kalavek came to a sudden halt, finding himself standing on a high ledge above a swift stream that leaped down the steep hillside in a series of tumbling rapids and short falls, descending almost sharply enough to be thought a single narrow waterfall. The green branches of the forest reached up to enclose the passage of the stream like a tunnel, the way beneath too narrow and low for a dragon or a Shadow to fly, certainly while descending so sharply, but perhaps not for the two dragonets.

"Do you think you can do it?" he asked Ayesha as she stood beside him, staring down into the rapids.

"We have no choice, do we?" she asked in return.

Kalavek knew that already. He leaped out from the ledge and snapped out his wings, drifting down more than actually flying. Branches flashed by almost in his face and he sometimes pushed himself away from stones that loomed up below him. It was all he could do to hold to the center of the way without crashing into the trees and the rocks, he was so shaky and uncertain on his wings. His flight would have been more steady with a little more speed, but things were moving past him too fast as it was. The descent was not very far, only some two hundred yards, but it seemed to last forever. Kalavek came out at the bottom so suddenly that he nearly dove straight into the small river below, but he turned sharply at the final moment and began to climb up the river with strong, quick thrusts of his wings. The trees still closed in close enough to make passage difficult for the larger Shadows, and the way promised to become even narrower as it ascended into the ridges ahead.

Soon the way beneath the trees became too narrow, the climb too steep, even for the little dragons. Kalavek landed on a large flat stone beside the stream and waited for Ayesha to join him.

"Are they still behind us?" he asked.

"I cannot say," she said. "I have not seen either of them since before the waterfall, but I still sense them."

"So do I," Kalavek agreed. "We have to go on, before we lose our lead."

They ran again, turning to ascend the slope until they climbed up and over the top of the ridge. The other side was no less rugged, and the young dragons found themselves weaving a twisting path through a maze of trees and great piles of grey stones. The forest was dense and dark, the deep canopy above allowing sunlight to penetrate only in occasional shafts of misty white light fading away into the blackness that seemed to grow along with the shrubs and ferns. It was as if the night washed into these woods to stand in deep pools hidden from the day above. The little dragons ran, small, swift shapes that hurtled past in a scattering of leaves and twigs, disappearing again into the darkness.

Kalavek had to choose his course quickly and carefully, for he was moving quickly and could see only a short distance ahead. He was slowed somewhat in finding a way through one area where whole groups of large round stones, dark and covered with moss, stood together in tight piles. Coming around a large cluster of rocks, Kalavek suddenly found himself face to face with a Shadow, leaping back almost on top of Ayesha just as sharp teeth snapped before his startled eyes. He looked quickly to either side for an opening and darted swiftly to his left, only to leap aside as a second Shadow made an abrupt lunge at him. Too late he realized that he had run into the middle of a trap. The Shadow drew back its head for a second darting attack, and Kalavek seized the moment to sit back on his tail and spit a tongue of dragon flame directly at its face. That startled the Shadow enough that it leaped back, and the little dragons took advantage of that moment to rush almost between its legs.

After that the way seemed open, and the rugged, uneven nature of the land and its crowd of trees and stones was more to the advantage of the little dragons than the large, heavy Shadows. They had escaped the ambush and were still alive, but Kalavek hardly knew what else they were accomplishing. He was frantic with fear, knowing that he should be doing more, perhaps thinking of some trick to throw off the pursuit. He saw the black shape of a Shadow racing to intercept them from the forest to his right and he turned again, hoping to slow this new pursuit in the trees and stones.

He saw another group of dark stones ahead and made a quick dash for a narrow opening through the middle, hurtling through as fast as he could run and right into yet another Shadow. Whether the creature of dark magic was waiting for him or not, Kalavek was running too fast and the encounter too sudden for him to stop, and the path gave him no room to turn. He tried to stop himself, frantically bracing his legs, but in the next instant he bounced off the Shadow's armored chest and was sent spinning half-senseless through the twigs and old leaves that littered the ground. He lay panting for a long moment, then lifted his head and shook it fiercely.

When he looked up, he was frightened and amazed by what he saw. Ayesha had placed herself between him and the Shadow and was standing her ground fiercely, her small back arched and her head well down as she growled in raw fury. Kalavek could not have been more surprised. Considering her initial reaction to him, he would have expected her to leave him to the Shadows. Then he allowed his head to fall weakly to the ground, as if he had been dazed or injured by the impact.

"Turn him around," he said very, very softly, the weight of his message carried telepathically. "Turn him around!"

If Ayesha heard him, she did not for the moment know how to respond. The Shadow snapped at her, and she sent a rather feeble blast of flame almost into his face. The Shadow drew back in alarm, then shot a sudden, brief blast of his icy breath at her. Ayesha leaped well to one side, again resuming her furious stance, but she had forced her adversary to turn nearly a quarter of the way around to face her. Kalavek watched tensely, knowing that they had to escape before the others could arrive and knowing that they were near. The Shadow snapped at Ayesha yet again, daring to stretch out his long, slender neck to its limit.

Kalavek hurtled himself forward in a single sudden leap, attacking swiftly and silently. He threw his entire weight against the back of the Shadow's great armored head and held on tight to the black horns. The Shadow had been crouching with his hind legs folded beneath him and his slender forelegs braced wide, caught in the middle of an awkward stance. Unprepared for that sudden impact, the Shadow was thrown off balance and crashed heavily on his chest. Kalavek had already released his hold and leaped clear.

"Follow me, quickly!" he shouted to Ayesha, hoping that he had not caught her by surprise as well.

The little dragons had run out of time. Kalavek saw the vague dark shapes of other Shadows rushing through the forest to intercept them and he knew that the one they had just fought could not be far behind, so he turned his course for the deepest, darkest part of the forest that he could find. They had been lucky yet again, but Kalavek found no comfort in that thought. They still had a very long way yet to go back to the dragon caves, fifteen miles at least; a distance the young dragons could easily run, but he doubted that they would survive so long. He knew that some of the Shadows would be taking to the air, flying ahead to find yet another ambush. He was becoming desperate enough to consider that perhaps he and Ayesha should try to fly. They could stay low, down in the tops of the trees where the large, heavy Shadows could not easily get at them.

The forest parted without warning and Kalavek found himself in a small, round clearing like a deep well in the darkness of the woods, a misty place where shafts of silver sunlight hardly penetrated. There, across the clearing, stood the most remarkable creature that either of the two little dragons had ever seen, even though they knew it at an instant for a mortal man. He was standing with his legs braced as if he stood ready to fight, although he was holding a long, straight stick in his hands and looking down its length in a way that seemed menacing for some reason that was not obvious. Kalavek and Ayesha pulled themselves to a sudden stop when they saw him, uncertain of whether this was a completely new attack. Then the Shadow was behind them, snapping his teeth almost in Ayesha's ear. The two little dragons leaped forward, running toward the man, for his attention seemed not to be centered upon them but the Shadow.

Suddenly there was a sharp crack like thunder breaking immediately overhead and the air was filled with thick grey smoke. The Shadow stopped short in his attack run and jerked back his head sharply, for he had been stung in the armor of his cheek by something that he had not seen, and he was more surprised than actually hurt. All the same, he obviously did not want to press his attack again until he knew for certain that the mortal and his stinking smokes could not seriously hurt him. He was outraged that a mortal would dare to confront him, and outraged all the more by his own fear of this weapon that he did not understand. The man was already doing something with the weapon, poking powders and other curious objects into the hole at one end and ramming them down with a long, slender rod. The two little dragons, quick to adopt an ally, rushed over to stand behind his legs.

"Now just you keep your distance," the mortal declared. "If you come any closer, the next time I will shoot you in the eye."

The Shadow hesitated, wanting to attack and aware that he could bring this mortal down in only two long bounds, and yet fearful of the weapon that the man once again held up and pointed straight at his head. Then the moment was lost, for there was movement in the underbrush on the far side of the clearing and a large draconic form stepped out to stand quiet and motionless, facing him. This was not the menacing black shape of a Shadow but a burnished silver that seemed to shimmer in the hazy light, and Kalavek knew at a glance that it was Halahvey. Selikah joined him in the next moment, an even larger shape in the deepest green that stepped out of the darkness of the forest, and a brown dragon that was Kalavek's mother Kalfeer. He hurried to her, hiding himself between her legs.

A second Shadow bounded out of the forest into the sudden clearing to join the first, stopping short when it saw the dragons. Even as the Shadows stared in surprise and slow rage, other dragons stepped quietly out of the darkness one by one, surrounding them on almost every side. The Shadows glanced about apprehensively, finding themselves in a trap they had never expected.

Halahvey took a step toward them. "Go back. The contest is at an end, at least for now."

"Old fool, the time of the dragons is at an end," the largest of the two Shadows hissed. "You have no place in this new world. This age belongs to us. Go back to your caves and die in peace."

"If that is so, then it hardly seems worth your effort to seek to hasten our end," Selikah answered. "We still hold that in doubt. But even if it is true, it is not in our nature simply to die without a struggle. You would expect no less of your own kind."

"You are doomed, all the same," the Shadow said coldly.

Selikah took another step forward, his head lowered, a gesture that was subtly menacing. "The dragons will live or die in our own good time. Go now, while we are still prepared to be charitable."

The Shadows hesitated only a moment before they turned and disappeared silently into the darkness beneath the woods. Halahvey stood for a moment longer, then turned to the other dragons. "I think that we should be on our way quickly. They might think to gather their numbers for a quick strike against us, as a last hope of getting at our young."

He turned then to the mortal, who was standing well to one side with his hat in his hand and his weapon on the ground beside him, a gesture that seemed friendly enough and even a little submissive. Halahvey walked slowly over to where he stood. "You still remember the dragons."

"I have heard about dragons," the man admitted. "I had also heard that there never were dragons, so I just wanted to see if you were real. I knew that I might have been taking too much upon myself, but when I saw that black dragon chasing the little ones I knew that it meant no good."

"That was a Shadow," Halahvey corrected him. "They look very much like true dragons, but they are creatures of evil. Who are you?"

"I am Einar Myklathun, if you please, Herr Dragon. A forester."

"The forest took care of itself a long time before your kind ever came into this world."

"That may well be so," Einar agreed. "The King pays me to go out and look at it, all the same. Foresters mostly keep people from coming into the woods and doing such things that they should not, but that has never been a problem here."

"Do you then consider yourself a friend of the dragons, and do you also promise to keep our secret?" Halahvey asked.

"I cannot say anything about my being a friend," Einar said, choosing his words carefully. "But I can promise you that I will never say a word about you to anyone, and I will likely convince myself that I never really saw you just as soon as I leave here. I have no wish of anyone saying that I'm a liar or a fool, beginning with myself."

"If such thoughts satisfy you, then let it be so."

Of course, Halahvey had not been listening just to Einar's words but to his thoughts, so he knew that this mortal meant even more than he was able to put into words. Einar was frightened of the dragons but only in the way that one would be afraid of something grand and dangerous and not as one would fear a natural enemy. He was far more afraid of the consequence of saying that he had seen dragons than he was of the dragons themselves. When he said that he would keep this matter to himself, he meant it. Einar Myklathun was, as were all Norwegians, a very practical man. Halahvey sent him on his way.

The dragons were sent out to hunt, and that night they roasted venison and mountain sheep over the fires outside the dragon caves. Kalavek knew this to be a celebration, although he could not guess whether it was for the joining of the two tribes or for the fact that he and Ayesha were still alive. He was still a dragon, even if he was very young, and his inability to protect himself from the attacking Shadows had annoyed him greatly. There were many things about what had happened that he did not understand at all. He had been told to fear mortals, and a mortal had fought for his life. He had been so eager to meet other creatures of Faerie, and the Shadows had disappointed him greatly. They looked just like dragons, except of course for their color, but they possessed a most unfriendly attitude.

"Why do the Shadows want to hurt us?" he asked as he sat that night with Halahvey and his mother.

"You were warned that the Shadows are dangerous," Kalfeer admonished him.

"I remembered that," Kalavek insisted. "I have been wondering why they are dangerous. Is there a reason they want to hurt us, or is it only their nature?"

"There is generally a reason for everything that happens," Halahvey told him. "To say that it is their nature to do this or that indicates only that their reasons must be essential to their very being, whether you know that reason yourself."

"Is that the answer?" Kalavek asked, confused.

"The Shadows have their reasons, which they have never told to us," the old dragon said. "All that is certain is that they seek the destruction of all true dragons for reasons that they find very important."

Kalavek thought about that very hard for a moment. "Is there any reason that you can imagine?"

"Only that they must hate us—or fear us—very much."

"Why would they?"

Halahvey regarded him with a thoughtful expression. "They might hate us or fear us, or both, because we are real dragons and they are not. They are newcomers in the world. Their origins are not known to us, and perhaps not known even to themselves. But they have not been here long. Perhaps they believe that they will become the only true dragons once we are all gone from this world."

"Are they right?"

Halahvey looked profoundly surprised. "Whatever do you mean by that?"

Kalavek had to consider his words very hard. "They have only just come into the world, while we have been dying away. The Shadow said that we have no place in the world, that this age belongs to them. What if they are right?"

"We do not think of that," Halahvey insisted. "Sometimes it seems as if there really is no place left in the world for us. But we live, and we wish to continue to live, and that is reason enough. It is not in our nature to simply die."

Kalavek rose and walked slowly over to the nearest fire as he thought about that. Being so young, he had not yet learned to take the unexplained for granted, to say that this or that was simply the way things were because he did not know the reason why. And it certainly seemed to him that there were too many questions that did not have answers. What had happened to the magic? Why were the dragons dying? Where did the Shadows come from, and why did they seek the destruction of the true dragons? And above all else, why did the dragons themselves never seek the answers to such questions? Kalavek thought that if he only knew why these things were happening, then he would be better able to change things. For the first time, he realized that the other dragons were doing little else but waiting, and hoping that things would get better. It seemed to him a little late to do that any longer, and he was well aware that the others were expecting him to eventually find those answers.

He sat for some time, staring into the bright flames of the large watch fire and thinking about things. Suddenly he became aware that someone was coming up behind him, and he turned to see Ayesha.

"I am not sorry that I pushed you into the water," she told him. "That was fun. Perhaps I would not have done it if I had thought that you were going to fall on top of me."

"Do you like me any better?" he asked.

"I like you just fine, I think," she said, sitting back on her tail before him. "Racing with the Shadows was also fun, at least to think back about it. It was not very much fun at the time, I remember that. You do seem to be very clever."

Kalavek felt tremendously pleased by that unexpected compliment. "You did not leave me, when I was down."

"I have been told that dragons always stick together, no matter what," she said. "You did not run away and leave me."

"No," he agreed cautiously, trying to remember whether he had done any such thing. All he could remember was running for his life, and he did not consider it to have been any fun even in retrospect. He was still suffering from wounded pride over the incident.

"Just do not expect that I love you, or anything like that," Ayesha declared suddenly.

"No, of course not," Kalavek agreed amiably. "Not yet, at least."

Ayesha glared at him for a moment, but he just stared back at her without the slightest hint of expression. At last she sat well up on her haunches and smiled, looking extremely satisfied. "You even have a sense of humor. I think that I might like you just fine."

⮞ THREE

FOR AS LONG as dragons lived, they seemed in a terrible hurry to grow up. By the next spring, the two young dragons were already quite big, fully as large in the body as a small deer if not as long of leg, and yet still perhaps an eighth or less of their adult weight even yet. They both possessed the handsome and noble features typical of dragons even at that young age, with the slender, thoughtful faces and deep, full chests for flying, narrow of middle and tail. Even the graceful double arch was already to be seen in their necks when they sat or stood at ease, as disproportionately long as their necks had grown in the past months. Kalavek kept his colors of burnished golds and deep browns like polished wood, while Ayesha was subtle shades of misty brown and dark green like a forest morning. The one and only thing that they had in common was their large eyes of deep blue.

Even dragons were not perfect, although they were beyond any doubt the greatest and most noble of all the creatures that have ever called this ancient world their home. They had been a very old and wise race even before the coming of the first of the Faerie Folk. Although they had always been private and secretive, habits that had since become their best defense, they were also true and loyal to those few who were ever their friends. They were defenders by instinct, champions of the weak and the disadvantaged. Their compassion knew no bounds and they were generous with all they had to give, both wisdom and magic as well as their formidable fighting skills. They loved their world and all life so deeply that it seemed that their very spirits must be the spirit of nature itself.

Even so, dragons could also be dire and deadly, their moods slow to change but nearly impossible to guess. Their anger was cold and calculating, and utterly relentless when fired by the flames of vengeance. They had often been called remote and aloof, both because they were jealous of their privacy and also for their regal pride and dignity. They could be as obstinate as stone and just as cold, or abandon their friends and allies without warning if they felt slighted or presumed upon.

Like most dragons, Kalavek was private and self-contained, enjoying more than anything to sit in some quiet place as he enjoyed the world and his own thoughts. He liked to ride the winds, to sit on some high, barren peak under the stars or in some deep, dark place of the forest. Even at such an early age, Kalavek possessed many of those qualities that were best in dragons. He was curious and bold, and yet his curiosity was guided by caution and reflection. He was proud, but his pride was tempered by wisdom and compassion. He was also a dreamer, and that was something completely unexpected of a dragon. He thought about the way he wanted the future to be, and all the things he could do to make it come true. If magic made the dragons strong, he thought about ways to find more magic. If wisdom was their defense, then they would be wise enough to know everything they needed to know and never make a mistake.

Ayesha also was curious, quick of thought and action, bold and impatient. While it was the nature of most dragons to dwell in their memories and dreams of the past, she lived for the moment. She wanted to know everything that could be known and to see everything there was to see. And she was a fighter, fearing no challenge and recovering quickly from any fright or adversity. She was like Selikah, her sire, and in curious ways more like Kalavek's mother Kalfeer than her own son. It was a dragon's world for all she was concerned, and Kalavek's worries for the future meant little to her at that time in her young life.

On a time it happened, while the two dragons were still very young, that Selikah took them upon their first great journey together. Far to the north, and then nearly a long day's flight out across the sea, was an island which held one of the last decaying pieces of the lost Age of Faerie. Indeed there were several such places, if a dragon only knew where to look. For only a few hours flight to the east of their own caves, hidden beneath a great mountain with its walls of stone and its cap of snow, lay Behrgarad, in its time one of the most important of the underground cities of the gnomes. But Selikah would not take the young dragons there, saying that there were evils in the darkest levels beneath the city.

So it was in the fading light of a spring evening that the small group of dragons descended through the mists and found before them a great green island of dense forests and steep hills rising almost to a low mountain near the very center. Indeed the dragons had been flying very high, riding the winds above some very wet and cool weather that lay over the sea, and it seemed to Kalavek from that height that the whole island was only the upper ridges and slopes of some vast mountains rising from beneath the waves. Then, as they came around one spur of the mountain, the little dragons saw on a small plateau before them the remains of some ancient city. It was not a large city, indeed only slightly larger than the village at the opening of the fjord where they lived but far more compact. Many of the large, pale grey stones of the buildings had been tumbled by time and the forest had encroached until it all but hid the city from the air.

Selikah circled around once and then came straight down to land in an open space near the center of the city. The two young dragons were right behind him and Halahvey, the last of the small group, brought up the rear. The dragons folded their wings slowly as they stood looking about, their long necks lifted high. Kalavek sniffed the cool air.

"Smoke!" he exclaimed softly. "There is smoke in the air. Have mortals come here?"

"I certainly hope not," Selikah said. "I had hoped that there might still be elves living here. Although I do admit that I have not been here in the past two hundred years, and I am beginning to reflect that even that can be a very long time."

"And I have never been here at all," Halahvey added. "As you can see for yourself, the great ice never came here. The seas changed at the time of the great ice, and a stray current kept this island warm and green while the ice was laid thick only a day's easy flight from here."

"And it is true that a colony of elves lingered here," Selikah said, and now he was speaking very softly. "You have been told that the elves changed greatly in the decline of magic, becoming small and secretive, and in many cases strange and erratic of thought, even quite stupid. These elves are most like the High Elves in the early days of the Third Age, and yet even they have changed. They have become shy and even distrustful. Ask them no questions, for they will tell their stories only in their own good time and only such things as they want you to know. And by no means will they give their names, except perhaps to us out of their love and respect for dragons. But we will not ask."

The elves did not remain secretive for long, not once they saw that there were little ones in this group of dragons. They immediately took that as a sign that magic might be coming back into the world, and their delight was boundless. They praised the dragons and made a great fuss over Kalavek and Ayesha, and that night fires were lit in the last great hall and the dragons were treated to such a feast as there was to be had. There were a few deer on the island but meat was still scarce, and so the dragons were gracious guests and dined upon fish that the elves had brought from the sea and cooked for them. But when all were gathered, Kalavek was disappointed to discover that there were less than two dozen elves in all. They were not doing as well even as the dragons, for they certainly had no young.

The elves looked very much like the mortals, or at least they had once. One might have called them willowy, but the fact was that they were thin, frail and wasted. Indeed, they looked almost as if they had spent the last few centuries hiding in the dark, for their skin was the lightest chalky grey and their eyes had become large and pale. Their long hair was either silver or white, although often with a metallic cast of gold, green or even blue. They were a quiet folk, shy and even furtive in their habits, a simple people compared to what they had been in the past. The dragons were smaller and more delicate than they had been, but at least they had kept their beauty, their wisdom and their nobility.

Kalavek expected that he would at least hear stories of the ancient realm of the northern elves, more intimate and detailed than the somewhat remote and aloof visions that the dragons mostly knew of the lives of the other races of Faerie. The elves begged such stories from the dragons, but they did not seem inclined to relate any of their own. As the night progressed, Kalavek finally came to realize that the elves hardly even remembered any time before the way they lived now. In their time they had been lords and captains, great seafarers and the finest craftsmen of all things delicately wrought on metal, wood and stone. But that had all faded into only a vague memory of a dream, and now they were only half-wild children haunting the lost ruins of their own past.

Very late that night, as the fires burned low, Halahvey led the two young dragons away to a nest that had been prepared for them. The elves had mostly grown too feral to abide for long in their own places of stone, and they had been disappearing into the darkness beneath the forest even though the night was damp and cold.

"We will leave in the morning," Halahvey said softly. "Have you enjoyed your visit with the last elves?"

"I would not have missed it," Kalavek said. "All the same, it has been a very sad and disappointing visit as well. In all the stories that I have ever heard, the elves were wise and noble."

"And you have now seen the wisest and most noble elves left in the world," Halahvey said. "There are still small bands such as this scattered throughout the lands, running like packs of wolves and digging for roots in the forest or stealing what they can from mortals. Some, I have heard, wage a constant war of petty mischief upon the mortal folk, whom they blame for usurping their world. Some even steal the young of mortals and invoke what remains of their own magic to change these mortal children into elves. I have never heard that it has worked, and I would be very surprised if it did. The fact of their own slow death, or perhaps their decline from their former greatness, has driven them all to their own form of petty insanity."

"They seem to me more like talking animals than people," Ayesha said. She was less sympathetic, for as she had come to guess the truth, she had found the elves increasingly frightening and disgusting.

"That is a fair qualification," Halahvey said. "Now, tell me what you have learned from this visit."

"That I do not want to become like the elves," Kalavek answered without hesitation.

"Is there really any danger of that?" Ayesha asked, her doubt and, to a certain extent, her indignation plain.

"That I cannot say," the old dragon answered. "Our pride and nobility has been very much a part of our nature for all the history of our race, and those qualities have sustained us during the decline of magic. The elves have tried to survive at any cost, and they have allowed themselves to forget what they were. Perhaps they do not regret the price, but a dragon would. The very essence of what you are is more important even than life itself, for you will take that with you into your Long Sleep Between the Stars. There may well come a time when you might have to decide that death is preferable to the type of hopeless decay that you have seen here."

The dragons departed early the next morning, claiming the excuse that they had a long flight over water before they would return to their own lands. They would have left sooner, but the elves insisted that they remain for a meal of fresh fish cooked quickly over an open fire. The poor elves were desperate in heart and spirit for something that they could not put into words even to themselves, for they had seen the little dragons and believed that there was hope that magic might be returning to the world. They were frantic for some reassurance, but all they could think to ask the older dragons was to implore them to return often. Many wept quietly, for the stories that the dragons had told the previous night had stirred vague memories of their long-forgotten pride. Kalavek pitied them at the same time that he was deeply embarrassed for them, and Ayesha would hardly even look at them.

But Selikah would not be delayed for long. The weather had been turning bad during the night and threatening to storm by daybreak, and he knew that they would have a desperate time if they were caught by a storm while they were still over the waves. It seemed to be a considerable relief to them all to leave the elves behind, and Kalavek understood now why the dragons would only visit every two hundred years or so. Given another couple of centuries, he doubted that the elves would still be able to remember them.

As he flew, Kalavek recalled the words that Halahvey had spoken to him the night before. He had indeed learned something important during his visit to the island, or at least he had been made more fully aware of something that he already knew. If survival in this new world meant change, then the dragons would not be afraid to change. They had already changed much since the decline of magic had begun, but the essence of what it meant to be a dragon had always remained the same. Kalavek was not afraid to change, but he already knew that he could never tolerate being less than he was, in the way that the elves had lost so much of what they had been. They wanted to live and they certainly still lived well past their own time, but they no longer remembered what it meant to be alive.

What it mostly came down to was the fact that, as young as he was, Kalavek already knew that death was by no means a loss of either identity or pride, and the possession of those two things was enough to satisfy him. This was not something that he had simply been told and had to accept on faith. He was an immortal, a creature of magic, and certain knowledge was his by right to hold even if most of the specifics were still hidden from him. The Long Sleep was a time of waiting for the Return at the same time that it was a period of transition with a fullness and being all its own, not a limbo of unconsciousness nor even dreaming as the name might suggest. He also knew that life was his gift and he had the right to hold to life for as long as he was willing to fight to possess it. The only regrettable and distressing part of leaving this life was the separation from those things that he enjoyed about life.

It was entirely a matter of instinct that demanded that he live, and that he keep the race of dragons alive even at the cost of his own life, yet even those things were transitory. The dragons were by no means in danger of dying away completely and forever, only that they might disappear from this world. That was hardly the catastrophe it might seem; the dragons would endure, and it might very well be that this world was no longer any part of their destiny. But Kalavek was not afraid, for the prophecy insisted that he and Ayesha were adapted to life in their new world and they would thrive and prosper, and that they would be the parents of a new race of dragons whether Ayesha wanted to lay that many eggs or not. The two little dragons were strong and growing quickly, their colors bright and their young magic promising, so there seemed little reason to doubt Kalfeer's prophecy.

By late in the morning, the dragons were having to climb higher and higher to stay above the weather, and even that did not spare them from fighting the unpredictable gusts of wind. The little dragons were tired already from long hours of flight, and they no longer had the strength left to struggle against the wind. They were reduced to soaring when they could and saving their remaining strength for catching themselves when sudden gusts upset their flight by buffeting them from the side, or forcing their way against steady headwinds and the fierce updrafts and downdrafts that moved through the hearts of the clouds. Inland, this would come to no more than one of the long, slow heavy rains that were common in both spring and autumn. Over the sea and fed by the warm currents, storms such as these could rage for days.

"The time has come to find the nearest land," Halahvey called, for he had been flying close to the two young dragons.

"Due east, then." Selikah bent his neck to look back beneath his wings. "We will find no land nearer than the coast."

"How much longer?" the older dragon asked.

"We have been heading south and east on a path to take us directly home," Selikah replied. "At our speed, we would have found land in another three hours at least. By turning east and heading directly toward land, we might save an hour of that time."

That was not encouraging news to the little ones, but two hours was much better than three. Kalavek did not yet have a sense of time that could tell one hour from two or even three, but by flying on top of the weather he could still see the sun at least occasionally. Coming down in the sea was certainly no option, for swimming in a rough sea would be far more tiring to a dragon than flying in a troubled sky. His only hope was to stay in the air until he found land, so he had better do just that.

But as time passed, the clouds became thicker and higher until the dragons could no long fly above. They were often pelted with icy rain and sleet, a matter of no consequence to their armor but sometimes cold and stinging on the leather of the wings of the little ones. But the worst was when they had to fly into the clouds, for it was dark inside except for the sudden flash of distant lightning. Once they went in, there was no way to know whether they would come out again in a few seconds or several minutes, or perhaps not at all. The dragons had no trouble at all flying blind, for they could not lose their sense of direction and they were flying too high to worry about running up against the sides of mountains. But the two little dragons found it very frightening. Ayesha was flying just before her sire Selikah, while Kalavek stayed close behind Halahvey's tail.

"We are over the storm itself now," Halahvey said, speaking loudly so that Kalavek could follow his voice. "I suspect that we will be within the clouds all the way to land, now."

"I thought that we had been above the storm for a long time, and that it had only gotten worse," Kalavek protested.

"No, that was all very ordinary rain and wind," the older dragon insisted. "It might not seem like very much when you are on the ground, safe and dry in your cave watching a good, heavy rain in a driving wind. When you are above such weather, it can be very bumpy flying indeed. A storm is another matter entirely, as you can see for yourself."

"When I am older, I suppose that I will know more about flying in storms," Kalavek said.

"When you are older, you will know better than to fly about in storms if you can help it."

Kalavek knew that well enough already, and he was to learn that lesson even better as they progressed deeper into the storm. Now clouds, no matter how thick and heavy they might be, are never as solid and heavy as they seem from the ground but more like thick fog. As long as he stayed fairly close to Halahvey, he could always see the older dragon easily enough. Perhaps he was feeling a little more bold and clever than he should have been; for as much a challenge as it was, he was beginning to feel satisfied that he could ride the storm and find land. Suddenly the entire world disappeared in a fierce white glare as lightning leaped through the clouds all around him. Startled and blinded by the flash, Kalavek lost his balance and fell, tumbling down through the fitful winds as he struggled to get the air beneath his wings, blinking from the flash of lightning and shaking with the tremendous crash of thunder that had followed and with fright.

The dragons had been flying very high, and he knew that he could fall a long way before coming anywhere near the ground. His greatest concern was for losing the others in the clouds, and each second that he fell only took him farther and farther away. At last he was able to get himself turned so that he was facing into his fall and he spread his wings to catch himself. Then he began to climb as sharply as he could, all the time calling out as loud as he could in the hope that the others might find him. He was thoroughly frightened now, for the wind was roaring, the rain was driving in his face and the roll of thunder was almost constant, sometimes all about him and sometimes miles and miles away. He knew that the others were not likely to hear him. And they would certainly never see him, for the clouds remained thick about him now, going on and on without any break.

He fought the wind, which now seemed determined to push him back and away from land. The rain was cruel and relentless, so cold that there was ice on his face, and the lightning seemed almost to be looking for him. All he wanted now was to find the others, or at least to reach the coast so that he might discover some sheltered place where he could wait out the storm. He had to suppose, as he thought about it, that the other dragons would have had to continue on with the hope of finding him later. If they had circled to wait for him, they faced too great a risk that they would themselves only become separated from each other. Perhaps old Halahvey had stayed behind, while Selikah had led Ayesha on in search of land. That was really the only hope that Kalavek had, and he doubted even that. Even magic would not have been much help to Halahvey for finding him in this storm.

Kalavek had no idea how much farther he would have to go to find land. He was now so tired that he could no longer climb back to the same height that he had been flying before he had fallen, and that would make it even harder for the others to find him. All he could do was to go on, stroking his tired wings against the unforgiving wind as he tried not to think about how far he had come or how much farther he might have to go. He knew well that he was in dire danger, and yet it still seemed impossible to him that his life should have been to no better purpose than to simply disappear in a storm.

He never even saw the lightning until it was upon him, a single great arc of blinding white that leaped through the clouds to catch him suddenly like some silent predator. He felt no true pain but a great, oppressive sense of heavy discomfort and he was unable to move, for his wings were locked straight out, all four of his legs were stretched out beneath him, and his back was arched and rigid from the top of his neck to the tip of his tail. His eyes were blinded in the glare and all he could hear was a heavy, droning buzz. He felt as if he had been held suspended in that arc of white flame for a very long time indeed before the lightning released him abruptly, and he fell. His armor was scorched and smoking and his wings were in shreds, but he was still alive. No mortal creature would have likely survived what he had just endured, but he was a dragon and a being of magic. Even so, he was badly burned and exhausted. All he could do was to pant heavily while he fell, while the icy rain cooled his burns.

But the will remained within him to live, and a relentless instinct told him that he must do something to save himself. A fall from this height, even into water, would certainly kill him at the best of times, even if he was not already half-dead from the lightning. He was no longer afraid, as if he was too tired and hurt to care, and he knew instinctively that that was wrong. Fear would have given him the will to try. Since fear would no longer serve him, all he had to serve him was cold determination. He opened his eyes and found that he was falling on his back while the wind forced back his wings until he could look up and see them, burnt and ragged above him, and he wondered if he even had enough of his wings left to fly. He rolled himself over and then forced his wings down with a great effort, even though he cried as the wind stretched the burnt leather to give him lift. The pain and the sight of himself told him that he was going to die and he wondered why he did not feel his call to his Long Sleep Between the Stars. All dragons heard their call when they were going to die.

But he recovered his flight at last and leveled out into a wild, hurtling dive and he wondered what he meant to do now, for he found that he did not have the strength to stroke his stiff, aching wings. Then something solid hurtled past him in the thick, dark fog, nothing more than a vague black shape in the mist at least a dozen yards away. He wondered if it could be one of the older dragons, for they could carry him to safety and he might just live even yet. Then another passed him even closer and he saw that it was the top of a tree, one of the tall pines of the high ridges. If he could have seen the ground, then he might have landed himself without further harm and then he needed only to wait until Halahvey found him. But the clouds came right down to the ground, and he was flying blind. Suddenly he was crashing through the branches of the forest.

The dark, stormy evening passed into a deep, cold night. The clouds at last began to break apart and great pieces of the storm seemed to move off inland into various parts of the mountains, still flashing with lightning and grumbling with distant thunder. Three-quarters of a bright, silver moon came out and cast her pale light across the forest, where the trees and the grass were still wet and heavy with the rain. Kalavek lay quietly on a bed of fern where he had fallen, and his eyes were closed and his ears laid back as he slept as still as if he was dead. His wings lay in ruins across his back and on the ground beside him, burnt and frayed from the lightning and now broken and rent from his fall. The plates of his armor, once golden and brown, were blackened from his burns.

The night deepened, as deathly still as if no creature still dwelled in the woods, not even a squirrel or the smallest bird. But as the moon rose higher into the night and the silver moonbeams crept across the forest floor, then there could be seen the shape of a dragon standing over Kalavek's broken form, as silent and patient as stone. She was larger than any dragon who yet lived in the world, her armor all shades of deep grey and the darkest blue like stormclouds against the sky, but she was a creature entirely of magic and without substance, and her form shimmered in the moonlight. She stood over Kalavek protectively, and her proud pose and concerned, watchful eyes would have reminded any young dragon of its mother. Her duty was to watch the storms for little dragons who had become lost, and lead them home once again. But she knew that Kalavek would be making only one last journey, and she expected that they would begin before dawn.

A sudden breeze stirred through the forest, where there had been no wind at all since the passing of the storm. It danced lightly through the leaves and when it died away, there sat the dark form of yet another dragon. This one was larger still and as black as the night sky between the stars, although she was no Shadow, for her eyes were bright but not hard. She lowered her long neck slowly and it seemed that she sniffed delicately at Kalavek's burnt and broken form, even though he lay some yards away.

"Are you so impatient to have him that you have come for him yourself?" the Dragon of the Storms asked, spreading her wings protectively as if to hide the little dragon from sight.

"There are so few dragons left that the whole world seems to hold its breath when one of them is dying," the Dragon of the Night said. "It is not the time for this one to come to me, and I do not want him. But I fear that he will come to me very soon, whether I call him or not."

"He still fights to live," the Dragon of the Storms protested.

"Yes, he fights to live. You gave him the strength of will to bring him forth from the storm and the lightning. Can you now give him life?" Her black form faded away into the night. "That is no gift that I might grant."

The Dragon of the Storms lowered her head, then looked down at the little one who lay nearby. Once that had been her own gift, in a time when the world had been younger and there were dragons in every mountain. Once was the time when she could have easily given life at a whim, but there had been so many dragons in the world that she had seldom felt the need to interfere in the struggle between life and death. But now the magic had faded and the dragons were almost gone and she was herself reduced to a pale ghost when she came into this world, stripped of powers and substance, even though she remained as strong and magnificent as ever in that place where the spirits of the dragons had gone. She and her sisters were elementals, given to the race of dragons to watch over and protect them. They had been there when the first dragons had been born and they would still be here when the last dragon died, and then they would themselves never return to this world.

So she sat through the night and waited for Kalavek to die. She wished that she might do something as simple as straighten his broken wings, but her touch was too insubstantial. It had always seemed to her so strange that one whose spirit was so strong should also be fading into death, for the greatest part of the life of any true creature of magic such as a dragon was its spirit and its magic, and far less of the substance of the mortal world than it might seem. Kalavek's breath was quick and shallow although he remained still and motionless, too far removed from consciousness to be even remotely aware of his pain. There seemed to be little hope that the dragons might find him in time to help him, and it was doubtful that their magic would do him any good if they did come. It would have been better for him if the Dragon of the Night had called to him, except that he did not seem to suffer.

Lightning flashed regularly in the clouds that lingered in the heights, and now a cool, wet wind moved through the forest, brushing softly through the branches of the trees. The moon passed behind the clouds, its cold silver light fading gradually to permit the blackness of night to creep back beneath the forest. The storms were threatening to return; Kalavek's curious guardian had ridden the storms of this world for a hundred million years, and she knew the feel of it beyond any doubt. Then a new, pale light began to grow, an icy light with a pale blue cast, not in the sky but there beneath the forest. The Dragon of the Storms looked up. There was nothing to be seen except the light itself, casting long shadows from the branches and ferns, but she knew that she was not alone. Indeed, she knew exactly whose company she now kept.

"I welcome you, Aeravys," she said. "I had not believed that you still endured."

"You know what I am," a soft voice replied. "The passing of magic has only weakened me. I will live for as long as there is life in this world."

"Have you come to offer help, or only to observe? You are life, and the gift of life is yours to bestow."

"I have been debating this matter with myself," Aeravys said. "I know that you would have me save him. Even your sister wishes that he should live, and she has always been a jealous guardian of the spirits of the dragons. His kind struggles to survive, but what is that to me when so many have died away into time already? Death of the old is often a necessary part of the origin of what is new."

"They want to live. Is that wrong?"

"He is the very turning point of destiny, and the dragons know it not," Aeravys declared. "When magic began to fade and the Faerie Folk declined, then mortals came slowly into being to fill the loss. If the faerie races are to survive, the dragons must bring magic back into the world as they brought magic forth the first time. But if magic returns, then mortal folk become superfluous in the greater schemes of nature. The matter is not as simple as it might seem. Will there be magic in the world, or will there not? Will mortals keep the world that they have inherited, or will the faerie races return to claim what they have lost?"

"Which is best?"

"Even I am not permitted to know the future." The light came closer and brighter. "Awake, little one."

Kalavek lifted his head and yawned hugely, then blinked like a lost owl. Standing over him was the greatest dragon he had ever seen, or at least the form of a dragon. All he could see clearly was a well-defined outline of a dragon in bright, misty blue light, as if this dragon stood between him and some brilliant source of blue radiance. But of course the light came from this curious dragon itself, bright enough to cast long shadows beneath the forest. Kalavek rose quickly and shook himself, then snapped his wings onto his back. Then he paused as if he had only just remembered something important, and he bent his neck around to look at himself.

"I thought that I had been hurt by the lightning," he said.

"You were all but dead, little one."

"Aeravys!" he exclaimed softly, looking up at the strange glowing figure in awe, remembering well Halahvey's stories of how she would appear to the dragons. Aeravys was the faerie name for the world itself. "Did you make me well?"

"It was not yet your time to go," she told him. "I wish that it were so easy for me to save all the dragons, and all the races of Faerie. But that would require bringing magic back into the world, and only you can do that."

"But the prophecy says that we have adapted," Kalavek protested.

"There is no prophecy that I know, only that you will not thrive in this world as it is now," Aeravys said. "The Dragon Lords brought magic into the world long ago, and only the dragons can find it again."

"But I do not know how," Kalavek protested.

"There is not much that I can tell you," Aeravys said. "When you are older, then you must do what the Dragon Lords did long ago. You must find the Fountain of the World's Heart and descend into its depths. I do not know what you will find there, for it is not a part of this world and so it is no part of my experience. Likely you will understand better when you go there and see it for yourself."

"I will try," Kalavek insisted.

"There are only two things that you must promise me," Aeravys said. "The first thing is that you must not begin your quest for several years yet, until you are fully grown up to be a very strong and wise dragon. The second thing is that you must have strong magic to protect yourself. The older dragons will be able to tell you where you will find such magic."

"I promise."

"Guard yourself well, little one," Aeravys said as she began to draw away, fading into the night. "Remember that the Shadows will oppose you at any cost when they discover the object of your quest."

Then she was gone. The frosty blue light died away, leaving Kalavek sitting alone in the darkness. Lightning flashed, closer now but still so distant that its glow barely penetrated the cover of the trees, and thunder echoed through the night. The storms were returning, and this time Kalavek meant to be well under cover. Then the dark form of a dragon descended through an opening in the trees, braking with quick sweeps of its wings as it prepared to land just before him. Kalavek hesitated, fearful of the Shadows after what Aeravys had told him; then he saw who it was and eagerly stepped out into the open. Halahvey had come to take him home.

For Einar Myklathun the forester, that same spring had not been so good. Anne-Marie had been ill all during the winter, never seriously and never in any way that you could say what was wrong. She just never felt very well, and she never had quite the strength to do anything she tried to do. Things were certain to be better once spring was settled in, everyone was quick to say. Frau Myklathun herself was the first to say that it was probably just a cold that refused to go away. A few dry and sunny days would be sure to do the trick. But spring came about as bright and warm as anyone could wish, as long as one did not have unreasonable expectations, and Anne-Marie only seemed to get worse in a hurry.

At last there was no hope for it, and Einar insisted that the doctor would have to come in. Now there was of course no doctor in that village, but every few days a doctor from a town up the coast would come down on the mail boat, stopping at every village along the way. In the winter he had only been able to come about every two or three weeks, but now that it was spring he could be counted upon to appear with the boat about every three days, which was as often as the mail boat itself came. Some of the older folk just shook their heads and insisted that this doctor was too young to know very much of anything, although they would never say that to his face since he was the only physician they had. But Einar, who was a very firm believer in education, suspected that younger doctors were likely to have been taught new things that the older ones would never know, and that suited him well enough.

And so the doctor went into the house with Anne-Marie and closed the door behind him, while Einar sat on the bench beneath the tree outside and cleaned his old musket. He waited a very long time, and he found that he was thinking about things that had never seemed very important to him before. That gun of his, for one thing. The old forester had told him one night about going all the way up the coast to Bergen to get the gun, and that had been in the year of seventeen and ninety-one, a good thirty-five years before Einar himself had even been born. The old musket had been a trustworthy servant of two foresters for nearly seventy-eight years, and Einar wondered how many times that gun had been shot in all that time. When he considered that he cleaned it more often than he shot it, he fully expected that it would last another seventy-eight years at least.

That led him to think about all the things that had changed. His friend Young Thorson the shopkeeper was now Thorson the Elder, and the venerable Mayor Thorson besides. Schoolmaster Berg had quickly become an old man in just the last few years, withered and bent with painful joints and contemplating his retirement, when he would go back down the coast to Stavanger to live with his younger brothers. Einar had been in the service of the King for the better part of twenty-five years already. He had married Anne-Marie these eighteen years past, and his son Carl had been born twelve years before. As he thought about it, Einar suddenly realized that he was no longer young. Now that might seem like a strange thing to just suddenly become aware of, as if the idea had never crossed his mind before that very moment. But Einar was a busy man in all the right ways. He had never thought about growing old, and so it had never occurred to him that he was.

Now as far as it went, Einar had in some ways been an old man for quite some time, at least by his own definition of being old as wise, patient and congenial, and he had never understood why so many people were afraid of growing old. Now he thought that he saw becoming old as they did, for it only meant losing all the things, youth, strength and optimism, friends and family, that are given to you when you are young. And from that moment on, Einar was no longer quite the man that he had once been. He had expected so much of life, and he had never anticipated that life would not be as delightful and exciting as he expected it to be. That had all collapsed in a single instant of disillusionment.

After a long time, the doctor came out of the house and walked over to sit down beside Einar on the bench. He did not seem inclined to say anything in a hurry, which was a generally good indication that he had no encouraging news.

"I suppose I wish that I did not know what is wrong," he said at last. "Then I could hope that I could do something about it. But I know what it is, and I know that I cannot help."

"I know that you cannot work miracles," Einar assured him. "I do not expect that even from the Parson."

The doctor nodded. "Anne-Marie has not been especially honest about her condition for these last few weeks, as hard as it might be to fault a person for such dishonesty. Still there was nothing that I could have ever done, no matter how early I had known. I fear that it will not be very long, perhaps no more than a few days. And I fear also that it will not be pleasant."

"Then it is perhaps just as well that it will not be long," Einar said.

"I will certainly ask around some physicians I know when I get back to Bergen in a few days," the doctor continued. "You never can know when some new ideas come along, and I must admit that I am away so much of the time. But I am afraid that it would take nothing short of magic."

Now for whatever reason, that word magic stayed right in the front of Einar's mind, for it happened that he knew one thing about magic that no one else in that part of Norway even suspected. It had been about that same time, one year earlier, that he had seen dragons in the mountains above the fjord. He had really not thought much about the dragons in the year since, preferring to put them firmly out of his mind. He certainly was never going to tell anyone that he had once seen dragons in the forest, and it seemed good to him that he should not believe it too strongly himself since the incident probably had never happened anyway. But herbs and wives' tales had done Anne-Marie no good in the past weeks and now the doctor admitted that he was helpless to offer any advice, so it seemed like a good time to think about dragons.

Einar thanked the doctor and saw him on his way, then walked slowly back to the house as he weighed whether he should make a journey in search of dragons. They had done nothing particularly magical and he could not recall that they had said anything about magic, although he admitted that he had been in their company hardly more than two minutes and both he and they had been anxious to send him on his way. But it still seemed to him a good bet that if there was any magic to be found, then they would know what to do. And since he had saved their little ones from the thing that had looked just like a black dragon even though they had insisted that it was not, it did stand to reason that they owed him a favor. He did not feel particularly hopeful that the dragons would help him or that they would even allow him to find them, his greatest fear being that they had left the area completely because of either him or their quarrel with the black dragons. Dragon magic was simply the only hope that he could find for Anne-Marie.

When Einar went inside, he found Anne-Marie sitting in a chair beside the fire and working at her knitting, still acting as if nothing at all serious was wrong. Indeed, she looked up at him sternly. "The King pays you well to watch over his forest."

"And has the King ever come to look at his forest?" Einar asked defensively out of habit. Then he caught himself. He had wondered how he might attack the subject of undertaking a long journey, for he was feeling guilty enough for needing to leave at this time. The dragons would not come to him. "Ja, I suppose that I should take myself all the way up the fjord for a look around. I have not been that way this year."

"I should think that you might need to make all of your long trips right away and be done with them for a while," Anne-Marie said. "It might be that soon you will not be able to get away for a while."

That was all that she intended to say on the subject, a brief acknowledgement that she knew the truth of the matter. Einar nodded. "This is the only long trip that I need to make, but I might be gone several days."

"You really should consider getting that dog that you have always talked about," Anne-Marie added. "I do not like the thought of you going off into the wild all alone."

Einar put a good supply of provisions in his pack and took up his musket, his hat and his coat, and soon he was away. The path leading inward along the fjord was perhaps the most pleasant walk he knew, and certainly his favorite. He could look down on his right and see the water just below him, while on his left the forest climbed steeply into the heights. Einar felt better for it within the first hour, or at least he found that he was clearer of thought and more determined of purpose. He actually had never come this way often, partly because there were no villages for many miles all around in this direction but also in part because he liked to save this, his most favorite trip, for rare occasions. And he had not been this way at all since he had seen the dragons, thinking that he had better make himself scarce in their territory.

As it happened, Einar thought that he had a very good idea of just where to find the dragons. He was going to look first along the low, steep mountain that stood immediately at the back of the fjord, since that was where the two little dragons had been going during the chase when he had found them, and all of the dragons had gone in about that direction when they had left him in the clearing. He knew at least that they must have lived west of the place where he had found them, nearer to the fjord. He suspected that this would be not so much a matter of him finding the dragons as the dragons finding him, and that he should be fairly obvious about the fact that he was looking for them. If they were willing to talk to him, they would come to him. If not, then he would have to find some better way to make himself known. He was determined that, at the very least, those dragons were going to answer him.

Night had already settled in as he reached the back of the fjord, and he would not have gone any farther that day under any circumstances. He made his camp in an open place in the forest where he would be in plain view of the mountains and lit himself a very large fire, which seemed to him a very clear way to announce his presence. Einar certainly did not expect that the dragons would come looking for him on that first night; he considered his fire to be only an overture, a statement of his presence, and that the dragons would watch him for a while yet before they were sure that he was looking for them. Therefore he was especially surprised when not one but two dragons stepped out of the darkness into the light of his fire.

"You have been looking for us," the larger of the two said simply. "That is obvious enough from your thoughts."

Einar had jumped up in fright, for he had forgotten just how large and fierce the dragons looked from this close, even if they were small compared to the dragons in the stories he had heard. He pulled off his hat and tried very hard to look respectful. "You must forgive me, Herr Dragon, but I had hoped that you would remember me. We met about this time last year when the black dragons were chasing your little ones. I saved them by shooting the black dragon with my gun."

"The Shadows," the dragon corrected him, obviously taking some offense at the comparison.

"That was the word," Einar agreed quickly.

"And now you have come to request some reward?"

"I would not want to give the impression that I am trying to force you to do anything for me," Einar insisted. "I just want to ask."

"Ask, then."

"It is for my wife, for Anne-Marie. She is very ill, you see, and the doctor says that he can do nothing for her and that she has only a few days left. So I had wondered if you dragons might know any magic that would help. I had to ask."

"The dragons pay their debts when they can, and you do not ask for yourself." The larger dragon paused, and looked toward the other one. "Halahvey?"

The smaller dragon walked over to the fire and sat down like an immense cat on the side across from Einar. His neck was bent in a great bow and he was staring at nothing on the ground, obviously deep in thought. "I am not certain that I can do anything. It is easy enough to mend the occasional injuries of dragons, but we are creatures of magic. The very substance of our being is different from their own."

"Is there nothing you can do?" Einar asked fearfully.

"I cannot say," Halahvey admitted. "I will need some time to search my memories. Go back home in the morning, Einar Myklathun. If there is anything I can do, then I will meet you there."

At least the dragon had remembered his name after a whole year, and that seemed to be an encouraging sign. Einar was not at all satisfied with having to leave without a definite answer, but he could see that the dragons were not going to go too far in obliging him. He had their word that they would try to help, and he could only wait to see how well they would keep their promises. Einar, of course, knew nothing of the troubles of the dragons. To him it seemed that they were very old and proud, but also very willful and arrogant and quite probably very dangerous. But the two dragons disappeared into the night without another word.

Einar packed himself up first thing in the morning and started back toward the village, wondering all the time if the dragons would come. The journey home seemed even longer, and the way that was only a few short miles by boat was about three times as far going in and out along the shore and over hills and ridges. As hard as he tried, Einar still did not find himself coming near the edge of the village until darkness had settled deep beneath the trees and warm yellow lights shone in the windows of the houses.

But Einar hesitated as he came nearer to the village, then paused as he came to the top of a small rise and could look down at the lights below him. Although everything looked just the same as it always had and always would, still there was something very different about the way things felt. The night was awake. That was how he described to himself the sense of alertness and expectancy that seemed to fill the air, and the light wind had a biting edge to it even though it was only cool but not cold. As he came nearer, Einar felt his hair wanting to stand on end, and he was shaken by a sense of great urgency. Something was happening, and he knew that he should hurry home.

The door of his house was standing open, and he was surprised that the doctor was waiting for him. He had expected that the doctor would have left again on the mail boat yesterday afternoon.

"We had not thought that you would return in time," the doctor said as he helped Einar remove his pack. "Anne-Marie became much worse almost as soon as you left. I thought that I should stay."

"Things do not go well?" Einar asked.

The doctor shook his head sadly. "I fear that it could well be any moment now."

Einar frowned fiercely. Even if the dragons did come, they might not get there in time. He stepped inside and put his coat and hat on the pegs. "What about Carl?"

"Frau Haugen has taken him home for the night."

"And Anne-Marie? Does she hurt much?"

"I have given her all the medicine I have," the doctor said. "I do not believe that she will need any more."

So much for dragons and magic. So much for all of his foolish hopes that he could have his way with fate by begging dragons to give him what no other mortal was permitted. He regretted now that he had even tried, but he still knew that he would have regretted having never tried even more. But those dragons had been so grand, noble and strong that the very sight of them had once led him to believe that anything was possible.

Einar stepped into the bedroom quietly, but Anne-Marie still knew that he was there and she opened her eyes to look at him. She had been growing thin and frail in the past weeks, but she seemed to have grown old and wasted only in the hours since he had seen her last, the very morning before. Then Einar found that he was frightened, not of her but of himself. Had it not been for his own determination, he would have turned then and run away. He did not want to see Anne-Marie like this, when in his own mind she had always been the prettiest girl in all the village. If he was going to lose her, then he did not want to lose his memory of her as well. Instead he smiled and sat down on the edge of the bed beside her, and he took up her small, fragile hand in his.

"So what did you see in the forest this time, Herr Myklathun?" she asked, her voice as soft as the breeze flowing through the leaves.

"I saw dragons, Frau Myklathun," he said before he was aware of his words.

"Ja, dragons?"

"Two big ones," he said, thinking that it hardly mattered. "One big and green as the leaves, and the other all silver and grey like sunlight on a clear stream. They said that they would try to bring you some medicine, but they have not hurried."

"You must not be so angry with your dragons, Herr Myklathun," Anne-Marie told him.

"Ja, vel," he agreed grudgingly. "They were just so beautiful, I never thought that they would not keep their promises."

Anne-Marie closed her eyes, but she smiled. "Off consorting with dragons, and never a word to me. You always were a curious man, Herr Myklathun. When you had first come to the village, I used to think that you had walked right out of the old stories. You would walk along under the trees with that musket on your shoulder as if you were a king who never knew that he had a kingdom. Then, when you would sit outside the tavern with your friends, you were more like a wise and crafty wizard plotting some dire adventure. It surprised me so when you agreed to marry an ordinary girl like me."

"Ja, every king should have his queen," Einar said. "You have been the best."

She smiled again. "You were always so kind."

"And you were so beautiful."

But Anne-Marie said no more.

"No," Einar protested weakly, but he knew that it was too late. He patted her small, cold hand gently and laid it back on the cover. "It was kind of you to wait for me to come home."

Einar rose slowly and stood for a long moment with his head bowed and his hands deep in his pockets, hardly knowing what to do, and then he walked slowly out of the room. The house suddenly seemed so close and oppressive, and he thought that he wanted to step outside for just a moment to breathe the fresh night air and see the trees. The forest had always been a comfort to him, perhaps because it never changed and it never promised to be more than it was. He stepped out the kitchen door and stood for a long moment behind the house, there at the edge of the woods.

He had forgotten the night and how strange and alive it had seemed as he had come down from the forest into the village. That same feeling was still there, as if it had been waiting for him. The light wind was cool and fresh, and it seemed to follow a will of its own as it moved in and out through the trees, singing some vague and distant song. Einar paused a moment to listen, and he was certain that there was music in the night that he could just almost but not quite hear. The tip of every leaf and needle held a tiny spark of pale blue light so that it looked like a frost reflecting the moonlight of some distant winter's night. It seemed to Einar that this small part of the world was awake this night, or at least caught in vivid dreams of an ancient time when the world had been young, bright and alive. A large, dark shape stepped silently out of the forest.

"You came too late," Einar said, his voice soft but cold with accusation. "What is the good of all your magic now? You came too late."

"We have been here since the time when the shadows had grown long and the night was at hand," Halahvey told him. "I had told you that our magic can do little for mortals, but our debt to you demanded that we try. Now our debt to you is doubled, but we still did everything that we could. For the last two hours, all twelve of the dragons of my tribe have been singing."

"Singing? What is the good of your songs?"

"Our songs are how we combine and focus our magic into a single purpose," the dragon explained. "Do you think that I would have brought every dragon in my tribe, even the little ones, to the very edge of your village if it had not been important? We have given you all that we could. We have done our best to keep our promise to you, and it was not enough."

"This is hardly a matter of simple promises," Einar said.

"I never promised you that I could help you," Halahvey said, restraining himself from anger. "I promised only that I would try, and I told you at the time you asked that this was a matter beyond my knowledge or abilities."

"Ja, you dragons are so great and wonderful!" Einar shouted as the dragon turned and walked slowly back into the forest. "What do you know of mortal life and death? Everything you want, magic brings it to you. No doubt you sit on your mountain and watch the world roll by for thousands of years with never a thought of need or concern. What good are you? If ever I should see your kind in the forest again, I will likely just shoot you!"

Then Einar fell silent, for the dragon had disappeared into the night.

✦ FOUR

THE SEASONS PASSED and Kalavek grew quickly into a large, slender dragon. Although he was yet to reach his full weight by the spring of his twelfth year, he was quickly reaching his adult proportions. He was promising to be the largest of all the living dragons, larger even than Selikah, long-limbed and large of wing and very powerful in his chest and neck. His colors of brown and gold deepened to a metallic sheen as the plates of his armor grew to nearly their full size and thickness. Ayesha was only noticeably smaller, and yet she also promised to be as large as her sire Selikah. Her own colors were the shades of the deep inner forest on a sunny morning, deep browns and greens.

That spring of their twelfth year made a very big difference to Ayesha. She began to feel such things and entertain such thoughts as she had never before experienced in all her life, and it all seemed to have something to do with Kalavek. She detested the very sight of him so much that she could kill him, and yet she missed his company so much that she could hardly stand to be alone. Some nights she would lay close beside him in the chamber they shared and sleep content, while on other nights she would feel so anxious and restless that she would fly and climb the high ridges until the sky turned pale with dawn. She felt as if she was being pulled in every direction all at the same time. Those final frantic stages of growing up were not easy for female dragons. Kalavek had been going through this himself for most of his life, but at a much slower and more manageable rate.

Then, one afternoon, Kalavek found Ayesha lying curled up on the turf beside their little pool, her neck and tail looped around as if she slept. She rolled her eyes up to look at him as he drifted down into the dell, but she did not stir. Kalavek folded away his wings as he glanced at the pool and the narrow waterfall that had never failed in all the time that they had been coming here. There were no rainbows this day; the sky was filled with the towering clouds of threatening storms.

"You look sad," he observed.

"I came to swim," she said, and she sounded sad. "But the pool just keeps getting smaller and smaller, and it shrank so much during this last winter that I can hardly swim in it anymore at all."

Kalavek sat back on his tail, looking quietly amused. "I have noticed that sort of thing happening myself. If the world gets any smaller, then we will be able to head out to sea and fly right around the world faster than the sun. We are no longer children, my friend."

Ayesha lifted her head and rubbed the side of her muzzle against his own, but she seemed even sadder than before. "Time passes too quickly."

"We have all of our lives before us."

"Even if we live a hundred million years, we will never ever be young again," she complained. "I often wonder about mortals. They know all their lives that they do not have very long. They even have a vague idea of when they are going to die. How can they endure that? They must be incredibly sad creatures indeed. Einar is the only mortal that I have ever met, and he seemed so sad."

Kalavek bent his neck well around to look over his shoulder, although only the grey stone of the valley wall lay behind him. "Have you ever flown over the lower fjord early in the night? Sometimes in the distance you will hear bells or music, or even singing. The lights of their village always seem to be so warm and comforting. I am not so certain that they are very sad. They are not creatures of magic, and not even immortal. But they are perfectly adapted for their own place in this world, perhaps better so than ourselves. For one thing, they have their own scheme for being prosperous and happy."

Ayesha lifted her head to look at him. "What is that?"

"They keep themselves very busy." He glanced at her. "You should see the way they live. They need so much to survive. Put them in the woods and they starve. They are slow and awkward and possess no natural weapons. Take away their wrappings and they die. Nature has made it impossible for them to live as we do. They have to stay busy all the time doing the things and making the things they need to stay alive."

Ayesha sat up on her haunches. "You've been down to their village to watch them."

"No, I have never approached them so closely," he assured her. "But I have watched them when I could, especially when they are out on their boats. And there is an easier way to find answers."

"You asked Halahvey," she assumed. That was Halahvey's favorite saying on the subject. The easiest way to find answers is to ask; the surest way is to find out for yourself. Ayesha elected to take that advice on its face value. "We could go and spy upon them. We could hide in the trees and watch them."

"What, now?"

"Certainly. If we wait any longer, we will be too big to hide."

There was just enough logic in that to satisfy Kalavek. He had been wanting another close look at the mortal village for a very long time himself and he was surprised to find Ayesha in the mood for it; she had always professed to have absolutely no use for mortals. "If you really want, this might be a very good time for it. The boats have all gone out to catch fish, so there might not be too many of them about."

Now this was something that the two young dragons knew they should not be doing. Perhaps the only danger they faced was the danger of discovery, but that was danger enough. Selikah's tribe had lived in this land before the coming of the first Norsemen, before even the Lapps had arrived to follow the wandering reindeer. But it was a lure that no dragon could resist. Dragons were immortal. The things in life that were most important to them would seem inconsequential to most men, while the things that men cherished often had no meaning to dragons. They cared nothing for wealth or possession, things they did not need or could not use, or would only burden them in their travels.

No, the treasures of the dragons were abstract things. Magic they hoarded jealously. Wisdom and knowledge were two things they cultivated with perfect care. Above all else, dragons lived for new experiences. Measured against eternity, it was the only way to keep so long a life from becoming tedious and dull. They nibbled at the richness of life; they never tried to do everything all at once, but would savor an experience or anticipate some important event for years or even centuries. For mortals, who lived their short lives in such a hurry, it often seemed that the dragons never did much or accomplished anything. But dragons could spend many happy years just sitting beneath the stars as they walked and flew, sang and loved in their memories, which remained as clear and fresh to them as the living world around them even after a million years.

But it was hard for young dragons to be so patient.

The village itself sat atop the bend where it seemed that the broad fjord widened out just before it joined the sea. The little town occupied the only large area of fairly level ground to be seen—and even that was not much. This was a fishing village of some five to six hundred sturdy wooden houses, most of them clean and white with bright trim, and so a somewhat large settlement for the southwest coast of Norway. The largest part of the village was grouped together in a tight knot along the piers, together with a couple of small warehouses and most of the shops. The rest were scattered loosely along the lower edge of the steeply climbing slope that rose immediately behind the village, the eaves of the forest washing down over their roofs.

The two dragons thought that they might be best able to stay under cover if they approached through the forest and then remained on the outskirts of the village, higher up the slopes of its eastern end and deepest within the fjord. Stealth and cunning were their native talents, but these two young dragons were quickly approaching their full growth and already quite as large and heavy as horses. At least their keen sight and hearing permitted them to keep their distance and still see and hear all that they could want. And being creatures of magic, they carried very little scent that any mortal nose could catch; they were not likely to upset the village dogs as long as they were careful about the noise they made.

It did seem that Kalavek had been right about the fishing fleet, for there was no one about. The two dragons crept along the edge of the woods, passing close by several rather rustic-looking houses built of heavy planks. Patches of gardens had been tilled but it was still too early in the spring and the nights still too cold for anything to grow. Kalavek wondered briefly what manner of plants men might like well enough to cultivate. Dragons were fond of berries and fruit, when they could find enough to serve them for a bite, and they gathered herbs of many types to cook with their meat and fish. But they would not dig for roots.

Ayesha suddenly paused and lifted her head, breathing deeply with closed eyes. "What is that delightful scent?"

"Hush," Kalavek warned, reminding her to speak very softly. Then he turned his own long nose to the breeze. Although their elders had told them of the feasts of the Faerie Folk in ages now long past, the two young dragons knew nothing of hot bread and pastries. Already they had found one aspect of mortal life that had caught their interest.

Kalavek pushed farther into the opening, already entertaining thoughts of following that scent to its source and helping himself to certain delicacies that did not belong to him. Dragons possessed no real concept of property, and their attitudes toward food were absolutely predatory. He pushed his way very slowly and carefully through the last line of brush until he stood in the open yard behind a large rustic house. This was the last house in the line along the narrow road, on the very edge of the village just before the road dwindled to a trail that disappeared into the woods. Suddenly Kalavek knew that he had been here before, many years ago, for this was Einar's house.

If Kalavek had known more about the ways of men, he would have been better aware of his danger. This house was very large; unlike most of those farther down in the village, it was only a single story, with a high, steep roof and deep eaves. There was a large yard behind, enclosed by a rough wooden fence, and a long, narrow outbuilding like a small barn and stables. There were hens and geese in the yard, and a pair of sleeping dogs near the back door. The beasts curiously took no notice of the two dragons.

Kalavek just stood for a long moment, his head lifted high and heedless of his danger. Dragons were creatures of magic, and he had thought that he knew all there was about magic. He had certainly believed that magic had been disappearing from the world for a very long time. Now he found himself standing on the edge of a pool of magic unlike any that he had ever known.

He had always thought of mortals as the opposite of Faerie Folk, creatures lacking in any magic, dreary and shallow. But they possessed a curious magic all their own, completely different from any other magic that had ever existed in the world. He must have missed it on that first and only visit to the mortal village years ago, for the dragons had been so involved in their own song of magic. It was a magic that did nothing, serving no purpose, offering nothing that could be used to any effect. It just was, like a bright flower standing alone in the dark places of the forest. There was a comfortable sense to this place, the sense of what mortal men would call home. Bright shafts of silver sunlight filtered down through the trees, and a cool breeze stirred through the trees.

"Magic," Kalavek said softly. "Mortals have magic of their own, and they probably do not even know it."

"Who would have thought?" Ayesha asked in wonder. "Why, they might even have souls."

"Quietly," he warned. "Someone is coming."

He looked around quickly, but he saw no better place to hide than the forest behind them. Ayesha was more inventive. She hurried to a large tree that stood over the road, then rose to her hind legs and pulled herself up into the thick lower branches. She intended to miss nothing, if she could help it. Kalavek considered it madness, but he had only a nervous moment to consider the alternatives. He pulled himself into the branches beside her. The two young dragons climbed as high as they dared, holding to the branches to either side of the trunk, then took a firm grip with their hands and held themselves completely motionless. Dragons were used to sitting for hours without moving at all, but they generally did not climb trees.

The last branch had stopped shaking and the last leaf had just settled to the ground when a pair of mortal folk appeared around a turn in the road. They were both very young, a man and a woman, talking quietly together as they walked along very slowly. The man was very tall and thin with hair that was golden yellow. The woman was also tall and slender and she was very beautiful, although not in any fancy or delicate manner. Her long, loose brown hair was almost the same color as her long brown skirt, but her features were still those of a girl not quite grown up.

"What of it, Carl?" the woman was asking, pursuing some conversation that they had been having. "You have been working for this so long, saving your money and all. Is it really so much longer?"

"No, Anna. Not so long now," he admitted, staring sadly at the ground as he walked slowly beside her. "Another year and then my studies at the University will be done, and I will be an engineer. And yet two years might as well be forever, and now I hardly see any need even to try."

"But why?" Anna asked anxiously.

"What is the purpose in working so hard?" he asked in return. "At that great university in Christiania, there are every year several dozen young men who have come from all over Norway to study to be engineers. Every year, several dozen young engineers go back out to all parts of Norway looking for work. Norway is a poor country in one respect, for there is just not all that much industry here. The shipyards in Christiania and Stavanger, even in Bergen, have all the mechanical engineers the university can produce, and all the rest go begging for work."

They stopped beneath the very tree where the two dragons were hiding. Carl set his bags on the ground, and they sat together on an old wooden bench that stood before the trunk of the tree, much to the surprise and consternation of the two dragons perched in the branches above. If they had happened to look up, they would have seen something that might have taken their minds completely off the very serious discussion they were having.

"Is there no solution?" she asked.

"There is only one that I have found," he said. "I would have to go to some place where great things are happening, where there is much industry and a need for engineers. I would have to go to America."

Anna glanced over at him sharply, a gesture that was hard to interpret whether it was just surprise, or displeasure, or perhaps even hope. But then she saw that he did not seem to believe in the possibilities of what he had just suggested, that it was an end to hope rather than a beginning. "What is the problem with that?"

"What is not the problem with that?" Carl asked in despair. "For one, there is my father. He cared little enough when I went off to my studies at Christiania the first time, and he made his thoughts plain enough when I had to return home last fall. He believes that I should stay here and lead the type of life that he has led. He can imagine nothing else in life."

"You cannot so easily give up all that you have ever wanted and dreamed to please the fancies of someone else, not even your father," Anna told him. "One day your father will be gone and you will be an old man yourself, and then you will look around and ask why it was so easy to cheat yourself of everything that your life should have been. But to make your life a copy of everything that your father has been! Carl, he belongs to a world that has nearly passed away. He belongs to the past, to a time when life was simple because it had so few choices to offer and the outside world was a million miles away. But the world is changing quickly. Today we are free to choose so many ways of life that did not even exist when your father was young. But I have seen that the only choice that we do not have anymore is to keep things the way that they have always been."

Kalavek leaned his head well down, listening intently. Even the mortal world was changing, and they knew it. But they also seemed to know some way to survive and thrive, although they were sometimes reluctant to change. How could they do that, and was it something that dragons could learn? He only wished that he knew more. The branches beneath him protested even this small shift of his weight, and he paused.

"Yes, I do understand that," Carl admitted. "It is something that is not possible for me to do, and yet it is hard for me to refuse. If I do go away, then he will have no family here. None at all. And he has never been the same since my mother passed away."

"But what would you do?" Anna asked. "Stay here to tend your father, after all that you have done? He may grumble and fuss about you going away, but he is happy for you in his way. If you do not go, then he will think you a fool and feel like a foolish old man himself, and then you will both be very miserable. Besides, Widow Haugen has not yet given up on him."

Carl smiled, grimly amused to consider the unlikely chances of the worthy Widow Haugen. It would do his father good; which was also to say that it was the last thing he would consider.

Then Carl frowned, staring at the ground. "Perhaps that is, in its way, the least of all problems. If I go, then it will be such a long time before I ever see you again."

Anna glanced at him briefly, a look that said a lot but one which Carl did not notice. "What do you mean, such a long time?"

"Years, I suppose," he said, and shrugged helplessly. "First I have to go back to college. Then I must go to America and find work. It will take some time to make a little money, to get a comfortable place where I can bring you to live. But that would all take so long. I would not ask you to wait, and I certainly have no wish to leave you for so long. There is nothing more to discuss, I suppose."

The day suddenly turned dark, as if a black cloud had passed over the sun. Kalavek glanced up briefly, remembering how the afternoon had been threatening to turn to storm. He hoped not, at least until he had seen how this odd affair would turn out.

"No, I suppose not," Anna said as she stood and turned away. "There is a simpler solution, but one that it seems would not occur to you."

She began to walk away, turning her back quite pointedly. There was a distant rumble of thunder and the storm threatened. But this time Kalavek paid the weather no notice; he was watching Anna. She was not walking away too quickly and she was also going in the wrong direction, away from the village. But Carl just stood there, watching her.

"Well, go after her," a slightly deep but smooth and lyrical voice told him, coming as if out of the air itself.

Carl did not hesitate. He took a couple of quick steps forward before he slowed. "Anna!"

She stopped, and looked at him over her shoulder.

He paused shyly, kicking at a small stone on the ground. "What other solution would you have in mind?"

Anna turned to face him. "You are asking me, Herr Carl Myklathun who knows so much?"

He shrugged. "If Herr Carl Myklathun knew so much, then he would have everything planned well. But what business is it of mine to plan anything for you? We have not spoken yet of what you think. All I know is what people say, and what I have seen and heard tell that other people do. It is often done that a young man will leave first, to find his living and make a comfortable home before he calls for his girl."

"Yes, and I have heard such tales from the other side," Anna answered. "All too often a girl will wait for years for the young man who never calls for her, and then she is no longer young herself. So there I have two complaints for you. I do not see that already I am such a grand lady that you must go before and attend to my comforts. And I certainly do not see that I should be expected to sit meekly in this village waiting for you to decide that it suits you to have me. I will tell you now that I would rather get on with my own life, with you or without you."

"Good for you," Ayesha remarked quietly, and her approval was very plain. Kalavek glanced up at her, and his expression was one of surprise and just a little uncertainty.

But Carl remained silent on the subject for a long time, as he reflected upon that. "Ja, I see your point exactly. It is not that I am trying to leave you here. It would be different if we were married already."

"Well, even that fault can be cured."

Carl waited in silence. Anna walked back over to join him beneath the tree and they sat again on the bench.

"We could be married now, this summer," she explained. "Then I would go with you when you return to school. I would work at something while you finish your studies and we would save all the money we can. Then we would have the money to go to America right away, as soon as you are finished with school. Perhaps we would even have something left over to live on when we get there."

Carl glanced up at her. "Is that what you would want to do?"

"I have no fear of such a life," she said. "Indeed, I welcome it eagerly. There are things that you want to do in life. Well, there are things that I want to do as well. Perhaps it will not always be easy or comfortable. Life here for me is easy and comfortable, but it is not very interesting. When you face a challenge and win, then you have this feeling that tells you why you were ever born to this life. Many people learn to be afraid to face the challenge, and that is the biggest mistake in their whole lives."

"Anna, you are a wise lady," Carl said, with a sad smile. "Are you now wise enough to know what to do about my father?"

"Wise enough perhaps to mind my own business," Anna told him. "Your father is a sad, tired old man who has become weary and disinterested in life, and there is nothing really that you or anyone could do to change that. Not if you stayed here and did everything you think might please him, and certainly not if you take him away and expect him to be content with the type of life you want."

Carl thought about that for a long time, and at last he nodded reluctantly. "Ja, you are right. There is really nothing else I can do. But this I will do, when we have been in America for a time and are settled in. Then I will write to my father often and remind him every time of how welcome he would be to come and join us."

"I cannot imagine your father ever leaving Norway, for he is as much a part of this land as it is of him," Anna said. "But I think that he would appreciate the offer, all the same."

"Even so, it will be a sad parting. I have worked so long and so hard to make this dream come true. Yet now that it is coming true, that wonderful, happy dream is in part sadness and disappointment. Is that the way that life must always be?"

A sudden wind rushed through the trees, a warning of a rainstorm that would not be more than just a few minutes to follow. The tree above the bench swayed slightly, a slow, graceful bend first with the wind and then back. The branches where the young dragons sat creaked alarmingly. Kalavek and Ayesha clung motionless, not daring to move, with expressions of quiet dismay frozen on their long faces. They rolled their eyes to look at each other. If Carl and Anna did not go away soon, the two dragons were going to have to come down in spite of them. And if they did not get out from beneath the tree before the wind became any stronger, then their troubles might come to a very sudden and unexpected end beneath a falling dragon.

Carl stood and offered his hand. "That is how it will be, then? We will be married now?"

Anna accepted his hand and rose with a small curtsey. "I could not very well refuse such a practical offer. Shall we have a big wedding, do you think?"

"The biggest, certainly," Carl agreed as they walked slowly toward the house, arm in arm. "We will be married on a bright, sunny day in the middle of summer. Everyone from the village will come to our wedding, and people from every village a hundred miles in each direction along the coast. Perhaps even my father will be there too."

"And his dog, no doubt," Anna added.

He nodded. "And then we will find a ship to America, and we will endure our poverty in bliss."

"See, perhaps you are a smart man after all, Carl Myklathun."

A cold, wet wind swept through the woods, shaking the trees fiercely and whipping up swirls of dust from the road and waves of old leaves from the ground. The storm that had been threatening for the last few minutes seemed about to break at any moment. Carl and Anna disappeared into the large house that stood at the end of the lane. As soon as they were safely gone, Kalavek and Ayesha climbed slowly and carefully down from the tree. With the wind rattling and shaking the trees so fiercely, they could no longer trust the swaying branches to hold their weight.

Kalavek stood for only a moment, staring at the house. Then he ran across the small clearing between the houses and leaped into the sky, fighting the fitful wind with long, powerful sweeps of his wings. Dragons could ride almost any wind once they were in the air, but it could be a difficult matter for creatures so large and wide of wingspan to get themselves off the ground in restless crosswinds. Being lighter for her size, Ayesha was nearly blown into the trees before she was able to find clear sky. But once they were well above the trees, they were able to ride the winds rather than fight them. They climbed quickly into the heights, letting the winds rush in beneath their wings and carry them upward.

Even as they flew inland along the fjord, the dark clouds continued to build swiftly into mountains and towering columns of storms. The two dragons kept to clear sky, soaring through passages like the chambers and halls of some immense cavern with walls of white and grey and deep midnight blue that flowed and billowed with the wind, illuminated by the occasional flash of distant lightning. Far up the fjord they climbed, into the stony mountains high above the storm. They raced the wind with long, powerful sweeps of their wings, two young dragons delighted with life and with each other. They were proud, graceful creatures of fierce beauty, their every movement and sudden pose as smooth and elegant as the motions of some ancient dance. Shafts of afternoon sun cut through the clouds, bathing the dragons in an almost magical light that almost seemed to sparkle upon the rich, deep metallic colors of their armor.

Kalavek saw something as if from the very edge of his vision and he turned his long neck for a closer look, then dived in close beside Ayesha. "Look! There."

Ayesha glanced sharply to her left, following his gaze. There not so very far away was a sight unlike anything that either of the two young dragons had ever seen. As fond as she was of rainbows, Ayesha had never guessed that such a thing could be. A great shaft of sunlight reached deep inside a pocket of the storm, passing through a curtain of rain almost like mist whipped by the fierce winds and casting a perfect rainbow. Not the vast watery arch of a rainbow as one can only be seen from the ground, but a small rainbow of bright solid colors in the form of a perfect circle.

The dragons circled around sharply for a better look. Then Ayesha began to move forward with strong sweeps of her wings, as if she meant to fly right through the middle of that ring of light and color.

Kalavek hurried after her. "No, do not approach too closely, or it will go away. Rainbows can only be seen from a distance."

Ayesha seemed to hesitate a moment, as if undecided between his logic and her own desires. But she knew that he spoke the truth. Some things of joy and beauty could be held and cherished and were as durable as time itself, and some things could only be glimpsed. Rainbows were like that. She had spent many hours of quiet fascination in her younger years watching the little rainbow that formed in the mist of the narrow waterfall of her pool, wondering what trick or magic would allow her to capture it. But it had proven itself a delicate and elusive thing, for only a tilt of her head or a shift of the wind would cause it to disappear. It had been a hard thing for her to learn that she could never have something she cherished so much.

Then the clouds began to shift. The light was broken and faded, and the rainbow melted away into the shadows. Ayesha lowered her head, and there was sadness in her large, dark eyes. But when she looked up, she was surprised and even somewhat embarrassed to see that he was staring at her. His gaze was steady and even, speaking clearly his concern and compassion. She lifted her head and returned that gaze firmly with an expression of challenge and amusement in her stern eyes, and yet there was also something that hinted of a hidden uncertainty.

She turned suddenly and darted away, quicker than Kalavek was able to follow. She was smaller and lighter and also faster, at least in a short race. She was not trying to evade him; if she had really wanted to be alone, she could have simply told him and he would have respected her need for privacy. She needed something, and she did not know what. She was afraid of something that frightened her unlike any fear that she had ever known, and dragons feared very little. Something was happening to her that she did not understand. She knew it for what it was and she had anticipated its coming for some time, and now she found reality to be far more than she had ever expected. Nothing seemed as simple as she had imagined it must be, and now she did not know whether she wanted to flee in fright or to embrace the inevitable. For now she only flew, knowing that he would follow.

Strong, cool winds swept over the land in waves, running before the clouds like heralds warning of the storms that followed. Those same winds swept her higher and higher into the mountains, flying low and swift over treetops that swayed and danced before the tempest, climbing suddenly over sharp, rocky ridges where the wind shrieked in the

stones and descending again over wide valleys that har-
bored meadows of deep grass and slow, placid brooks and
small forests of trees as tall and ancient as the world itself.
Suddenly she knew where she was going. In such a place
there was a forest as old and musty as antiquity where the
trees stood as tall as any in these lands, flowing like a skirt
over the steeper middle slopes of one of the great peaks. She
found an opening in the woods and drifted down on arched
wings around the trunks of trees so massive and tall that
their lower branches were three wingspans or more above
the floor of the forest, carpeted in dry leaves, and the storms
that shook the tops of the trees so fiercely were sensed only
as the sound of a restless wind overhead.

Ayesha turned and settled atop a great platform of stones,
great rounded boulders tumbled together in the deep woods.
She folded away her wings as she turned back around, then
sat back on her tail with her head lifted high as she sat
listening to the wind and testing the scent of rain in the
air. There was a feeling of being safe and comforted here
beneath the forest as if the wind and the storm were probing
the canopy of the trees looking for her and were unable to
penetrate her protection. Sudden flashes of lightning would
momentarily illuminate some portion of the leafy ceiling
above in white and shades of deep green, and occasional
wisps of the stronger winds that roared restlessly in the
treetops would find their way to the floor of the forest,
chasing through the drifts of old, dry leaves.

Ayesha lowered her head and looked down at the ground
below the boulder where she sat. Why was she frightened?
If she was so afraid of losing something, then what was
it she had to lose? She had watched the older dragons
closely enough in the last year, sometimes when they did
not even knew she was watching. Sometimes when perhaps
she should not have been. They never really seemed to have
lost anything, but they seemed so very happy with what
they had gained. They were waiting for her to bring their
race back to the strength of their former days, and in her
earlier years she had imagined that they had meant for her
to bear brood after brood, a dozen or more at a time all the

time, like some hapless fox or badger in the woods.

She looked up sharply, thinking that someone was there, watching her from behind. But there was no one. She was reminded immediately of the stories that her mother used to tell her, of the Dragon of the Storms. She was a true creature of magic, an elemental spirit as old as the world itself, lacking any substantial form. Most often she passed quietly and unseen in the dark places of the forest or in the barren heights, but when the clouds gathered dark and violent and the winds became fierce and restless, then she would fly swiftly in the edge of the storm. Not as a herald of the storm, but seeking little dragons who had become lost, to find them shelter from the wind and the rain and later guide them home again to their mothers. Or if a dragon died and became lost on his way to his Long Sleep, then she would lead him high above the lightning and clouds and on into the stars of a clear night.

The Dragon of the Storms was a friend to the lost, and Ayesha certainly felt lost. But the spirit calling her at this time of her life was the Dragon of the Dawn, who joined the hearts of dragons who loved and who gathered the magic that brought forth little dragons. The Dragon of the Dawn had stolen her heart and given it to Kalavek, and she loved him. But there was also the Dragon of the Night, as black as any Shadow but with soft eyes, who watched over the spirits of all the dragons who had ever lived and died and who was now more powerful than any of her sisters, for the dragons were nearly all dead and she was jealous of those few who still lived.

But Ayesha was no longer a simple child. She knew that the Dragon of the Storms and her sisters had faded from the world long ago, like so much else that was magical. Ayesha was nearly a grown-up dragon, facing the first and most important mature decision of her life. She knew already what the answer must be.

She looked up to see that Kalavek was weaving his careful way through the maze of trunks. He circled around wide to come up behind her, settling gently atop the boulder beside her own.

"I could leave," he said, his head cocked inquisitively, his expression eager and hopeful.

"I cannot elude you this night," she told him. "I have no wish even to try."

Kalavek settled back on his haunches, encouraged and inordinately relieved and yet fearful to presume too much. He knew that he had been invited to court her, to entice her to sharing with him their first mating. He tried to think of all the things that he had seen the older dragons try but there seemed to be no pattern for him to follow, no rules to guide him, no simple tricks that promised success. The other dragons made it seem so simple and playful, something they enjoyed as a part of their lovemaking. Kalavek was not himself old enough to know that their experience spared them the fear of each other, the fear of failure and the fear of what must follow even if they succeed.

"It . . ." he began hesitantly, and faltered. "It looks like rain."

"Is that a fact?" Ayesha asked, glancing at him with wry amusement.

Kalavek bowed his head and turned away. "I have no words for such play. You must think me a poor, inexperienced child."

He began to climb into the higher group of boulders behind them, perhaps to launch himself into flight. But when Ayesha saw that he seemed determined to leave, she turned to him quickly, sitting up on her haunches and laying a hand on the shoulder of his wing to restrain him. "No. Please."

He turned his head to look at her, and there was amazement and some confusion in his large eyes. But then he lowered his head sadly. "What does it matter? I hardly know how even to begin to court you properly."

Ayesha drew back from him somewhat, turning her head aside in a gesture that was hesitant and demure. "What do I know about being courted? Have you not yet realized that we are both afraid? Please, stay with me a while. Talk with me."

Kalavek stepped back down to sit beside her, facing her across a distance that was intimate but not yet too close. "These words are not easy for me to say, but I do not mean them any less because of that. There are perhaps a thousand deft phrases and flattering remarks that I might invoke to capture your fascination and possibly even your heart, and I wish right now that I knew just one of them. All I know to do is to tell you what I think, and what I feel."

"I can find no complaint with that," Ayesha told him. "I would rather have one simple, sincere word from you than all the flattery in the world. This is no game of teasing between dragons who have known one another for whole ages out of time. We are not discussing games, but the consummation of our joining as mates, perhaps for as long as we will both live in the world. We have never had the chance to completely understand each other, as mates."

"You told me once that we would never be mates," Kalavek reminded her.

"Until this day, we were children," she said. "Now we speak of matters of grown-up dragons, so that is what we must be. What do you want of me, Kalavek? What do I mean to you?"

"Only that I love you, for now and for as long as I can foresee, so much that I could fly to the moon and shout your name to all the world," he declared.

He had taken his hint from her, for she had asked him a direct question and he had answered her frankly. But such sudden candidness surprised and frightened them both, and they turned away in embarrassment until they were sitting almost with their backs to each other. Kalavek sat musing for what seemed like a very long time, blaming himself for being a fool and wondering what he should do. He looked up. Either the day was ending and night had begun to fall, or else the storm had brought an early twilight. The trunks and branches of the trees disappeared into a roof of darkness, illuminated frequently by flashes of lightning through the leaves that brought no thunder.

"I often think of that day we first met, and you pushed me in the pool," he began to speak almost absently. "Then the Shadows chased us for miles and miles, and you did not seem to be afraid at all but spoke to me of how much fun it was. I was afraid of you from that first day, thinking how wild and brave you must be when I felt so small and timid. I was very afraid that you would never forgive me for making you so angry that very first time you ever saw me. I was afraid that I could never be bold and adventurous enough to win your approval. I was afraid that I had fallen so far short of your standards and you would never love me, but laugh at the very thought."

Ayesha glanced over her shoulder at him, and it was a surprised and rather fond glance at that. But he just sat there looking forlorn, and she sighed to herself. "I remember being chased by the Shadows. And I also remember, whatever you might say, that I was so frightened and furious that I hardly knew what to do. But you were there, and you led me away from danger. And I remember thinking what a bold and clever dragon you must be, and I have loved you ever since. I just never knew it until now."

She lifted her head and looked up, thinking of stars, but there was only the roof of the forest over her head, and the flash of lightning that she could not see. "Sometimes I would lie in my nest in the night and imagine that the Dragon of the Dawn would come to me. I used to be so furious because everyone had already decided that you and I would someday be mates and bring great numbers of little dragons into the world. But the Dragon of the Dawn would soothe me with words, the way my mother would stroke my neck and wings so softly when I was young. She would remind me how handsome and clever and kind you really were, and how loving you would be the most wonderful thing in the world if I would only allow myself."

"And what would you say?" Kalavek found that he had to ask.

"I would remind her that I had precious little choice," Ayesha declared. "But hearing her say that would always make my heart feel warm."

Kalavek looked over his shoulder at her, thinking of all the secret hopes and fears that they had each held for so long. He had never dared to think that she would want what he had wanted for so long, and he had despaired. But Ayesha was there before him, graceful and beautiful as the sunlight in the depths of the forest or the cold bright stars in the sky of a moonless night, and he thought that the very sight of her would break his heart with joy.

"A fine pair of fools we are, it seems," he said softly.

Ayesha smiled shyly. "We have so much in common."

She stepped over and sat close beside him, and rubbed her cheek slowly against the side of his neck. Then Kalavek sat up on his haunches and wrapped his arms around her shoulders and neck, drawing her close. And so they sat warm and close in each other's embrace, while the night deepened and a cold, damp wind shook the branches in the deep shadows of the trees above and danced through the dry leaves that carpeted the forest floor. They watched the almost constant flash of lightning in the treetops and listened to the distant, muffled rumble of thunder, as their love grew strong in the depths of the night.

And then it began to rain.

❦ FIVE

IT MIGHT HAVE seemed a time of happiness and contentment for the two young dragons, but it was in fact an anxious time. Three years had passed since their first mating, and yet Ayesha was yet to bear young. That was hardly to be wondered, for they were both still very young and dragons might pass through whole centuries between the bearing of their young. But the dragons could no longer afford the luxury of such time. They were counting upon the offspring of Kalavek and Ayesha to reestablish their race to a new age of glory, and they had to regain at least a shadow of their old strength before they were crowded out of this ancient world by the race of mortal men. And yet time passed and Ayesha bore none.

Now Kalavek worried about such things, and he had been quietly assuming the weight of responsibility for the fortunes of the dragons since their first mating. There might yet be no problem except that they were still very young, but he wanted to be prepared for all events. The making of a new life of the race of dragons began in magic, for they were creatures of magic. Magic was the substance of their powerful spirits and far more essential to their existence than their physical self, which was only a convenient cloak to clothe and serve their innermost selves. That obstinate core of magic was the reason why no dragon could ever completely die.

To Kalavek, there were only two answers. He could try to find a source of magic to serve as the substance for his young yet to be born, but that was at best a temporary solution. More likely, he had to undertake the quest that he had been given by Aeravys, to descend into the Fountain of the World's Heart and find the source of all magic. Such a journey would be a long and dangerous one, all the more so because he had no idea what to expect; the Dragon Lords who had first brought magic into the world had never returned and there was no way to know what they had done. In all the long years since, no dragon had ever descended even part of the way into the Great Well. Kalavek could not forget that the return of the old magic would likely mean the end for the mortal world. But if he only had the chance, he would still do it. The Mother of the World had herself told him that he must.

And yet there was one other thought that had lingered in Kalavek's mind. He wondered if he might find a new magic for the dragons, a type of magic that was not passing from the world, different and certainly more subtle and inert than any known before. A magic so alien to the dragons that they could not yet even sense it clearly in its native form. He was reminded always of the mortal magic that he had sensed in the village, and his surprise upon finding that men were themselves learning to adapt to a changing world. He often wondered how they had learned to survive.

And yet these were still happy times for the last tribe of dragons. For the first time in centuries they lived with hope, after all the time that they had lived without hope for any future but passing their final dreary years in their dreams of ages past as they waited to die. Kalavek and Ayesha were so large and strong and colorful, so curious and full of life, that there seemed little room for doubt that Kalfeer's prophecy was true. A new age of dragons surely must be at hand, because the heralds of that age already lived and prospered.

Perhaps the dragons were even able to forget that nothing was perfect in this new world, and that nothing lasted for very long. They had not given much concern to the Shadows since the two young dragons had been hatched, but now the Shadows suddenly attacked with only a few moments of notice. One summer evening they were gathered on the small plateau before their caves as they roasted their meal of venison over fires, when they suddenly sensed the presence of the Shadows moving swiftly toward them. Kalavek stood up swiftly as he listened with his inner spirit to a dark magic unlike anything that he had ever known. Halahvey and Selikah hurried to the edge of the cliff, staring into the night.

Halahvey turned back to the others. "Shadows, and they will be here in a moment. They mean to fight, I am sure."

"And we will fight," Selikah added. "If we do not defeat them, then they will never leave us alone."

The dragons knew that to be the truth. The Shadows were ever a dark and dangerous enigma, their manner and motives unclear. They were devoted to the destruction of the true dragons, but they had never given their reasons. From time to time they would attack and, after a defeat, disappear again without a trace for years.

Ayesha moved up close to Kalavek's side. "They are here for us. They intend to prevent us from breeding. There is no more certain way to destroy our race."

"That may well be so," he agreed. "If it is, then the greatest part of the attack will be aimed at one or both of us. We must be careful that we are not overwhelmed by their numbers."

"We will be watching," Selikah assured them both. "You will not fight them alone. Everyone get to cover now. Make them land before we try to fight them."

The dragons hurried back to the caves and the rocks that surrounded the edges of the plateau, where the Shadows could not come at them from the air with deadly snaps of their tails. Dragons did not fight a defensive battle on the wing if they could help it, where their natural weapons were too effective and far too dangerous for either side to survive. They might seek their enemy in the air but they preferred to meet an enemy on the ground, one place where a dragon found it difficult to bring a battle but easy to defend. The tribe melted into the shadows of the stones and into the thresholds of the caves.

The Shadows dropped down out of the night, vast, dark forms that were seen only by the fierce lights that burned within their eyes and by the reflection of firelight on their black armor. They descended silently on cupped wings, which they snapped to their backs at the same moment that they touched the ground and leaped forward into battle. Kalavek had been watching from the darkness to one side, standing ready to spring out at the largest and boldest of the Shadows. But Selikah moved more swiftly, suddenly darting in low and catching his opponent, a black dragon larger than himself, in a deadly hold near the top of the neck, and the two rolled thrashing and snapping across the clearing.

Kalavek selected his own prey, a large male that seemed to be the leader of the Shadows, and leaped out to attack. Their impact was fierce, with the dull, almost hollow echo of armor against armor, and Kalavek drove forward relentlessly with his greater weight and strength. He thought that he could win on size and determination alone. But the mock combats in his younger years with Ayesha, even under Selikah's experienced and unforgiving teaching, had not prepared him for this. Perhaps he could have taken any other member of this tribe of Shadows as easily as he expected. But he had chosen their leader, a warrior as experienced as Kalavek was naive, old, fierce and cunning, and as determined as himself.

But Kalavek possessed some advantages of his own, for he was larger and stronger and he was also very clever and resourceful. Their first few moments of conflict were furious but indecisive, a series of bites and snaps as they rolled across the clearing, first one on top and then the other. The Shadow broke away suddenly, leaping back like a cat to put the largest of the fires between them. The two opponents began to circle slowly and coldly, glaring at each other through the flames. They both knew by now that they had taken on an enemy who was more than either of them had expected. They both wanted a moment to think, to measure themselves against their opponent and to consider new strategies. Dragons and Shadows battled fiercely all about them, in the light of the clearing and in the darkness of the stones, but they took no notice at all.

The Shadow made a sudden move, a quick swipe of his armored claw through the fire scattering sparks and bright coals at his enemy's face. Kalavek ducked his head to protect his eyes and the Shadow charged him right through the fire. Kalavek was lifted up and fell heavily on his back and the Shadow was on top of him in an instant, pinning his head down in a hold that he could not break. He could not get at his enemy with claw, fang or flame, nor could he find the leverage to pull himself free. But Kalavek thought that he knew exactly what to do. This had been a favorite trick of Ayesha's during all of their mock battles, until he had finally found a way to defeat her.

Kalavek arched his back inward to bring his tail completely over until its slender, flexible end wrapped itself snakelike around the long, curved horns of the Shadow's head. Then he pulled back in a sharp, fierce jerk, shifting both the weight on top of him and his own just enough that he was finally able to get the leverage he needed. They rolled again, each one fighting for a hold, until they came suddenly to the edge of the plateau and toppled over the edge into the darkness below.

That unexpected fall had caught them both by surprise, but Kalavek was the one to seize the moment. He spread his wings just enough to right himself, but he refused to release his tight hold on his enemy. Plummeting together, they fell more than a hundred feet to crash heavily into the boulders at the base of the cliff, but Kalavek was on top and he forced his full weight through his forelegs into the chest and belly of his opponent. The Shadow arched its neck and screamed in mortal pain. Dragons were hard to kill and slow to die, and the Shadows no less so. Kalavek kept the struggling black dragon pinned to the ground, then bent his long neck and took his enemy by the base of the throat, sharp fangs piercing dark armor in a hold that he refused to release. A time passed that he did not mark, whether an instant or whole long minutes in the depths of the night. But after a time the Shadow ceased to struggle, and its form swiftly dissolved into loops and trails of black mist that poured away into the cracks between the stones.

Kalavek lifted his head, finding that he was standing alone in the dark boulders beneath the plateau. The sounds of battle were dying away, and he looked up to see that the rest of the Shadows were fleeing into the night, black forms passing before the stars. He spread his wings and lifted himself with long, slow strokes to the top of the plateau. The dragons of the tribe were still scattered about the clearing, some standing on guard as they watched the Shadows disappear into the night. Halahvey and Ayesha stood with his own mother Kalfeer over the supine form of a dragon. Kalavek landed and came forward softly and slowly, pausing when he saw that it was Selikah.

The older dragon bore no obvious sign of injury that he could see, and at that very moment Selikah rose slowly and unsteadily to sit up on his haunches and shake his head cautiously. And yet there was something different about his appearance, something that Kalavek had never before seen in a dragon. He looked very worn and tired. There was a faded look to his armor, the color dull and dusty, and the edges of his crest and ridges no longer looked so bright and sharp.

"Selikah, you are hurt?" Kalavek asked gently.

"No, I do not believe it," he answered. "I chose the largest of the lot, and bit off more than I could chew, it seems. And yet I do not understand it. I was giving more than I got, for it seemed to me that he was young and very inexperienced for all that he was cunning. I thought that I would have him when it seemed that every trace of strength and magic went out of me all in an instant. He was about to put an end to me when the whole black pack of them suddenly turned their tails and fled. How did you manage?"

"I slew the one I fought," Kalavek answered. "He was old and full of many tricks, and he taught me several of his tricks the hard way. I was lucky. I think that he was their leader. The rest fled in a hurry the moment he died."

Selikah lowered his head and sighed heavily. Then he looked up to see that Kalavek and Ayesha were watching him closely. He bent his neck to rub his cheek against

Ayesha's, then turned to Kalavek. "Tend to my tribe, the two of you. Be certain that no other dragon has been hurt. Then put more meat on the fire, even if you must go out to hunt. I am certain that you will be safe enough, just do not go out alone."

He watched until they were gone, then lowered himself slowly and painfully until he lay upon the ground. He looked up at Halahvey. "I do not have to tell you that I am called. You have lived too many long years and seen too many dragons who have known that their time has come to die. I do not understand why, but the spirit is going out of me."

"It does not seem that you have taken serious harm," Halahvey protested. "Perhaps you should not answer the summons until you are very sure."

"Oh, I will not depart at once," Selikah insisted. "If I am going to make a journey from which I may never return, then I will be very certain that it is time for me to go. I thought that I should never die, that even if all the other dragons of the world despaired of life then I would linger on, the last of our race. I could never see any reason to die, and I do not even yet. Reason, it seems, has little enough to do with it, and I honestly have little doubt that I am called. You must be the leader of our tribes now, and look after the last dragons as best you can."

"That will be a difficult task in this changing world," Halahvey said. "I must refuse that charge. Give it to the one who was born to be a leader of dragons in this new age. Kalavek will now lead the tribe."

Selikah lowered his head nearly to the ground and closed his eyes wearily, but he seemed content. "Young Kalavek is a wise and cunning dragon. The other dragons will look to him, if you do. But I will go to my Sleep easier knowing that you will be behind him with your long experience and wisdom, and that he is wise enough to listen to you."

Kalavek sat on the rocks above the clearing of the dragon caves, watching as the last light of day faded from the sky. It was late spring in the northlands, and it already seemed that night would never fall. He was determined to keep watch during the night, fearful for the safety of the tribe. The older dragons insisted that the Shadows always fled after a defeat, never to return for years. In their place, he would have attacked again immediately, when the tribe would be unsuspecting and unprepared. But he could not predict the Shadows without knowing their true purpose, and that was something that the others could not tell him.

Kalavek lifted his head, looking up at the stars. The spirits of all the dragons who had ever lived and died were said to be sleeping amid the stars. As he had grown older, he had learned that it was just a saying. The spirits of the dead dragons were out there somewhere, under the care of the Dragon of the Night, although the dragons did not know where. Certainly not as far away as the stars. But they had gone somewhere. Kalavek could sense them, as if they were forever on just the other side of some distant mountain. How many had there been, through all the long ages that dragons had inhabited this ancient world? Millions at least. Tens, or perhaps even hundreds, of millions. So much magic, knowledge and wisdom, creatures so great and powerful that even he was only a small, pale shadow of what they had been.

If a new age of dragons had indeed come to the world, then why could they not help him now? Was it that things had changed so much that the magic of their spirits had reduced them to exiles in an alien world? Was it not so much that the magic had gone from the world, as it had simply changed?

Kalavek glanced down, and then he rose to stand attentively as Selikah stepped from the entrance of the main cave below. The older dragon paused and turned his head to glance up at Kalavek. After a moment he turned back and continued slowly toward the edge of the plateau. Kalavek leaped down from his perch and hurried after the old dragon.

Selikah settled himself gently, almost painfully atop a large flat stone on the edge of the cliff, looking down into the dark, pine-filled valley far below. Kalavek paused,

approaching him with slow, almost stealthy step and eyes
that were filled with surprise and concern. Selikah looked
so incredibly old, so worn and tired, as if the weight of
every year that he had lived had come crashing down on
him since their battle with the Shadows on the previous
night. His armor had lost its sharp edges and now looked
dull and chalky, as if it would crumble to dust under a sharp
blow. Kalavek slipped forward and seated himself silently
on a stone to one side.

"The time has come for me to go," Selikah said simply.

Kalavek glanced away, blinking back tears. "I had not
thought that your injuries were so deep."

"Neither did I," Selikah agreed. "Dragons are almost
impossible to kill, and many times have I taken worse
in battle than I received last night. But I am called, just
the same. Perhaps my magic has become that thin and
fragile through these last years, and I just never knew
it."

He glanced then at the younger dragon, who was still
staring off into the night to one side, and he smiled fondly
to himself. Nothing in life held his interest now, but if
anything could have called him back to life then it would
have been the tears of the two young dragons. They were
young and eager enough that death was an enemy to wound
their hearts, and not a welcome friend for those who had
grown sad and weary with the years.

"I will not be there to help you and Ayesha in the years to
come in all the ways that I would have liked," he continued.
"You have been worried that the two of you will not be able
to breed."

"I am afraid that there is not enough magic," Kalavek
explained. "We have tried to sing for all the magic we need,
and even that has not been enough. I know that there must
be a way, but I cannot find it."

"You have hardly had a chance to look for it very far
or very long," the older dragon told him. "In the old days,
there was a place deep in the mountains, a special place that
only the dragons knew. It was a place that was magic itself,
in the same sense that we are creatures of magic. We called

it the Fountain of the World's Heart, and it was the focus of all the magic of the world."

"I know of the Fountain of the World's Heart," Kalavek said, although he seemed confused. "The world's magic came into being there when the dragons released the magic long ago, and at that time the dragons themselves became creatures of magic. Years ago when I was lost, Aeravys Mother of the World found me and told me to seek the Fountain of the World's Heart. But you know that."

Selikah was silent for a moment, his reservations plain enough to be seen. "It has not been the way of dragons to interfere in the natural order of the world. You could argue that magic has been natural and even essential to the world for a very long time, but you could as easily argue that there never would have been magic except for the interference of dragons. The sad truth is that, in the world that this one is becoming, it is proper for the dragons to die."

"There is no good reason why the dragons should all die," Kalavek protested. "Would there be any harm in bringing back the magic?"

"That is a decision that the dragons have been reluctant to make, for the world has changed and it will change again if the magic returns." He glanced briefly at the younger dragon, then sighed. "All of your life, you have wanted not only to return magic to the world, but all that could be salvaged of all the faerie races. You are the first dragon ever to think that you should do something about it if you could, while the rest of us have only waited for what will be. Very well. What do you know of the Cores of Magic?"

"I know of the Cores of Magic," Kalavek said. "Ayesha and I have sung those into being before. They are just inert magic. Magic that can be stored against future need, at a time when it might not be possible to sing so much magic into being."

"But those were only your own small attempts," Selikah said. "In ages past on the longest night of the year, the Dragon's Night, dragons from all across the land would gather at the Fountain of the World's Heart to sing, and as they sang through the night they brought forth a Core of Magic. A true Core of Magic can only come from the Fountain of the World's Heart, and they are reservoirs of more magic than you might believe. All the magic that you will need to undertake your journey into the Fountain of the World's Heart. As I recall, Aeravys told you that you must wait until you were older and far more experienced, and until the time when you had strong magic to protect you. I believe I know where one might be, and not so far from here."

He glanced at the younger dragon, and he seemed pleased. But Kalavek only leaned forward, watching and listening intently, and that pleased him all the more. "In past ages, this was a favorite land of the mountain gnomes. Deep in the hearts of these same mountains, they carved and built their greatest cities, hidden deep within the stone from the rest of the world. Cities so vast and deep that they sealed themselves within to wait out the times of the great ice. The greatest of all, Behrgarad, has its main gate not far from this very place.

"Now in those days, the dragons were the kings of the world, and many of the other races were glad to serve our needs. I remember Behrgarad from when I was young, and indeed not so very long ago my tribe would still speak on occasion with the surviving gnomes. I cannot now say whether there are any of their kind still alive, haunting those vast, dusty halls. But it remains that deep within the lowest level, you may still find a Core of Magic, left there by the dragons centuries past."

"The gnomes would not have used it?" Kalavek asked.

"None of the other races of Faerie could ever use the dragon magic. But there is one thing that you must keep in mind. No creature of Faerie can touch a Core of Magic. We are living magic, and the touch of magic to magic causes the Core to dissolve in sudden, violent destruction. I do not know how you might retrieve the Core of Magic. It used to be that the dragons could sing a spell to move a Core of Magic where they wished. But you will find a way, I do not doubt."

"And then?" Kalavek asked.

"When you undertake the quest to return magic to the world, you will certainly have need of such magic. But remember your history. You may change the world if you wish and if you can, but the last time dragons descended into the Fountain of the World's Heart, they nearly destroyed it."

He lifted his head to look up at the stars, then rose and turned to step down from the stone where he had been lying. Kalavek hurried to follow him, and only then did he see that all the other dragons of the tribe had gathered about the clearing, watching silently. Old Halahvey waited just behind the stones where they had been sitting at the edge of the plateau. Selikah paused for just a moment, and the two older dragons looked at each other but said nothing. Then Selikah moved slowly to the center of the clearing.

Then he lifted his head a final time to look toward the stars. Kalavek looked up as well. The stars seemed so bright, but cold and remote, but the night itself was tense and heavy, as if any sound of wind, leaf or stone would have been buried beneath its weight. Ayesha moved silently along the edge of the plateau until she was able to move in close to Kalavek's side. He glanced at her and saw that she was weeping, and he knew that he could not contain tears of his own. Dragons did not fear death, but that made the parting no easier to bear.

Selikah spread his wings and lifted himself into the night sky with broad, deep strokes, climbing upward in a tight spiral. And yet it seemed that he was almost carried upward on a gentle breeze, no longer the massive armored form of a dragon but something that had become thin and light, almost fragile. As he rose higher, his colors grew lighter until his entire form was glowing softly in a pale, misty white. But he began to fly stronger and faster as he left behind pain and sorrow and saw his destination welcoming him. Then the light of his form faded quickly into a few ragged wisps of pale mist, and he was gone.

SUMMER

The Season of Life

❧ ONE

WHEN SUMMER CAME warm and bright to the fjords of Norway, when the slow, cold, dreary rains of spring were past and those of autumn were yet to come, when the days were long and life was easy, then old Einar Myklathun would come down to the village and sit with his friends the Mayor and the Parson outside the pub. Einar was a forester, a man who had spent his whole life walking through the woods and tending the wild things in the pay of the King, and it sometimes seemed that Einar and the King were the only ones who gave much thought about the forests of Norway, which had been there long before either one of them. But Einar had never met the King and it was quite likely that the King had never even heard of Einar Myklathun, and so they both went about their business.

Einar was a forester in a small fishing village, and that meant that he was something rare and different from everyone else he knew. Perhaps that was why his only friends, if such companions of convenience could really be called friends, were the Mayor and the Parson. They were all three one of a kind in their own professions, the only one in the entire village. There were many fishermen, three teachers and two grocers. Even Ole Brinson the baker now worked with his son Lars, so it could be said easily that there were two of them. But there was only one Mayor, one Parson and one Forester in all the village. There would probably be Parsons until doomsday, and Mayors long after. But there was only one Forester, and it seemed that there would be no one interested in taking Einar's place after he had retired his old felt hat and his musket.

No one bothered to talk to Einar Myklathun unless they knew him well, for that was considered a dangerous thing for the unwary to attempt. He was a good man in the sense that he was honest and honorable. He did not go to church, although he did spend as many hours with the Parson as anyone so long as they met on common ground. In his younger days he had been counted a friendly, even happy man, but he had outlived just about everyone who remembered those times. His years of his duties in the forest had made him a quiet, private man. The untimely death of his wife had left him a bitter man. And when his son and only child had gone to America nearly ten years before, he had become a disillusioned man. The world was changing all the time, but he had found every change a disappointment.

Einar's constant companion in his old age and in a way the only family that he had left was his dog Torsk. He was not much as far as dogs went, except ugly. That indeed was how he had come by his name, for he had a flat, wedge-shaped head like that of a big codfish. He was lazy and would invariably fall asleep like a stone at any time and place he came to rest. He was not stupid, at least as far as dogs went, but his lack of initiative more than made up for any virtues he might have possessed. But he was loyal, and as constant as the rain in autumn.

But now it was a warm, bright morning in late summer, and Einar Myklathun had hurried down the road to the pub to meet his friends the Mayor and the Parson and share with them the latest letter from his son in America. He looked forward to the letters from his son Carl, and they certainly came often enough to please him. But they also made him sad and so he found them easier to read in the company of others, not because he found comfort in such company but because he did not have the leisure of brooding in public.

They would sit about the little round table in the yard outside the inn, where the innkeeper or his wife would serve them coffee in the morning and beer in the afternoon, while tiny patches of sunlight would sink down through the restless leaves of the trees and dance nervously on the grass and the road. Carl Thorsen, now Thorsen the Elder, had been the Mayor of this village for as long as most people there could remember. He was a round little man with a round, jolly face, a friendly, engaging sort of face just made for big smiles and mirth. But contrary to appearances, the Mayor was an unhappy little man who never seemed to tire of complaining about everything that was wrong in the world and with his world in particular, and how many problems there were to solve and how people expected more of him than any one man had to give. Parson Ondurson, on the other hand, was a man who hardly ever spoke, except at some rare interval to offer some slow, ponderous word of wisdom that really said nothing. He was a tall, lean man who was no longer young but far from old, with a long, narrow face forever frozen in an expression that was at the same time sad and pensive, and also just a little bewildered. Unlike the Mayor's round, cheerful face, the Parson's reflected the character of its owner very well.

And yet these three, the Mayor, the Parson and old Einar Myklathun, were held by all the village to be the local founts of wit and wisdom. Which was perhaps to show that it was indeed a small village.

So it was that Einar Myklathun came down the road to the pub and found the Mayor and the Parson already there and seated before him. They were gathered about that same little round table in the lawn where they would always sit when the weather allowed, and there was black coffee and pastries on the board before them. They both were in exceptionally high spirits, and that came as some indication that they had not been at it for very long. The very sight of Einar's face would put them in a more somber mood soon enough. But this morning even Einar felt good, because it was such a fine day in summer and he had a letter from his son besides.

"Good morning to you both," Einar declared as he took his seat. "Ja, and a fine, sunny day it promises to be."

"Sunny days are all very well and good," the Mayor declared, with a note of admonition in his tone. "Just so long as we do not have too many sunny days all at once. Then the forests would get dry, and all the fjord could go up in one great fire."

"Fires are not so common in Norway," Einar reminded him.

"Of course, because it rains so much!" the Mayor exclaimed. "But it can happen, and we are overdue. That is what worries me. Something should be done."

"I may tend the forest, but I cannot make it rain. You must ask the Parson for help in that."

They both looked to the Parson, who was sitting back in his chair and smoking a long-handled pipe. He did not appear to have been listening to them at all but staring off into the distance, but he took the pipe from his mouth and leaned forward.

"Ja, I can make it rain," he said at last, and he seemed to be perfectly serious. "Making it stop again is another matter. You should never ask a man of faith for rain. Look at what happened to Noah."

"Ha, I cannot believe that!" the Mayor exclaimed. "For you it is not a matter of faith. Just convenience."

Einar took out his letter and began to open it, and that caught the attention of the other two quickly enough. He read aloud just about every letter he received. He certainly never tired of talking about his wealthy son in America, who always had new wonders of the modern world to discuss. He was also quite pleased to show off how well he had learned his letters, coming as he did from a time when that had been less common, and also that he could still see perfectly well even at his age.

"Great doings in Chicago?" Parson Ondurson asked.

"Great doings, to be sure," Einar responded absently as he unfolded the letter.

"Strange doings, perhaps," Mayor Thorsen remarked dourly. "One never knows what to believe. Your son talks about that place as if it was the very center of the civilized world. But by all the stories you read, hardly a person ever dies quietly in his bed of old age but for some Indian wanting to take off the top of his head. Floods, and tornadoes. And stampedes!"

"Many people from this country have gone away to America," the Parson said. "Minnesota, they say, and that is not so far from Chicago. And that young couple from down the coast. They went to Texas."

"Ja, and I should bet that you never heard from them again."

The Parson paused a long moment, concentrating very hard. "I do not recall that they ever talked to me before they left."

"That is it. So many people leaving their farms here and going halfway around the world so that they can start all over again with another farm just like the one they left. They could have stayed right where they were, and kept the tops of their heads as well." The Mayor paused, seeing that Einar was just sitting quietly and affording him a very hard stare. Einar's bushy mustache always seemed to droop when he was practicing a hard stare. Mayor Thorsen looked embarrassed, and shrugged. "I am quite finished."

"Are you sure?"

"Yes, I think so."

Einar held up the letter and peered at it closely. He had not yet read it himself. "Let me see. This letter is dated July the twelfth."

"A little more than three weeks ago," Mayor Thorsen remarked in quiet wonder. "Think of that! Three weeks for a letter to go all the way across the ocean from Chicago to Norway, and then up the coast to this very village. What a time we live in!"

" 'Everything is well here. Elizabet will soon be five years old. A fact that still comes to me with a great deal of surprise, since it seems like only yesterday that Anna and I were getting off the boat in New York. And young William is already three.' "

"Hvilliam," the Mayor muttered in disgust, having trouble with the name. "What manner of name is that for a young man?"

"A fine one, for an American," Einar said sourly without looking up from the letter. " *'The new house seems so big and empty, but two children can fill one up in a hurry. All the same, it is a little frightening for a boy from the fjords of Norway to get used to having these well-to-do Americans for neighbors. It might have been different, in Boston or even New York. But the people of Chicago are so friendly, even the rich people. We even have a live-in servant girl now, an Irish girl named Rosie, and she is very good with the children. Anna it was that insisted upon not having a Norwegian girl come in, as easy as they are to find. She says that if she must have a stranger in the house, then we can at least have one who cannot eavesdrop on our private conversations.'* "

"Did you ever ask your son about Indians?" Parson Ondurson interrupted, as if he had not heard a word.

"You had me ask him about that, four or five letters back," Einar reminded him. "He said that he has never seen an Indian. Remember? *'Rosie insists that she will go back to Ireland in a couple of years or so, when she has enough money for a dowry to marry a good man and perhaps a little besides. But I have been here long enough to know better. Except for the farmers who come to stay on the new land, they almost all believe that they have only come to America to make a little money for when they go home, to get married, or to buy land, or a boat or a business. They meet someone here, or something happens. But mostly they find that the lure to return home begins to fade, or the lure to stay becomes too strong.'* "

"Has he ever shot anyone?" Parson Ondurson interrupted suddenly.

Einar Myklathun stared at him impatiently. "Chicago is hardly the American frontier. From all that I have ever been able to tell from Carl's letters, it is a very quiet and civilized place not so unlike Christiania or Copenhagen."

He peered down at the letter again, which immediately seemed to give the lie to what he had just said. " *'The Anarchists riots that we had in May are all but forgotten now. It came at the end of the great National Strike. At first everyone felt at least some sympathy for the workers who were on strike, although I am proud to say that no one who works for me had felt the need to consider such a thing. There was a final large meeting in Haymarket Square, when an Anarchist threw a bomb at a group of policemen. Fortunately the riots that night were the worst of it, and also seemed to be the end of it. We were never even aware of what was happening at home, until it was in the papers the next day.'* "

"I have been hearing stories like that for some time now from Germany and England," Mayor Thorsen remarked quietly. "I am surprised to hear of such things from America, which is supposed to be a perfect place. If such things go on for long, then they will all be coming back here. That will make no one happy."

"Except the Indians," Parson Ondurson amended.

" *'There are some amazing things happening in the field of engineering these days,'* " Einar continued quickly. " *'As you know, my business has grown quickly because we make the most efficient and powerful steam engines as anyone in the world. Now the American Navy has approached us to build for them new engines for their ships, engines that could cruise perhaps thousands of miles on their own supply of fuel and yet fire up quickly to speeds that might outrun anything on the seas. I am told that the American and British navies are now making plans for the biggest, fastest ships ever, made perhaps entirely out of metal and with no sails or masts at all. Such a thing will have to be proven, of course. All of the old-time sailors would not want to trust a ship that is just a machine.'* "

"Well they would not!" the Mayor declared righteously. "Machines are complicated and likely to fail. The wind will never let a sailor down."

"At least not for as long as it chooses to blow," Parson Ondurson was quick to point out.

"The wind will take you anywhere in the world you want to go."

"But it hardly ever blows in the direction you are going."

Ordinarily Einar Myklathun could have sat with the Mayor and the Parson on the lawn before the pub all morning, arguing opinions and philosophies and even a certain amount of dark prophecies like a gathering of old sorcerers. They had played this game for years, time enough to practice it to perfection, and they each knew with reasonable certainty what the other would say on any given subject. They found that was no deterrent to conversation. Quite the contrary. If anything, a certain amount of predictability was the lubricant that allowed these three old men to hold forth like wise and learned scholars, pondering the problems of the world.

But this day, Einar felt the need to do something else. He had much to think about. Something was bothering him, some minor unease of either mind or spirit not unlike a vague itch, although he could not easily determine what it could be. He thought that he needed to go for a walk in the forest, and it was time for him to be about his business anyway. He hurried home to collect his pack, his musket and his worn leather bag of shot and powder, and then he and Torsk took the path west from the village, along the edge of the fjord.

As he walked, he read the final part of the letter. There was always that final paragraph, the portion that he would never read to his friends. His son could never write a letter without repeating that offer that Einar should leave Norway and join the rest of his small family in America. He knew that Carl made the offer only out of his sense of obligation, knowing that Einar would never leave Norway. This was the place where he belonged, but lately he had also been thinking that there were good, sensible reasons why he should go. He was growing too old for this sort of work, walking for miles and miles through these woods to make his rounds, most often in the worst weather. He was beginning to think that perhaps he did belong in Chicago, living out his final years in a comfortable home with his family.

But he was hesitant to go, and for reasons that had nothing to do with his reluctance to leave the only home he had ever known. America was a strange and different place. He did not speak a word of the language, and he did not know his way around big cities. He certainly was not used to so many people. Also he was somewhat uncertain about trying to fit in with the life that his son was leading in Chicago. Young Carl Myklathun had left for America a poor, young student more than ten years earlier. Now he was Mr. Carl Michaelson, the owner and chief engineering designer of a major steam engine company and a very well-to-do man who had changed his name to seem a little less foreign to his American friends and associates. There was really no place in his fine, big house for an old, weatherbeaten forester.

Einar felt the need to see something different this day, so he followed the path all the way to the back of the fjord and up into the mountains. This was of course the mountain of those deceitful dragons, but he had ignored them since that time when he had begged their help and they had certainly ignored him. This was a much older part of the forest, or so it seemed to him. It had been around for so long that it had learned to take care of itself, for it always appeared so well tended and it never changed. It certainly never needed his tending, so he came here only when he felt the need. This was his favorite place in the whole world, in spite of the dragons, and so he was careful never to come here except when he must. These woods and ridges were so special, so peaceful and magical, that he did not want it spoiled with familiarity.

It also reminded him of the dragons, which was often enough to put him into an ill humor. Of course, he had not seen wing or tail of a dragon in the past eighteen years, since the night that Anne-Marie had died, even those times when he came here to the back of the fjord where they dwelled. Perhaps they knew his thoughts and kept themselves hidden. Perhaps they had gone away.

As he and Torsk climbed steadily into the higher slopes of the forest above the fjord, he began to feel better about things soon enough. And not just better; he felt younger. Perhaps because he came this way so seldom, and not at all in the past three years that he could remember, it might have brought to mind without his really knowing the memories of times when he had come this way before. Happier times, by any account. The sunlight through the trees was just as bright and clear as ever. The air beneath the trees was cool and damp. It was even more than going home. He thought that heaven had better be just like these woods, or he was going to haunt this place.

The thought did have to occur to him that this might well be his last time to visit these woods, as seldom as he came. He was right on the very edge of becoming an old man. He might soon be too weak in the knees to climb the steep slopes, too old perhaps to make his rounds in the cold, damp rains of autumn or to force his way through the deep snows of winter. He might be in America by the winter after this next—he knew that he would certainly not be leaving as soon as the coming winter—sitting in a comfortable chair by the fire and telling stories to his grandchildren. As soon as he learned to speak English, of course, for he doubted that his own grandchildren spoke that much of their own language. Why, he might even be dead before the mood ever took him to visit here again, and by then it would certainly be too late.

Einar was walking along deep in thought and hardly watching where he was going, so it came to him as quite a surprise when he looked up and saw a dragon lying on a bed of grey stones not twenty yards ahead. This one was the largest of all the dragons that he had ever seen, just slightly larger in the body than the largest horse with a long, graceful neck and an even longer tail, and broad wings folded onto its back. It was colored all in golds and rich browns, not actually scaled but clad in large but flexible plates of armor. It just lay there on the weathered stone beneath the trees and surrounded by ferns, regarding him with large blue eyes that were calm and disquietingly steady of gaze.

For the moment, Einar was too surprised to think clearly. The only thing that came to his mind was the oath that he had made on the night his wife had died that he would shoot the next dragon he saw. He just stared for a moment, while Torsk sat down and panted with an annoying lack of concern. Then he lifted his old musket, fully as long as he was tall, cocked the hammer and shot. The report of the weapon was thunderous and a large cloud of thick, pale grey smoke obscured his target, but his shot was true. The musket ball bounced off the armor of the dragon's lowered head and disappeared into the trees.

The shot certainly did no harm, except to the dragon's mood. It suddenly leaped up and, in only two long bounds, closed the distance to Einar and bowled the old man over. Then it just stood over him, one massive paw holding him to the ground, with its long neck bent around to peer straight down at him. After a moment, Torsk shuffled slowly over and stared down into his face as well.

"What ever possessed you to want to try that?" the dragon asked. He seemed honestly surprised and perhaps even a little hurt by such treatment, but he was still very annoyed.

"Ja vel, I had told the old dragon that if I ever saw your kind again then I would shoot you," Einar explained. "I have kept my word to the dragons. That is something that dragons have never done for me."

"You are Einar," the dragon said. "I hardly recognize you. I was very young at the time, and you have changed."

"I am older, you overgrown lizard," Einar complained. "What would you know about that? You have probably been sitting on this mountain since before there were people in this land."

"I am not as old as you," the dragon told him. "It was only twenty years ago that you protected me from a Shadow with that same weapon that you have just used on me. It did my head no more harm than it did to his, but I am considerably less impressed. When you thought that you wanted to injure a dragon, did you ever contemplate whether or not it would do you any good?"

Einar just glared at him.

"Just as I suspected. That was too foolish of a thing for you to have thought it out," the dragon remarked as he released Einar, then picked up the old musket and peered at it closely. After a moment, he looked up. "Is this thing quite safe?"

Einar had picked himself up quickly and retreated a few steps, and stood brushing himself off. "Ja, ja. It must have more powder and shot before it will fire again."

"Will you show me?" the dragon asked politely enough, offering the gun.

Einar took the musket and stared at it, then glanced up suspiciously at the dragon. "You are not afraid that I would shoot you?"

"Is it likely to have any better effect?"

The point was taken as it was intended, and Einar opened his bag of powder and shot, then took the ramrod from under the barrel of the musket and began the careful process of cleaning and reloading the gun. He showed the dragon everything, including the tiny flint striker. It was the very latest design and quite advanced as far as muskets went, for things such as revolvers and rifles that shot bullets with cartridges were told about but hardly ever seen in this region of Norway. Then he shot at a pine cone that he had set on a large stone several yards away, and missed. The dragon was impressed in a way that he had not intended.

"Is this a good gun?" he asked.

"This is all the gun I need, surely," Einar explained. "But it is also a very old-fashioned gun, and there are better guns and cannons in the world. Big enough to hurt a dragon, if that is what you want to know. I think that they will not be happy until they build a gun that can destroy this whole big world."

The dragon seemed to be losing interest quickly. "As I remember, we owe you two favors. One for helping to save myself and Ayesha from the Shadows, and one for failing you when you had asked for our help. As one favor, I will promise you no harm and will even forgive you for your behavior."

"You are generous," Einar remarked, not nearly as sarcastically as he would have liked.

"Just do not shoot your gun at any other dragons you might happen to meet, Einar Myklathun. They have done nothing to deserve such treatment from you." The dragon turned to walk away into the woods. But then he hesitated, and turned back again. "Einar Myklathun. There is one thing perhaps that you can tell me, if you will."

"What do you wish to know?" he said, wondering what else might be on this dragon's mind. He did not doubt that the dragon was every bit as fierce as he looked, but he had also been very well-spoken and civilized in his behavior so far.

The dragon seemed to frown. "Several years ago, when I was still quite young, I was sitting in a tree outside your village when I had the chance to listen to the words between two mortals, one called Carl Myklathun and the other called Anna. Your name has brought that to my mind. They spoke of leaving for another place. What became of them?"

"Carl Myklathun is my son," Einar said. "He is now called Carl Michaelson and he is very successful and well-to-do. He and Anna live in America, in the new land beyond the western sea."

"Then he did find his secret for adapting to this new world?" the dragon asked, taking a few slow steps forward.

Einar frowned in his confusion. "I do not understand what you mean by that."

"They said that the world is changing. The dragons have known that for a very long time, of course, but we had not thought that it meant anything to mortals. From the things they said, I had the impression that many mortals have learned to adapt to the world as it is becoming, while many have not. I have wondered ever since how mortals have learned to adapt."

Einar just stared in complete mystification for a long moment, before he was finally able to make any sense of what the dragon was saying. "No, the world is not really changing, not in any real sense. But the lives that men lead and the ways that men think have been changing very quickly for some time now. Some, like Carl, are able to adjust to these new ways, even to use these things to their best advantage. Others, like myself, we belong to the past and we are only waiting for our time in this world to come to an end. But that is the only change there has been in our world, in the ways that men live and think. We brought this change upon ourselves."

The dragon lowered his head and turned aside, and he looked utterly disappointed. It was as if some deeply held hope, dearer and more important to him than life itself, had been ripped away in an instant. Einar had never in his life seen a creature look so unbearably sad and dejected, as if his very heart would break with some hidden grief. Einar could make no sense of it, but for the moment that did not matter. The dragon seemed to have forgotten him, and he should have been slipping away quietly into the woods. He was a loner; he needed the help of no one, and he minded his own affairs. He even reminded himself that he was at war with the dragons, but his mouth seemed to possess a will, or at least a conscience of its own.

"I am sorry," he called after the dragon. "Perhaps there is something I can do to help?"

The dragon paused and turned his head to look back at the old man, perhaps as surprised as Einar himself at that offer. "I was under the impression that you are not particularly fond of dragons."

"Well, no," Einar said, trying to sound sullen. "There just seems to be nothing that I can do about it."

"I will grant that you have some reason to be disappointed with us for having failed you in your need, although we honestly did our best for you," the dragon said, sitting back on his haunches. "Your regard for us seems more a matter of resentment."

"You are not mortal," Einar explained simply. "You never have to think about growing old and dying."

"And so you seek to remedy that situation with your gun?" The dragon rose and turned to walk away slowly. "Do you wish to live forever?"

"Me? Why should I like that? The life that I have led so far has been largely a disappointment."

"I, for one, enjoy my life tremendously and would like to continue living for a very long time." The dragon turned his head to look back. "Perhaps the wrong one of us is stalking about this forest with a gun."

Einar frowned fiercely, largely to keep from laughing. He had always appreciated wry humor, no matter the source, and the dragon had surprised him by that. Now that he knew one a little better, he was beginning to find that dragons were irresistibly interesting.

"Are all mortal folk like you?" the dragon asked.

"Like me?" Einar asked. "No, I doubt that. I am just one foolish old man. As soon as you leave, I will probably be certain that I am only having the delusions of a senile old mind. Perhaps that is why I found it easy enough to run about the forest hunting dragons. I have never been sure from the start of whether or not you are real."

"I am real enough, if my assurances can mean anything," the dragon said. "Fair well, Einar Myklathun. You are a kinder man than you believe yourself to be. And keep in mind what I said about shooting at dragons, even if you think they are not real."

"How will I know if dragons are real?" he called after the dragon, who had already turned away and was disappearing into the fitful shadows of the forest.

"Ask your dog."

Einar looked down at Torsk, who was sitting back on his haunches beside him. Torsk only looked up at him, wearing a rather startled look for a dog, and rolled his eyes sadly. Dogs are man's best friend for many reasons. One of the most important is the fact that they cannot speak, and are obliged to keep their comments to themselves. Torsk certainly looked as if he had something to say.

Kalavek sat alone in the night on the stones above the entrances to the dragon caves, watching the darkness with eyes and ears and with deeper senses that were even more keen and reliable. Ever since the last attack of the Shadows, now some years past, he had insisted that the tribe never be without a dragon on guard at all times, day and night. He believed that if the Shadows were going to attack again, it would be this night.

They might as well come, for all the good it was doing the dragons to endure the years with pointless waiting and foolish hope. The dragons could continue to live, but such life was only a form of lingering, accomplishing nothing but delaying the inevitable. Kalavek had been born for the sake of hope. He and Ayesha were supposed to be the promise of a dawn of a new age of magic. Everything about their appearance argued that they were. But they had yet to pass the necessary test; they had not yet been able to breed and bring forth new life. They were still young, but it was hard to be patient. It meant the difference in whether the dragons would prosper once again, or whether they would slowly fade away one by one on dark, clear nights, and the survivors of a changed world would forget that they had ever existed.

Perhaps he was a fool to have ever hoped, but hope was all the dragons had left to keep them alive. Once he had overheard words that he had not completely understood, but words that he had taken to mean that mortal men had found a way to adapt and prosper in a changing world. Now he understood the truth. Men had never needed to adapt to a world without the old magic, because they had been made for this world. There was nothing that the dragons could learn from how mortals lived and thrived. They had to find their own way.

The answer was becoming increasingly simple, at least to identify if not to implement. For the dragons to prosper, he had to find a way to bring magic back into the world. The time was at hand for him to attempt the task that he had been given, and make his journey into the Fountain of the World's Heart to restore magic to the world. He had hoped that it would not be necessary, for the consequences were too dire. He remembered too well the stories of how the Dragon Lords had nearly shattered the world when they had descended into the Fountain of the World's Heart. At the least, the return of magic would mean the end of the mortal folk. Kalavek was reluctant to accept the responsibility in either case, but he had very little choice. Kalfeer's hope had been in vain, for the young dragons had not adapted to the mortal world, and now he knew that there was nothing in the strange magic of mortals that would help him.

Now he had come to a time when his choices were limited only to the two that he had been given. Either he had to descend into the Fountain of the World's Heart and do what he could to restore the faerie magic, or he had to accept that the time had come for the dragons to die.

Kalfeer stepped quietly out from the entrance of one of the caves below and looked up at him. "Allow someone else to take the watch for now. Ayesha is calling, and you should go to her."

Kalavek slipped down from the ledge in graceful, catlike steps and hurried into the cave, slipping quietly and quickly through the dark passages to the most remote and secure chamber of the group where Ayesha had made her bed. He had been waiting through the night with all the patience he could manage for her to lay her first egg, knowing that it would not live and yet desperate with hope.

Halahvey moved quietly into a secluded corner of the chamber as Kalavek entered. Ayesha lay on the bed in the back of the chamber, the edges of her armor glittering faintly in the dim light cast by the single lamp, and Kalavek thought that no dragon more proud or beautiful than she had ever lived. Then he saw that she lay alone in the bed. That meant that the egg had not lived, and had already been removed. He lowered his head so that she could rub her cheek against his own.

"There was never a chance," Ayesha told him. "The magic needed to begin a new life was not there. I am sorry."

"The fault is not your own, not by any means," Kalavek insisted. "Do not blame yourself."

Ayesha sighed and looked away. "Perhaps next time."

"Next time will make no difference," Kalavek declared. "Or the next time, or the next. The old magic is all but gone from this world. Unless something is changed, then the dragons will never be able to breed and prosper."

"Then what indeed can be done?" she asked. "The world has changed, and all the dragons who have ever lived cannot turn back time or make the world the way it was."

"Really?" Kalavek asked, lifting his head. There was a hard look in his eye and a cold edge to his voice. "I suspect that they never tried. This will not happen again, I promise you. There is at least one option left to us yet. Rest now."

She laid her head on the bed and closed her eyes; he had seen that she was tired. Kalavek slipped quietly out of the chamber, and Halahvey followed close behind. But they did not speak until they stepped out of the cave into the cool night air of the clearing. Kalavek stood for a moment, staring up at the stars.

"Has anyone ever tried to determine why the old magic has been fading?" he asked after a moment. "Has anyone tried to bring it back? There is a reason for everything that happens, and knowing why is the only way to know how to set things right again."

"The dragons never tried to find those answers," Halahvey mused. "I wonder if it is too late to seek those answers now."

"I must try," Kalavek said. "It has come to mean life or death for the dragons."

More than three weeks had passed quietly since Einar Myklathun had met the dragon in the forest, and late summer was just beginning to fade toward the first days of autumn. He had never told anyone that he met dragons in the woods, and more than once at that. He did not want to be called a liar, nor did he care to be thought a senile old fool. And the simple fact was that he had never been so sure of the event himself. They always seemed real enough while he was speaking with them, but afterwards it all seemed like a confusing dream even if he still recalled clearly every detail. The only one who knew for certain was Torsk, and he still refused to say anything.

And if it had happened, then he did not know what to make of it. Why had that dragon left so utterly disappointed, even heartbroken? What had it meant by its question of how mortal men had survived a changing world? There was a mystery here, but he could make nothing of it and he doubted that he ever would. But he found himself worrying about that dragon more and more, even after three weeks.

And so he sat at the tavern late one evening as the day was growing dark, with his old friends the Mayor and the Parson. But he was mostly occupied with his own thoughts and paying little enough attention to what the other two were saying, except when Mayor Thorsen took a notion to hold forth knowledgeably on some subject. But the others tended to ignore it when he was in a mood; it happened often enough.

"No, this will be a bad autumn and a worse winter," the Mayor was declaring. "You just mark my words."

"But it was a fine spring, and a better summer," the Parson protested.

"Ja, that is just the point. Too good, if you ask me. Everything has to be paid for in the balance of nature. You can ask the Forester!"

"Eh?" Einar looked up. "A fair amount of nonsense, that is. And you should know better, Thorsen. Nature is unpredictable, and she is not to be held to any rules. If you want to predict the coming seasons, you have to approach it in a logical and scientific manner. You have to look for all the proper signs."

"Such as?" Mayor Thorsen asked as he settled back in his chair, a gesture that suggested that he was balanced between skepticism and learned agreement. He saw the wisdom of testing nature for signs; just now, he was waiting to see which way the wind was blowing on this argument.

"Oh, if the winter is threatening to be hard, then the wolves will come down from the mountains. All the birds with red colors would be heading south by now. And you will see foxes on the shores. When times are hard, the foxes know how to catch fish."

"Ja, whales," Parson Ondurson agreed.

The Mayor only stared. "Whales? What would whales know? Whales live in the water all the time, and they would hardly know or care whether it was raining or sunny. If you want to talk about signs, then I ask you this. When has Norway ever known a good autumn?"

"Relatively speaking, of course," the Parson amended.

"The only sure way to predict the seasons is to wait and see," Einar said as he rose from his chair. "If you philosophers will excuse me, I think that I should retire early this night."

"The infirmities of the old," the Mayor whispered rather loudly, and the Parson nodded sadly. "Rest well, old man. At the first snow, you are going to show me how foxes fish. Do they use nets, or lines?"

Einar said nothing more. He could see now that the debate about foxes and their abilities as fishermen would furnish the topic of discussion for many of their meetings, and he did not intend to reveal the truth of the matter any time soon. He walked quietly along the road as the evening shadows deepened beneath the trees, while Torsk marched stoically in front with his head and his tail down, filled with thoughts of home.

They came soon to the crossroads, where a short path went up to the last brief row of houses looped along the grey bluffs behind the village. Einar paused at the calling of his name, and turned to wait as Widow Haugen hurried down the path to meet him. She had been widowed these past twelve years, ever since her husband had gone out with the fleet to fish one spring and had never returned. She had soon come to think of Einar as a suitable replacement, but a decade of vigilance had not brought her very near to that goal. At least she had the support of three good sons and two daughters and the company of many grandchildren, and so she was quite comfortable.

Einar would endure her company as well as any, even accepting the invitation into her home—at rare intervals, to be sure—for coffee or dinner. He enjoyed the company more than anyone would have thought of him, but he was also very protective of his privacy. He waited now partly because he had seen the large pie she carried, a cloth tossed over the top of the pan to keep it warm. Widow Haugen was also his major source of life's amenities.

"Good evening, Herr Myklathun," she said, presenting him the pie. They always addressed each other by their proper names from old habit. "I had thought that you might find a use for this."

"It is welcome and appreciated, Frau Haugen," he said as he accepted the pie. "I thank you, and Torsk thanks you."

Widow Haugen cast an uncertain glance at the dog. Torsk sat back on his haunches, looking up at her, and he seemed to smile.

"Summer will be coming to an end any day now," she continued. "That will mean the first cold rains of autumn. You will watch out for yourself, Herr Myklathun? We are neither one of us so young any more."

"Not so old as that," Einar protested weakly, looking uncomfortable. "But I think that I shall not be spending so much time in the woods this autumn and winter. I mean, that only makes sense. The forest is not very likely to burn in the middle of a cold rain."

"That is right, Herr Myklathun," Widow Haugen agreed amiably. "You will be able to come to dinner next week?"

"I am sure of it," he promised. "Good evening, Frau Haugen. And thank you once again."

Einar took his pie and his dog and continued on his way toward home. The sun was gone from the sky and the day had all but faded into night. This was a rather awkward time of day, at least as far as Einar was concerned, and on a cloudy day in autumn it would seem to go on forever. Daylight is the time of bright colors and sharp detail, while night is an adventure of sharp contrasts and impenetrable blackness. But twilight is a dull and dreary time, when everything fades into a million blurry shades of grey. Einar did not like that time of day, when everything seemed so dull and uncertain. He was always impatient for night to fall.

The house was dark and silent when Einar arrived at last. He stood for a moment at the street, staring and thinking of how it once had been when he would come home and there would be lights in the windows, a bright fire on the hearth and dinner on the table. It had not been that way in many, many years now. Widow Haugen was willing enough to give him back a home like that, but he knew that things could never be the same. He supposed that he would have liked that, but at the same time he really did not want to try. His life was not entirely the life he wanted, but he was comfortable with it. The trouble with having something you want is the inherent risk of losing it in a world where nothing is promised, and he simply did not consider it worth the trouble to try.

He stepped into the darkness of the front room, setting the pie on a small table and putting his coat and hat on the pegs just inside in the dim light before he shut the door. He stirred up the embers in the hearth that he had banked that morning, encouraging a small fire within a minute. Then he used a long, slender strip of kindling to carry a spark of flame over to the lamp that hung from the ceiling in the center of the room, rolling up the wick until a pale golden light chased the shadows of night into the corners.

Only then was he aware that the golden dragon was standing in the wide doorway that led into the kitchen.

Einar stopped short, startled but not frightened. He knew well that this dragon was dangerous, the most deadly creature that he had ever seen, and he remembered that their first meeting had not been on the best of terms. But he found it impossible to be afraid. He was not even that startled, for he realized now that he had always known that they would meet again soon. The dragon just stood nearly motionless for a long moment, watching him with large eyes that glittered in the soft light, lowering his head slightly in a gesture that seemed benevolent.

"We meet again, Einar Myklathun," he said at last.

"I am beginning to recall what I do not like about dragons," Einar remarked. "You make free as if you owned the world."

"I must speak with you," the dragon insisted. "Do not be afraid."

"I do not feel particularly afraid," Einar answered, when it seemed that some answer was required. "Would it seem strange for me to say that I have been waiting for you to return?"

"Perhaps some things are fated," the dragon remarked vaguely, and he might have been quietly amused. "I am Kalavek."

He paused then, slowly stretching out his long neck, and tested the air with three deep, appreciative sniffs. Einar glanced over his shoulder, and saw the pie that Widow Haugen had given him. He looked back at the dragon, so large that he barely fit inside the house, and he sighed with no small regret. Frau Haugen always made a most exceptional pie, but Einar also knew well his duties as a host even if he was not known in the village for either his hospitality or his social graces. It also seemed wise to be congenial to a dragon, and especially to one who was very obviously interested in pies. He went to the fire to prepare a large pot of coffee.

"The dragons are dying," Kalavek said suddenly.

Einar paused on his way into the kitchen to fill the pot with water, so startled by that frank admission that he almost missed a step. The better part of two decades of his resentment of dragons had been based upon his assumption that they were immortal and largely immune to death and other misfortunes of life, and that had been the seed of his secret envy. Even more hidden was the fact that he actually cherished the dragons because he had assumed that they were eternal, and the only proud and beautiful thing in the world that he knew of that was so. Consciously he was still trying to be resentful, but deep inside he was shocked and alarmed. He was surprised that he actually had something in common with dragons: it seemed that life was a disappointment even for the creatures of Faerie.

"You do believe in coming straight to the point," he said after a moment, continuing on into the kitchen.

"Do you want me to be honest with you?" the dragon asked as he politely removed himself from the doorway, standing up on his haunches with his back hunched over to take the least possible space in the narrow confines of the room.

"Ja, I would prefer it," Einar called back. "I just never expect it."

"From dragons?"

"From anyone," he insisted. "I once had a very open mind where dragons are concerned, having no prior reason to expect a dragon to lie to me. But you dragons have insisted that it was all a misunderstanding."

"We are dying, and the magic has all but faded from the world," Kalavek said. "That in part might have been why our magic was unable to help you. We summoned all that we could, but we can no longer find enough magic to help ourselves. If that had been explained to you at the time, then perhaps your judgement of us might have been different."

"Ja, I can see that now."

Kalavek bent his head around to stare, his eyes as cold and bright as ice. "What do you know of the other dragons, the black ones who look like dragons but are not? They are the evil ones, full of mischief."

"I know hardly anything of black dragons who are not dragons, except that they do not seem to like you at all," Einar said as he filled the pot from the kitchen pump. "Until I met you, I had always believed what I was told, that dragons only existed in the old stories."

Carrying the filled coffeepot, Einar returned to the front room to put it on the fire. But he paused, glancing at the dragon. "These black dragons of yours who are not; they are the reason why the dragons are dying?"

"No, not at all," Kalavek insisted. "There seems to be no more of the Shadows than there are of us, and there are now only eleven dragons in all the world. The dragons began to die a very long time ago, long before the history of your race began. The world has been changing, and the magic has been fading for a long time. Dragons cannot live without magic."

"And that was why you asked how we had survived in a changing world, that first time we met?" Einar assumed. A few things were finally beginning to make sense to him.

Then Kalavek explained to him briefly a few things about the history of the dragons, especially of their origins and their decline. It was enough for Einar to begin to understand why the dragons existed, and why they had begun to die.

But Einar did not really understand, at least not as well as Kalavek believed he did. He was a simple man from a simple world, without the benefit of the great learning and wisdom of the dragons. He listened carefully as he waited for the coffee to brew and then poured cups for them both, one for the dragon in a large mug normally reserved for beer. Then he cut the pie, taking a large piece for himself and passing the rest, with a private sigh of regret, to Kalavek.

"The end of the matter seems obvious enough," Einar said. The dragon was making his first awkward attempt at attacking his pie with his fork, the first time that he had ever used one. "You intend to do something about the matter, and there is something that I can do for you."

"You are a clever man indeed," Kalavek said with some approval. He took a small drink of his coffee, and a brief, almost imperceptible shiver passed through his entire form. He cast a suspicious glance at the mug, and set it well to one side. "Would you be willing to help save the dragons, if there was something that you could do?"

Einar had to think about that for just a moment. "Will it be dangerous? I mean, you will not have to do something to me or make me have to do something that would not be to my good?"

"I have spoken of the Shadows," the dragon said, holding him with a firm, steady gaze. "If they know of my quest, they may well try to stop us. It is my intention that they will not know, and I believe that we are in very little danger. We face that danger, such as it is, at this very moment, even as we speak. I have come here, seeking your help, and so remarkable a thing as a dragon breaking our long secrecy to seek out a mortal will hold the attention of the Shadows, if they learn of it. That is the only danger you will face."

"It seems that I am involved enough already," Einar mused.

"Then know this," Kalavek told him. "Dragons keep their faith, and they pay their debts. If you will face the risk on my behalf, then if danger does threaten I will protect you from it to the very limit of my abilities, even above the guarding of my own life."

Einar considered that, and nodded slowly. "I will do it, then."

"Why?" the dragon asked suddenly.

The old man just looked at him for a moment. "What do you mean, why? You ask me to do something for you, and then you act suspicious about my reasons."

"Not suspicious, just curious. The first time we met, you tried to harm me because of your resentment of dragons for having failed you, and for our immortality. You seem able to adapt your moods and opinions very quickly."

"Ja, I do not have a hundred years to think it over."

"And what have you decided? Why are you willing to help me now?"

"Well, because you asked," Einar declared. "Heaven knows that there is not much in this world that I do believe in, and it seems foolish to begin to believe in dragons at my age. But here you are, and I find myself honored by your trust. Besides, I have reached a time in my life when I feel the need to see something new, and the danger does not worry me."

Kalavek seemed pleased. "I will tell you where you can find me. If you will come to the dragon caves when you are ready, then we will be on our way. If seeing something new and adventurous is what you want, then I believe that you will not be disappointed."

❧ TWO

EINAR THOUGHT THAT he must be getting foolish in his old age. He had every reason to have no part of this, including certain vague warnings and curious reservations on the part of the dragon himself. There was even the possibility that it was dangerous. So many of the old stories and fairy tales that he could recall warned against having anything to do with the Faerie Folk. The elves. The trolls and the dark folk that lived beneath the mountains. But most dangerous of them all were the dragons, magical beasts of prey without conscience or mercy.

But he suspected that such a description did not apply to Kalavek. He knew that the dragon was quite fierce and even cold, and that he could be the most deadly enemy that a man could ever meet. But Kalavek was also wise and reasonable and very honorable. If dragons were made out of magic, then nobility was the glue that held them together, and Kalavek was noble enough to have been the king of the dragons. Although Kalavek was quiet, even understated, still there was no doubt that his devotion to the cause of saving the dragons could not have been more complete.

Perhaps it was all of those grand, noble qualities that fascinated Einar, so much devotion and eagerness for life when he had only been waiting in a disinterested manner for the end of his own life. Perhaps, as he had said, he had just reached a time in his life when he wanted to see something new. For whatever reason, Einar and Torsk set out for the dragon caves only two days following Kalavek's visit, making their way up to the end of the fjord and into the mountains beyond. He thought that next time he was going to take a boat up to the end of the fjord. From the way the forest path looped about, up and down the slopes and around boulders and bluffs, he was most of the day walking to the back of the fjord. A fast boat with a full sail would have had him there in little more than an hour, with a good sea wind moving up the fjord.

From that point on, he had to make his way on his own. There were no paths leading up to the dragon caves, and he had only Kalavek's descriptions of the landmarks he needed to find his way. Night was falling quickly, and he was beginning to worry about losing his guides in the dark. He did not come here often and so he did not know this land at all well. But just as the night was settling dark and silent, he finally saw the black, massive form of a towering bluff standing before him, and he was certain that this must be the plateau below the dragon caves. If nothing else, he could smell roasting meat.

Remembering what Kalavek had told him, he followed the base of the sheer cliffs to his left until he had come nearly halfway around the circle of the plateau. Where the wall of the plateau began to merge into the steep mountainside that rose behind, he found a narrow cleft leading up. He sent Torsk on before him, knowing that he would have to boost the dog up some of the slabs and small boulders that formed rough stairsteps. The way was long and narrow, too small for the dragons to have used in any case, and with many a difficult step. But he made the top at last, and looked up to find himself staring straight into a dragon's cold, glittering eye.

"Excuse me!" he exclaimed, quickly pulling off his old felt hat to stand holding it rolled up in both hands. It was a shy, peasantish gesture. "I am expected, I hope. Herr Kalavek sent for me."

The dragon lifted its armored head, bending back its long neck in a graceful curve. "I will tell Herr Kalavek that you are here."

The dragon rose then and moved away into the darkness with that flowing catlike pace of its kind. Einar was not sure, but he suspected that he had witnessed the draconic idea of amused sarcasm. Dragons, it seemed, were not fond of titles, and he would do well to remember that. Perhaps they did come from Iceland after all, as the oldest legends said.

He looked around then, seeing the plateau illuminated as pale and cold as ice in the starlight. He was suddenly aware that there were at least half a dozen dragons gathered about, dark, colorless forms in the night, their very presence enough to be frightening in the size and power suggested in their lithe forms. A few were sitting around two of the three fires, cooking in some rude manner the carcasses of animals that may have been goats or small deer. They were all staring at him, patient and motionless, their stony expressions conveying nothing of either hostility or welcome. Knowing what little he did of the reserved nature of dragons, he took that neutrality to be an encouraging sign in itself. Torsk was less certain, and he sat down close between his master's legs.

Kalavek emerged from out of the darkness of the caverns a few moments later. There was no mistaking him, the largest and most noble of the dragons. There was just something in the way he moved that separated him from the other dragons, a surety and eagerness of motion. He was a dragon who loved life and seemed to possess the energy and perseverance to solve any problem. In many more ways, Einar found all dragons to be much alike. They did nothing, neither spoke nor acted, without careful consideration, each catlike movement part of a dance whose music only they could hear. It was not long before Einar came to realize the basic philosophy of dragons, the one thing that they had never quite recognized about themselves. They had never quite come to terms with the fact that they were at the mercy of a destiny that followed no predetermined path. They firmly believed that destiny should be guided by some intelligent force, and they felt themselves equal to the task.

Especially Kalavek. His enthusiasm and confidence were so boundless, he seemed to think that he could command destiny to his own designs.

"So, you did come," the dragon said. "You will keep your promise to help us?"

"You never expected that I would?" Einar asked, just a bit put off by the dragon's obvious surprise and delight.

"I never expected that you should," Kalavek commented candidly. "But I had to ask. Please, come over to the fire where we can talk."

More wood was added to the watch fire just outside the main entrance to the caves, and Einar soon found himself sitting in the company of the most wise and august dragons. His present company had been introduced to him as Old Halahvey, whom he had met before, Kalavek's mother Kalfeer and his mate Ayesha. Kalavek himself sat across the fire, nearly running over with delight and excitement, as hard as it was to tell on the outside. Einar felt a little ridiculous, as if he had been invited to a play tea party with predators, and he certainly felt very small and defenseless.

"I have heard that mortals have decided that dragons do not exist, that perhaps they never did," Halahvey commented.

"We have not had much reason to think otherwise, once the dragons began to hide themselves," Einar said cautiously. His acquaintance with Halahvey went back the better part of twenty years, and the old dragon obviously remembered they had had a rather serious falling out on their last meeting. "I mean, you dragons disappeared at about the same time that my people would have been able to learn to not be afraid of you. But Kalavek has also told me about the Shadows."

Kalfeer lowered her head. "In the lands of our ancient home in the east, dragons were respected and even revered by men, and I must admit that we held a more tolerable attitude about mortals in that time. The fear of magic was always there, in your superstitions and religions. But the Shadows caused the final estrangement, and that was the worst harm that they have ever done us."

A pair of dragons approached at that moment, bearing skinned and rather burned legs and ribs of meat on woven mats. These were quietly deposited within easy reach, and the pair withdrew into the night. Einar sat in careful silence, casting very furtive glances at the dragons, not even turning his head to look at them. Torsk, it seemed, had finally found some reason to feel far more amiable toward their hosts. He came out from the shadows where he had been cowering behind his master's back, staring at the meat.

"But there is never any evidence to be seen that dragons ever existed," he said quickly in his embarrassment. "You never see anything they have done. No scales or bones, although the old stories talk about such things."

"No scales to lose," Kalavek said, touching the heavy leathery plates of his armor.

"And certainly no bones," Halahvey explained a little disdainfully. "We dragons are creatures of magic, and when we die we return entirely to the magic from which we are made. Unlike you mortals, who leave the largest portions of yourselves lying about like carrion."

"As that may be," Einar muttered quietly. "For myself, I would prefer to be buried when I die."

This time, it was the dragons who afforded him some very curious and uncertain stares. Then they began quietly reaching for pieces of meat, giving the clear impression that they were working hard to maintain a polite and hospitable air in the presence of a barbarian. Einar Myklathun decided that it was time to stop these dragons shuffling the cards and play his hand. He reached behind him and brought forth his travel pack into the light, and began to untie the top.

"Widow Haugen made these just yesterday," he explained vaguely. "It took me a bit of doing to get them, explaining how I needed them in the wilderness. And there are only the three, but that still gives us a third each. So there you are."

He had set out three large pans of grey metal, with other pans inverted over the top to act as lids and tied down with twine. He cut free the lid of one pan and lifted it away, and the dragons bent their long necks forward for a deep breath. Kalavek had told them about Widow Haugen's good Norwegian pies.

"Cherry pie!" Halahvey exclaimed softly. "I cannot imagine how long it has been since the last time that I have had cherry pie, nor what manner of creature made it for me. To think that I have lived long enough to be given pies made by a mortal hand, when it seems that only yesterday they were the shy animal people of the woods and plains."

Einar was amused to think that all of human civilization could be summed up in a pastry. Was that the ultimate aim of all intelligent life, to eat well?

The dragons saved their pies until after dinner, proving that they were quite civilized in their own way. They were all greatly improved in mood after that, however, and even Halahvey laid aside his own misgivings to share Kalavek's enthusiasm for their quest.

"Kalavek has said that he has not yet fully explained to you the nature and extent of our problem," he began. "In as far as you can understand, it is this simple. The dragons have been dying because the magic, at least the type of magic that we need, has been fading from the world. That leaves us with only two real alternatives. Either we must learn to live without the magic that we have always depended upon, or else we must find a way to bring it back into the world. Since we are a part of that magic, it is extremely unlikely that we could ever learn to live without it. But it is by no means unreasonable to think that we might find a way to encourage it to return."

"We never thought to try to understand the nature of magic until it was almost too late," Kalavek added. "It simply was, like the air we breathe, just as essential but just as simple and just as endless. Is it like the air, all about us at all times and forever being renewed all about us? Does it have a source, as a stream may begin from a spring in the mountainside? Or was it simply a finite quantity, something created in the depths of time that has simply been used up or lost?"

"But you have told me already that the ancestors of the dragons released the magic at this Fountain of the World's Heart," Einar protested. He frowned fiercely as he thought that through. "So this is where you want me to go?"

"Not yet," Halahvey answered vaguely.

Kalavek glanced up at the older dragon, a look of brief impatience, before he turned back to their mortal guest. "Going to the Fountain of the World's Heart will do us no good until we discover two things. First, we still do not know for certain where it is. Nor would we have the slightest idea of what to do when we got there. We are still trying to figure out how to begin to solve our problems. And to do that, we have to have a Core of Magic."

"Oh," Einar remarked quietly. "And do you know what that is, or where to find one?"

"We are already ahead on that account," he explained happily. "A Core of Magic is a distillation of useful magic. Any group of dragons can sing one into being at any time, although by far the most powerful are created in the Fountain of the World's Heart. Do you understand?"

"Hardly a word."

"A Core is a whole lot of magic that you can save in a small package to use when you need it," Ayesha explained. The other dragons looked at her in surprise, but Einar Myklathun seemed to understand.

"We also know where a Core of Magic might be," Kalavek continued. "Just before he died, the dragon Selikah told me that a Core of Magic is to be found in the underground city of Behrgarad, not far to the north of here."

"Behrgarad?" Einar asked, confused. "Do you mean Bergen?"

"Well, I certainly hope not!" Kalavek laughed. "Behrgarad is the name of one of the ancient cities of the northern kingdom of the faerie race your people know as the gnomes."

"The Hall of the Mountain King!" Einar agreed excitedly.

"Well, I doubt very much that there have been any true kings beneath the mountain in centuries," the dragon said. "The gnomes themselves might still be there, a few pitiful survivors of what was once one of the wealthiest and most industrious of all the faerie races. Whether they are still there or not, Selikah insisted that we will likely find a Core of Magic somewhere beneath the city."

Einar frowned to himself, wondering how and where this discussion was going to lead to him. He did not think that the dragons were trying to hide anything from him; they were just slow to come to the point and he was not about to hurry them. He looked up. "This is where we are going this first time, I suppose."

"This is where we are going, just you and I," Kalavek agreed. He bent his head slightly to look at the dog. "And Torsk, if he will have us."

"Torsk insists upon going everywhere I go," Einar said. "I never ask; he just gets up and goes when I do. He has much better sense than I do in some things, so I never argue with him."

"There is perhaps little good sense in this," Kalavek told him plainly. "This is a matter of desperation. The dragons must survive. I will do anything required of me or pay any price to insure the survival of the dragons. The reasons for my devotion are obvious enough. I can only ask you to share in my quest for no better reason than I have asked it of you. Are you still resolved to help us?"

Einar did not have to consider that for more than a moment. He looked up at the dragon, his expression questioning. "I cannot say why, but I find that I am as devoted to your task as you could ask. You might be nearly as old as this world itself, but you are the first new thing that I have seen under this sun in a very long time. I ask you just the one question in return, the only payment I will ever ask of you. Why do you need me?"

"A fair bargain," Kalavek agreed. "We cannot touch the Core of Magic, nor is there any way I know that we can carry it forth from Behrgarad. We are made of magic, as we have said. If we touch the Core, the magic of both parts is released. We would be destroyed, and the Core would fall apart in a flood of raw, destructive magic. You are mortal. Magic is a part of your soul, if you have one, but it is no part of your physical being. We need for you to bring out the Core of Magic. My part in this is only to guide and protect you."

"That is no worse than I expected," Einar allowed. Then he afforded the dragon a hard stare. "What do you mean, if I have one?"

Einar Myklathun spent that night with the dragons, in better hospitality than he would have expected. The caves were rather sparsely furnished, but they were large, dry and warm. They smelled of dragons, but then dragons did not smell at all bad, a vaguely spicy scent that was completely beyond his experience. He was shown to a spare chamber deep within the caverns fairly early in the evening, although he was certain that the dragons would be talking and singing their magic for quite some time. They seemed to be inordinately fond of such behavior. He thought that he was going to give them barrels and teach them to brew beer, and then they would sit up all night making some real magic.

The dragons were creatures of many enigmas, but the newest mystified him beyond all others. The dragons knew so much of everything, of sciences, magic and history, but they never seemed to make use of anything they knew. Wisdom, magic and learning were the things of their wealth, carefully hoarded but never to be touched. They had nearly hoarded themselves right out of existence. Only for their first time in all the history of their ancient race did it seem that they had figured out that they could make their own end of their problem.

In that respect, Einar was just a little disappointed with the dragons. They were the oldest of races but not as wise as he would have expected. They knew so much, but for centuries they had clung to prophecies, empty hopes and blind trust in either divine intervention or just plain luck. In many ways they were as simple as the lives they led, the kings of the beasts, wise and learned predators but animals still and not quite people in the sense he knew. Kalavek might save his race by teaching them to reason, but they would never be quite the same for the tricks they had learned to survive.

Einar found it increasingly hard to dislike them any longer, they were so wise and so innocent at the same

time. He was left to wonder if they would be as great as
ever, once they learned to deal with a new world on new
terms, or if they would continue to be at a disadvantage in
a world that had no room for them. At least they would still
be alive.

Kalavek came for him at dawn, and they were on their
way very soon after that. It was a misty sort of morning, a
thin grey fog creeping the slopes from the fjord below. The
dragons of the tribe crouched on the boulders and on the
ground about the watch fire. They never said a word, watching in perfect, motionless silence as Einar pulled on his coat
and hat, slipped his pack onto his back and shouldered his
ancient musket. Then he and Torsk followed Kalavek into
the morning fog, hurrying down the cleft along the side of
the plateau after the dragon spread his wings and leaped
over the edge.

The dragon waited below until he arrived, then turned
without a word and moved with slow, deliberate steps
through the forest. They first had to make their way around
the mountain where the dragons made their home, a slow
and difficult task because of the forests, boulders and bluffs.
This was about the most wild and mountainous country in
all of southern Norway and they were moving deep within
a region where men had never been, not since the dragon
ships of the first mortals of that land had stalked the fjords.
Many of the races of Faerie had retreated west and north
and, seeing the way across the Great Sea closed to them,
had disappeared into this shadowed, rugged land to await
the inevitable.

In courtesy to his companion, Kalavek proposed to walk
the entire journey himself, fifty miles and more by wing
and at least half that far again on the twisting mountain
paths. This was no easy task, for dragons are somewhat
like cats in their build, their hind legs longer than their
front and tremendously strong for thrusting themselves into
flight. His broad, powerful wings, folded tightly atop his
back to either side of his plated ridge, made an awkward
burden indeed, sometimes catching in the branches. But
Einar never tired of watching him. In flight, the dragon was

slender and graceful. On the ground, he was massive and powerful, half stalking predator and half knight in armor, a frightening creature made for war and for the hunt.

Kalavek obviously was not used to walking; he thought of fifty miles as half an hour of easy flying, so it could obviously be walked easily in only a single day. Einar knew that they would be lucky to do it in three long days; he was expecting four. They would easily be gone a week and a half if they were gone a day, and he wondered what sort of company a dragon would be for such a length of time.

Kalavek did not speak much during the day. Dragons were always content with their private thoughts, and so they hardly ever noticed the silence. If nothing else, he was having to concentrate hard just on walking, for he was a large and ungainly form on the ground. If he regretted his decision to travel in this manner or if he was tempted to return to the sky, then he kept his thoughts to himself. He had asked Einar Myklathun to undertake this journey for his sake, so he thought it courteous to share its discomforts. He thought that his part could not be any worse than Einar's, who took smaller steps and had to walk only on his hind legs at that.

They stopped for a few minutes at noon, as the dragon thought only for a brief rest. And that was nearly all that Einar and Torsk got from the deal. Kalavek had said that he would provide what was needed, and Einar's own supply of food was rather sparse. Adult dragons would eat only once a day, usually just after nightfall, and Kalavek had certainly never heard or suspected that it might be otherwise with mortal folk. Fortunately Einar did have a few bits of dried meat and fruit in the bottom of his pack, as well as some bread. He also still had the extra fourth of a pie left over from the previous night, but he was saving that.

Kalavek did rather better for them both when they made camp that night. After asking Einar to build up a good, hot fire, he disappeared into the night on the wing, rising quickly through the clearing a short distance from the low bluff of grey stone where they had made their shelter. Einar used his hatchet to cut up a good bit of dead wood that he found lying about the area, hurrying to finish his task in the fading light of day. Kalavek had insisted upon a very large fire. The dragon returned only a few minutes later, carrying with him a small deer. They had it skinned and dressed out in short order, and on the fire to cook.

"That will take a very long time to cook," Einar commented as he and Torsk settled on one side of the fire to wait. He was not greatly concerned, but the dog was staring sadly at their dinner.

Kalavek did not answer. He cocked his head, regarding the meat for a long moment, then extended his neck and breathed a light tongue of flame over the carcass. He used only his thinnest flames, a nearly invisible mist of pale blue fire. Releasing his tremendous breath so slowly, he was able to sustain his flame for a surprisingly long time. At last he drew back his long neck and regarded the effect. The meat was already beginning to take on a cooked appearance.

"Ja, I suppose that our dinner will smell like your breath," Einar remarked. He was impressed, although not with the dragon's culinary talents.

"Does my breath smell?" Kalavek asked, pausing as he was about to settle to the ground.

Einar frowned. "I do not recall that I have ever noticed."

Kalavek responded without first asking if he should, thrusting his head in Einar's direction and opening his mouth. Einar nearly jumped; if the deer had still been alive, this was the last thing it would have seen. But the dragon only exhaled, a light puff of breath that still flipped Einar's old felt hat off the top of his head. With that, Kalavek gracefully lowered himself to the ground and arched back his head, striking a typically draconic pose.

"Well, nothing," Einar remarked after a moment. "I do not smell smoke or brimstone or anything. Perhaps your breath smells a little sweet, but that is all."

"Smoke?" the dragon asked, surprised and perhaps a little annoyed.

"Smoke follows fire, just as fire follows fuel," he explained quickly. "I expected to smell smoke or perhaps whatever feeds your flame, like kerosene. What is the source of your flame?"

"Magic, of course."

"Of course," Einar agreed. "Brimstone is another matter. Parson Ondurson would have told me to expect the smell of brimstone, for dragons are surely creatures of evil."

"We are evil," Kalavek said quietly.

Einar was putting on his hat when he paused and gave the dragon a very suspicious look. It was hard to say what Kalavek was thinking; that long, sly face was so completely expressionless. Then he noticed that the dragon was watching him very closely and he knew that he had just witnessed what dragons possessed as a sense of humor.

"I will say it for you, Herr Kalavek," he said after a moment. "This is going to take longer than you thought. Do not be worried about it. I knew that it would when we started."

"I am not worried," Kalavek responded. "You are the expert on walking."

Einar glanced at him. He had never yet figured out if the dragons were fitful in their manners, as obvious as it was that they could be aloof one moment and warmly polite the next, or if they were simply that candid. They did not think in any way that he found predictable, creatures of a far older world that was ruled by philosophy and honor, not harsh modern realities. It was those qualities that intrigued him most, the enigma that was an endless delight even if he never figured it out.

"Would you like to hear a secret?" he asked.

Kalavek turned his head. "Curiosity is the bane of dragons."

"It is a funny thing, really," Einar said, moving a couple of paces to one side so that he could lean back against a small tree. "This has all been so sudden and strange, it has not been very real for me. I guess that I have just been walking through it all in a daze, letting whatever comes happen to me. Until today. Walking all day has been so perfectly mundane, I would suppose that it has brought me to my senses."

When he paused, the dragon just stared at him expectantly. He shrugged to himself and continued: "What I suppose I mean is that it has finally just occurred to me that we are going to a real place, a place that I have never been and never thought existed."

"Ah, I understand," Kalavek said. "You want to know something more of where you are going, and what you can expect to find."

"Is that too much to ask?"

Kalavek glanced away, and it was the closest that Einar ever came to seeing a dragon laugh. In China, now centuries past, dragons had been known for their easy, eager humor, quicker to laugh than to anger and boundless in both. A colder, harsher world had taught them to be reserved and cautious, perhaps too cautious.

"No question is ever too much to ask, as long as you do not always expect an answer from a dragon," he said. "I had been wondering when you would become curious, or if curiosity was simply not that strong in your kind. So this time you may ask your question, and I will give you all the answer you could wish."

He paused a moment, sitting up on his haunches to turn the meat on its spit, then settled back again. "The gnomes were, in their ways, perhaps the most like mortal men of all the faerie creatures. They were certainly among the three most successful of the faerie races, their city-nations rivaling the kingdoms of the elves and the tribes of the centaurs. They were courageous with an undeserved reputation for cowardice, for they kept to themselves and would avoid any fight when they could, retreating underground to escape their enemies. On their own ground, they were hardly ever defeated. You might have thought that they would have survived, knowing all the tricks that have made your own people strong. But they were tied to the magic as much as any of us."

"They all died?" Einar asked.

"Their great cities beneath the mountains failed and fell quickly," the dragon explained. "They were vulnerable, and their greatest enemy took them without the need of battering down their massive doors of steel. The gnomes were dependent upon trade. They were the miners of the faerie races, and prodigious workers in metal and stone. They traded for everything they needed and their goods and services were in high demand for five thousand times the number of years that your people have kept your history. Then the decline began. The other races of Faerie fell into poverty as their magic faded and their numbers slowly declined, and then one by one they all went to exile into the west, seeking an escape that did not exist. But the gnomes stuck to their hidden cities like badgers in their holes while their every means of existence disappeared, and they starved by the thousands. Other races of Faerie may have been reduced to stray animals wandering the wild before the end, but at least they did not starve on their own perversity."

Einar listened in quiet fascination, then looked up when the dragon paused. "I remember you said before that they might not all be dead."

"Some have been lingering for thousands of years, that same furious determination that nearly killed them all now sustaining them beyond their time. The dragons still had dealings with them for a time, and we would help each other when there was need. But eventually our own numbers became so few, and we have not gone to the hidden cities of the gnomes in centuries. So you see that we really do not know whether or not any of them linger still. I have never seen a gnome in all my life, nor any other race of Faerie except a few half-wild elves living on a forgotten island. But they are still out there, the ragged ends of once-great nations haunting the wild places to protect themselves from the curiosity and ignorant fear of mortals."

He bent his neck forward to sniff at the meat, then turned to face Einar squarely. "There is this that perhaps you do not know. The dragons were the last to begin to decline, but we may be among the first to disappear from this world. There were never many of our kind, perhaps thousands of us to their millions even at the time of our height."

Einar sat in the firelight, frowning to himself and feeling guilty. He felt responsible, because his kind had usurped a world they had thought to be all their own. He felt responsible because his kind prospered while eleven dragons fought to stay alive. Above all, he felt guilty because he wanted to help and he had no answers, and he knew that it was because he simply could not begin to understand all of this business about magic and the changes in a world that was far more ancient than he had ever imagined. And he was very surprised at himself for thinking that it mattered, when he could be sitting by his fire at home rather than in the woods with a young dragon. But there it was. All he could do was to trust that the dragon had the answers, and to help in any way he could.

Kalavek was surreptitiously watching him in turn, and wondering about this odd little creature. Mortals were so flighty and insubstantial, their scattered thoughts tripping and leaping so quickly and endlessly. They knew of their mortality only too well, he decided. They tried so hard to live an eternity in a handful of years, and each day as if it was a year. They never took the time to look at anything or think anything through as a dragon would, for time was a luxury they did not have. They saw only the shapes of things, enough to determine the definition but never the essence. They thought things through enough to begin to act, but hardly ever enough to have complete trust in their own actions. There were limits to how far he would rely upon their reasoning or judgement. Even in Einar, whom he considered to be a wise and cautious man, he saw the tendency to give trust blindly in some instances and withhold it fearfully in others.

But in one thing he was certain, that Einar trusted the dragons completely and would do anything for them. And he would keep that faith, because he gave his trust against his will. Einar was an old man bitter with the hardships and disappointments of life, hesitant to believe in anything for fear of being disappointed yet again. But he was beginning to believe in dragons, in spite of himself. He had hated dragons for failing him when he had asked for their help, and he had resented them for their immortality. Now it seemed that he was beginning to think that creatures of magic were of a higher order than anything of the mundane world, incapable of breaking their promise of being anything less than what they seemed. But Einar was very wrong about one thing. He had not come along out of amazement for seeing something new, but amazement at himself for daring to try.

Kalavek continued to watch him in silence. Einar sat quietly on the far side of the fire, wishing hard for things that were beyond his power to give and blaming himself. He was staring into the fire, poking into the embers with a long, slender stick. Torsk lay on the ground beside him, staring up alternately first at the dragon and then the meat with large, wistful eyes.

"Are you afraid to die?"

Einar glanced up at him sharply, understandably startled by that sudden question. He made a long face or two as he considered the question briefly. "No, I stopped being afraid of death a long time ago. Why do you ask?"

"I had always wondered what it must be like for mortals, knowing that your time is limited," Kalavek explained. "I can imagine that it must be frightening at times to think about."

"Oh, it frightens you enough when you are young," Einar said, poking again at the fire absently. "Then you are full of youthful energy and enthusiasm and you think of all the things you would want to do. I guess what frightens you is yourself, knowing how you put things off and tell yourself that tomorrow is soon enough, while your guilty conscience reminds you that there are only a limited number of tomorrows. But as the years pass and you come nearer to your own death, then those things cease to worry you so much. You start to think that the things you used to want to do really never were so important, and you no longer seem to have the strength of will or body to care. Do you understand?"

The dragon dipped his head. "I suppose that I do."

"And what of yourself, dragon?" he asked. "Are you afraid to die?"

Kalavek lifted his head and stared. "Why do you ask that?"

Einar shrugged. "It just seems to me that you are trying as hard as any mortal to stay alive while time is running out for you."

"I suppose that I am," he agreed. "But how shall I answer that, when there are so many questions wrapped in those same words? For myself, I am not afraid of death because dragons never die but pass into another form, one less solid and less tied to this physical world. But I am very afraid that the dragons will die and pass entirely from this world. Perhaps it is pride, when we were in this world long before anyone else, to think that we should then simply fade away and pass forgotten from a world that we have ruled for millions of years. Perhaps it is only a baser instinct that all creatures share, to secure the future of our race at any cost. But for myself, it is for Ayesha. I will do anything I must for her."

His meaning in that was not immediately clear. Einar waited patiently while he sat for a long moment with his head down, while the fire snapped and a light, cool wind moved through the trees.

"What is the treasure of dragons?" he asked at last, although he still did not look up. "We keep no possessions. Gold is only metal to us, and diamonds only stones. Wisdom, learning and magic are the things that we have hoarded and cherished through the long ages. Other races—in their time, even men—would come like beggars to our doors for any crumbs of wisdom or understanding that we could be persuaded to share. I realized a long time ago that it was all hollow. All of our wisdom and knowledge could do nothing to help us when our time of need was at hand. The magic has burned slowly away like the embers of a fire. All that was left was love, and I love Ayesha dearer than any hoarded thing. I will not lose my only treasure."

He lifted his head high, staring up at the cold stars as if he faced the spirit of every dragon who had ever lived and died. "Where is my time? Where is my happiness? I do not want to die. Dragons of the faded ages lived for millions of years, content and unafraid that the future would be anything but kind and generous. Now my time has come and nothing is left, but that does not mean that I desire or expect any less. I want to live, and to be happy."

He sat there for a long moment, his head held high and proud as the light of fierce determination burned in his eyes. Then he lowered his head again to stare absently into the fire, his eyes cold, hard and sullen. "But there are no promises made to any of us when we come into this world. I will accept the inevitable with grace. I will not die in anger and bitterness. But I will fight to the end for the future I desire; that much at least is my right."

Einar said nothing. He reached into the shadows behind and pulled up his pack, and took out his pipe and tobacco. It was a wooden pipe with a large, richly-carved bowl and long, sensuously curved stem. He measured out a very precise amount of tobacco and packed it into the bowl with the touch of a true master. Then he kindled a twig in the fire and used it to light the pipe, puffing clouds of blue smoke furiously into the firelight. Obviously quite satisfied, he sat back and blew a large smoke ring. By that time, he had the dragon's complete attention.

"What is that?" Kalavek asked.

"A bad habit," Einar said, dismissing the matter. He puffed on the pipe a couple of times more, his expression thoughtful. "It seems to me that we are all afraid of death, each of us for our own reasons."

"Except for you," the dragon observed.

Einar thought about it for a moment, and shrugged. "I ran out of reasons for being afraid long ago. Life has been largely a disappointment to me; I do not believe that death is going to disappoint me, since I expect so little. But it will find a way, I suppose."

He puffed on his pipe a moment longer, then cast a thoughtful glance at the dragon. "The point of this entire expedition is that no more dragons are going to be dying for a long time."

❧ THREE

THE DISTANCE WAS fortunately not as great as Einar had anticipated when the dragon had spoken of a fifty mile flight, and it was late in the morning of their third day of travel when Kalavek announced that they were near. The land had been less rugged for most of the second day, for now they were moving again into the heights. Directly ahead was a mountain that Einar thought must be the largest in all Norway, and it looked to him that bright morning like the largest mountain in all the world. Its single massive peak was capped in snowy white, even though it was late in the summer, and slopes of brown-grey stone descended into the forests.

The stoic dragon had walked the entire distance, as much of a trial as that obviously was for a creature not built for walking. He paced in long, carefully calculated strides, moving through the forest and over stones like some immense golden cat. Einar followed close behind, and found that he was perhaps not so old as he had been thinking lately, for he had not made such a long journey in years. Torsk came last, following resolutely with a singleminded determination and lack of enthusiasm that he exhibited for all necessary tasks, except for eating and sleeping. At least he seemed to like the company of dragons, and his politeness exceeded the usual manners of dogs.

"There is one matter that has been bothering me of late," Einar said as they walked. "If the gnomes shut their doors and locked out the rest of the world long ago, then how will we get in? Are they likely to come if we must knock?"

"Doors were made to be opened," Kalavek answered in his usual, indirect manner. "Even doors that are locked will always have a key. The gnomes gave the keys to their doors only to the dragons, a rare matter of trust even at the time of their strength. We will see."

"That tells me very little," Einar complained.

"You will see when you get there." Which was, of course, the correct answer in the first place.

They came suddenly upon a clearing like a small meadow on a hilltop in the middle of the forest, the far end blocked by a wall of bare grey stone that was the base of a steep, tumbled slope. Einar had been expecting something in most ways like the dragon caves, except that there were no cliffs guarding the approach but a gentle rise leading to the top of the clearing. There were also no caves. In fact, Einar could see nothing at all, certainly no indication that they were standing on the doorstep to one of the largest and more powerful of all the cities of the gnomes. There were no roads, not even a path leading in across the meadow, which was as plain and pastoral as a cow pasture.

"It has been a very long time," Kalavek said, as if guessing his thoughts. "Once there were great roads linking all the cities of the gnomes through the mountains, and leading south to the kingdoms of the elves. There might have been guardhouses here, and a paved yard, and certainly stables and barns for the beasts of the caravans of wagons that would come."

"Has it really been that long?" Einar asked, finding it hard to imagine.

"The winters of the world have returned time and again in this later age," the dragon explained. "The decline of the races of Faerie was already well advanced before the last ended, and when the ice retreated there were none left to restore the damage, nor any reason. By that time, their great cities had become the tombs of their race. Those few gnomes that still survived wished only to hide in the eternal darkness beneath their mountains."

Although he had never been here in his life, Kalavek found the way easily enough. He approached the dark shadow filling a recess in the broken stone wall, and only then could Einar see that it was the oval opening of a cavern of fairly large size, although lower than the dragon caves. Kalavek paused only to test the air with his long nose, then bent his head low and, crouching slightly, entered the passage boldly.

Einar had his misgivings, but he followed without hesitation. He expected that the way would have been dark, but there was a pale golden glow that he realized came from the dragon himself, a trick that Kalavek had never demonstrated before this time. There might be a few gnomes left in these caves as Kalavek said, reduced by decline and poverty almost to furtive animals, and there might not be. After meeting dragons and hearing so many stories of the Ages of Faerie, Einar could now believe that all manner of dark creatures might have wandered into these deep ways. A dragon was formidable protection, but Kalavek was only one. Einar took powder and a ball from his bag and began to load his ancient musket.

Kalavek paused, affording him an almost droll expression. "Is that thing likely to be effective?"

"It works well enough against anything except your hard head," Einar said as he used the ramrod to pack the powder.

They continued slowly, the dragon leading the way, until they came suddenly to the end of the tunnel in a wall of smooth stone. The cavern had widened somewhat into an oval chamber, just large enough that the dragon could finally lift his head. Einar frowned when he saw this, but he trusted that Kalavek had not led them false. Kalavek only stood for a long moment, running his head up and down and back and forth with his nose only inches from the stone as if testing for some scent, although he was not sniffing but staring.

"It is indeed as I was told," he said at last. "The main gate is here, a massive portal of stone and iron more than a yard thick and only to be opened from within by the mechanical devices that lock it. There is a second door to one side, one meant to respond to the magic of one who knows its secrets. If the gnomes have not blocked that door, then you must go through and open the gate for me."

"And if it is?" Einar asked.

"Then we must knock."

Einar slipped the ball into the barrel of his musket, then used the rod to poke it down. "And if the gnomes are all dead?"

"If the gnomes do not answer my summons by this time tomorrow, then I will seek more direct means," Kalavek said. "I command a magic that will open that gate, but it will not close again. I will be certain before I commit such a violent trespass."

He stepped then to one side, sitting up on his haunches and staring closely at the stone wall for a long moment. He closed his large, bright eyes and his mouth began to move as if he spoke words to himself, although they did not seem to Einar to be quite the chant of an incantation as he would have expected. Then the dragon reached up and pushed against the stone and a section of the wall in the shape of a small door, deeper than it was wide, moved back smoothly under his great strength. He finally had to lean well forward to push the door to one side, then thrust his head through the opening all the way to his shoulders, as far as he could go. He drew back quickly after a moment.

"The gate is unlocked already," he said, surprised and suspicious.

"Does that mean that the gnomes are all dead?" Einar asked.

"Only if someone who knew the magic to force the door has been this way since," Kalavek remarked. "More likely is the possibility that the survivors here have gone to join their kind in some other city."

"You do not believe that any better?"

The dragon turned his long neck. "By all that I have heard, the gnomes were creatures of firm habits, as fearful and secretive as they were greedy. They would not leave the door to even the least of their homes unlocked, even if they meant never to return. More likely is the thought that others have come this way since."

Still standing up on his haunches, Kalavek stepped awkwardly over to the center of the wall and pushed firmly against the stone. Considering well the strength that the dragon applied to the task, Einar knew that he could not have opened that gate alone. The massive portal moved back slowly but smoothly and without a sound, until Kalavek pushed it well back against the wall. He leaned through the opening for a moment longer, peering into the way ahead, before he stepped in through the gate.

Einar followed quickly, holding his musket tightly before him, although the fact that neither the dragon nor the dog seemed at all concerned was at least somewhat reassuring. Kalavek seemed more curious than anything, the student of ancient history and the architecture of a lost age.

When Einar stepped through the gate, he found himself peering about with as much curiosity. He had expected more of the same as the tunnel outside, a rough cavern of bare brown stone. That was only a deception to discourage the accidental visitor from realizing that this was anything more than just another cave in the mountains leading nowhere. Inside was a passage carved as smooth as glass, walls meeting floors and ceiling in sharp, perfect corners, wide and high enough for any two dragons to walk side by side. The stone was no longer brown but dull grey and washed in a pale light, although Einar could not have said if the light came from out of the stone or the air itself.

"How does it seem?" he asked softly.

"I have never met a gnome, and I do not know their smell," Kalavek replied as he closed the gate. "There is something alive in this place, a scent that I do not know. There is something of it familiar, something that I am tempted to say is the essence of faerie life, but I admit that I am only guessing. I expect to find a few gnomes about the place, all the same, but not many."

"You seem to be supposing quite a lot," Einar observed suspiciously.

"I am supposing very little," the dragon said. "I smell smoke, fresh smoke, but not very much of it. I also smell the blood and meat of deer, mountain goat and rabbit. Someone is living in here and pretending on the outside that they are not. I do not smell mortals. That suggests gnomes."

"Clever dragon," Einar remarked in mild disgust.

Kalavek did glance at him briefly. "Almost anyone can learn how to think properly. Only dragons, it seems, make a habit of it."

"You always missed the most important point."

Kalavek did stop then, bending his head around to stare in mystification.

"Now that it has come to this point, there is one thing that you should keep in mind," Einar told him, taking something of the tone of the wise elder lecturing a child. Whether it kept the dragon's attention, it helped Einar to focus his determination into his words. "You dragons hold such great value in knowing all there is to know. You knew for thousands of years that something was wrong with the magic in the world. Why did it finally have to come down to you to figure out that you should try to do something about it?"

"It would never occur to dragons that it is our business to interfere in the ways of the world," Kalavek answered. But his slight hesitation, his sad eyes and his laid-back ears showed that he knew it to be true.

Einar nodded. "You made it your business. Something had gone very wrong in your world. Dragons just sat and did nothing for the longest time, hoping that this old world would take care of them before it was too late. After all that time, it finally occurred to you that your world would not take care of you unless you did something to take care of it. In all the time that dragons have been in this world, you have had the minds and souls of philosophers and scholars and lived like beggars. It never occurred to your kind to turn all the things that you have learned into any practical use. My kind has learned that lesson well and we have used it to very good advantage, admittedly at a price when we are not careful."

"I understand what you mean," Kalavek said guardedly.

"Ja vel, then keep it in mind," Einar told him. "It is the only thing you have that can keep you alive."

Kalavek hesitated a moment, as if he was about to say something. Then he lowered his head in a reluctant gesture of agreement. "Although you cannot begin to understand the philosophies of dragons, the essence of your judgement is correct. When the Dragon Lords first brought magic into the world, they nearly destroyed it. We have been fearful of the consequences of trying again. But when I was very young, Aeravys who is the spirit of the world herself came to me and told me that I am the one who must bring back the magic. With her endorsement, I am not afraid to try."

"I suppose that I can see your point," Einar admitted. "But my judgement of dragons stands."

"At least that is an improvement in your attitude," Kalavek commented; then he spent a long moment contemplating something very hard. "There is one last matter that I must discuss, for I cannot bring myself to deceive you even passively. This cannot be a mortal world and a world of magic at the same time. If I do restore the ancient magic, then the mortals will themselves be changed in some way that I cannot predict."

"We will ourselves fade away?"

"Nature is not wasteful if it can at all be helped. I strongly suspect that your kind will itself become magical."

Einar waved all such concerns away impatiently. "You would be doing us a favor."

"I had thought so," the dragon remarked. "I just wondered if you would agree."

He turned then, continuing on his way into the heart of the underground city. The passage ran straight and even into the mountain, changeless and unbroken. The dragon picked up his speed to what was a fast walk for them both, and still long minutes passed in the silence. Einar knew that they must have come two miles or more; it was hard enough to judge any distance in the featureless tunnel, both beginning and end disappearing into the vague, misty grey light. The suspense of uncertainty seemed to hang in the dusty air, and he felt bent beneath its weight. But he never felt actually afraid, and that surprised him just a little. He had seen enough these last few days already that the mysteries of magic held no more terrors for him, and the dragon at his side was a formidable reassurance.

In the dim light, Einar could not see the end of the tunnel until he was nearly upon it, less than two dozen yards. Even the dragon slowed as they neared the end, and Einar was content to allow him to thrust his head beyond the end of the passage for the first look. Kalavek seemed content and moved slowly into the open beyond the tunnel, stopping again just beyond. This time, Einar hurried to join him.

The chamber beyond was vast, as if the entire heart of the mountain had been carved away. Einar had never seen or even imagined anything like it, an immense pit that rose hundreds of feet above and descended into the blackness of unseen depths. Again there was no native stone to be seen anywhere, every inch that he could see smoothed into sharp angles and flat surfaces. It all looked not to be carved at all, but built of square and rectangular blocks of the same grey stone stacked together, some seemingly thrust out precariously high overhead or leaning out over the unseen depths below. Long, slender tongues of bridges leaped unsupported across the entire span, some above and others in the darkness below. As enormous as this one tremendous shaft was, Einar could see identical ones opening to either side and a third directly beyond where they stood, all linked together by open square passages just above their own level, small in the scale of this unimaginable work and yet large enough for the flight of an entire tribe of dragons.

For Einar, it was all confusing in its complexity, the random arrangement of blocks and shafts into patterns vast beyond his ability even to see, much less comprehend. Color might have helped, but all detail was hopelessly lost in the monotony of dull grey stone and black shadows. The very size of this place was in itself staggering, arguing that it had once teemed with light and life. Now it was only a tomb, a lingering monument to a time that was long dead and passed away, claimed by darkness and death.

"This is a dark, sad place, dragon," he said softly.

"I am told that it was once very different," Kalavek said. "Once a soft blue light filled this place. Lanterns broke through the shadows of the endless night below the mountain, bright little lights of gold, green and red, and thousands of windows that you cannot now see shone bright and comforting with the warm lights of home. Now the gnomes have all but died away. The lanterns have been unlit for centuries, and the magic that once gave this city its light has faded away to a dreary grey."

For a moment Einar saw a vision of this place exactly as Kalavek described it, images shared by his magic. The darkness took on a different shade, just as soft but friendlier and broken by the twinkling of hundreds of sparks of bright light. The silence was lightened by the sounds of voices and laughter, of quiet industry and gentle play. But these visions were only the dragon's imaginings of something he himself had never seen, and not true memories.

Kalavek glanced suddenly to one side, then turned to face the shadows that filled the wide avenue along their left. Einar turned to stand at his side, both hands on his old musket. Torsk hid behind his legs, peering around with uncertainty.

"Peace, oh great dragon, High Lord of the realm of Faerie," a thin, high voice came from the shadows nearby, although Einar could see no one in the thick darkness.

"You name me Lord of a realm that has nearly faded into the light of a new world. I claim it not," the dragon answered. "I am Kalavek, sired of Halahvey the ancient and born of Kalfeer, and leader of the last tribe of dragons. I call upon you to remember, as do I, of the peace and trust that has existed unbroken between dragons and gnomes since before the dawn of the Third Age of Magic."

"Such things are remembered, as faded as the memory has become," the voice returned, although the speaker still did not step forth from the shadows. "It is also remembered that Selikah was the leader of the northern tribe, the last time that any dragon passed this way. He was a bold and mighty dragon, and we would be grieved to hear that he is gone."

"Grieve then for one who was great among dragons."

A long moment passed before the sad, frightened voice spoke again. "Then even the dragons are passing away. The world of Faerie is all but dead."

"That is not so," Kalavek insisted. "Young dragons have been born even in these final days, and they are strong and eager for life. I am Kalavek, leader of my tribe, and I stand before you less than three decades in age."

"You speak of hope?"

"Hope for us all," he insisted. "I propose to return the magic to this world. If the magic can be returned, then we will all begin to thrive and multiply. I believe that I have found a way."

"A bold plan for a young dragon," the voice said.

A small, dark form stepped out from the shadows of a passageway a dozen yards or so from where they stood. Einar peered closely. He was not himself a large man, old and wiry, but the figure that approached stood no higher than his own shoulder. It stood on legs that were short and thin, but with arms that were long and shoulders that were wide and heavily muscled. As it came nearer, he was surprised to see a face that was more alien than he had ever expected. The long, oddly feral appearance of its head, he realized, was because its brain was almost entirely behind its face rather than mostly above as in a mortal.

Then Einar saw that other small forms were moving out of the shadows to either side, approaching slowly yet keeping a cautious distance. He had the uncomfortable feeling that they were being slowly surrounded, and he held his musket close. But Kalavek seemed completely unconcerned, and he could only trust the dragon's judgement.

"You want something of us, or you would not be here," the gnome said, the odd game of words apparently at an end. "You certainly are not here to boast of the cleverness of what you propose. Dragons were never given to such vain habits, and we have become such impoverished creatures that you would get no glory of it."

"I have come only for what the dragons gave into your keeping long ago," Kalavek said. "Before he died, Selikah told me that a Core of Magic was once hidden here. I must have it back."

That certainly surprised the gnomes, and Einar thought that they were also very alarmed and frightened by that request. He was given to wonder for a moment if they had somehow lost the Core of Magic over the years, or if perhaps they had gotten rid of it in fear of such magic. The spokesman of the gnomes cowered back a couple of steps toward the safety of the shadows he had just left, but then he gathered his courage and approached the dragon even closer than before.

"The Core of Magic will show you the way to return the ancient magic to the world?" he asked. "Clever dragon."

"Clever gnome," Kalavek said in return. "Such a great task is worth the expense of a little courage. I see that in your response."

"Gnomes have faded into the vile creatures that nobler kinds always held us to be, fearful as rats," the gnome told him plainly. "Courage is now dearer to us than any treasure; we hoard what little we have left. But I like the price of what you offer. And you have brought a mortal, whose hand alone may safely touch this thing. Clever dragon indeed."

"The day has come that we must be as clever as we are courageous, or we are doomed beyond any doubt. Is the Core of Magic here?"

When the gnome hesitated and actually began to shift and shake nervously, then Einar knew that something was wrong.

"We have grown so few in number. In a city once of a million, there are now only the thirty-seven of us left," the gnome explained obliquely. "Dark creatures, the dregs of dark Faerie, have crept into the depths to hide and to die, and we have not dared to go there in many long years. They are content with the depths, and we keep near the gate. But you are a dragon, greatest and most powerful of all the faerie creatures that ever was, and you are still young and vigorous besides. In your need, you might dare in safety ways that we have not seen in centuries."

Kalavek did not answer at once, but bent his long neck well around to look at Einar. "Your danger is far greater than my own. Dragons are not easily destroyed. It is for you to decide."

"If I do not go, there is no point in you going," Einar mused, speaking mostly to himself, and the dragon did not answer. "You know these things, and you are better able to judge how matters stand. If you think that we can do it, then we have to try. Otherwise you should go and fetch all of the other dragons, and we will go down there like a regular army."

Kalavek turned his cold gaze to the gnome, who cowered and shook and made some odd gesture of appeasement. "There is little enough for you to fear. Only dark and frightened things, too weak to bear the pure light of day."

"Then you will show us the way?"

The gnome leaped back in fear, then fell to his knees. "Oh, great High Lord of dragons. . . ."

"As far as you dare go, at least," Kalavek told him in a voice hinting of impatience and resignation. "We have spoken that the price of life is courage. Now the time has come for you to help in paying a share."

The gnome hesitated. Perhaps the sight of the dragon, the most noble and powerful of all creatures of Faerie, reminded him of a time when his own kind had been less fearful and desperate, or perhaps the dragon worked some subtle magic of his own. The gnome drew himself up straighter than he had stood yet, slowly and stiffly as if pushing against the weight of centuries. He was no true king, only the forgotten servant of a king who had been dead since before mortal men had tamed the horse or first shaped metal. But he was the last leader of a race that had once been strong and proud.

"It is said by the gnomes that our death is down there," he said at last. "For a very long time now, more of us have died from the things that hide in the darkness of the depths than from all other causes. From time to time, some dark and evil thing will move up from the shadows and take one

of us back into the abyss. For you, and for the value of your
quest, I will dare to go down into those dark reaches. But I
cannot promise that I will go all the way."

"I will ask no more than what you are willing to give,"
Kalavek said.

The leader of the gnomes turned then, taking a heavy
spear that one of his fellows offered him. Without a word or
glance at the dragon, he hurried to the edge of the immense
pit and peered for a long moment into its shadowed depths.
Then he walked with long, quick steps around the edge,
seeking their path in the confusion of massive grey shapes
until he found a narrow set of stairs leading down. The
dragon had to take this way cautiously, bracing his massive
weight carefully with his forelegs and stepping down with
his haunches low to the floor. Einar followed behind with
Torsk, thinking that he preferred this place in line, between
the fear of monsters below and the dragon becoming over-
borne by his own bulk. He glanced behind occasionally,
but it seemed that none of the other gnomes possessed the
courage to accompany them.

There was no straight path down. There were many sets
of blocks that were thrust well out into open space over
the pit, others that were deeply inset like dark ledges, and
smooth expanses of featureless stone that must have been
the true face of the pit. Brief runs of steps would lead only
from one level to the next, and then they would be forced to
seek another set nearby, hidden in the shadows beside some
other massive block of grey stone. It was a very long way
down indeed and not an easy one, with all the cutting back
and forth to find the next set of stairs. Einar had to wonder
what this place had been like in the past, and how so many
thousands of gnomes had all lived together in these caverns,
what they had all eaten, and how long it had taken them to
get anywhere. The largest city perhaps in all of Norway,
hidden beneath a mountain in the middle of nowhere and
unknown to anyone.

He also spared a thought or two on the way down to
reflect upon how amazed he was to find himself here,
following a dragon who was following a gnome into the

heart of a mountain. Mayor Thorsen and the Parson would have had something tart to say, if they had known. But he doubted very much that either one of those two worthies would have agreed to help the dragons, much less come near such a place as this. He wondered if anyone he knew would have come. He was beginning to think that Kalavek had been very lucky to have happened across old Einar Myklathun. The biggest fool in the village, it seemed.

Then he wondered if it had been luck indeed. The dragon employed his magic very seldom. But when he did, it was quite subtle in its workings. It could very well have told him who would have been willing to help him. Mortals had to rely upon far less precise guides in making their decisions: their own judgement and intuition.

"We are now coming near the bottom of the western shaft," the gnome said after they had been descending for quite some time. Einar could now see the bottom even in the dim light. He thought that they had come down well over a thousand feet, perhaps as much as fifteen hundred. The gnome spoke in a low voice, but not yet with extreme caution. "These were once the most desirable regions in which to live, with great houses filled with light. Still you can see the many stone bridges that were once hung with many bright lanterns and banners."

"Here at the bottom?" Einar asked. "I would have thought that the great foundries would have been down here, near the source of the ore coming up from the mines."

"It would have been less effort to take finished metals rather than raw ores up to the top," the gnome explained. "But smoke rises, and that is why our cities are built about wide shafts. And the foundries create the greatest smokes and fumes, so we put those on the top. There, they are also nearer to the gates."

"For wood?"

The gnome turned to stare at him. "Wood?"

"For the foundries," Einar explained. "To feed the fires that melt your metals."

"Oh. No wood. Magic," the gnome said as he continued on. "The problem always was getting rid of the wastes from our mining and refining, and the rock removed from the opening of new shafts. Near the top is a long, straight tunnel that leads far away from this mountain, until it meets with a great river that runs beneath a valley where a river of ice once flowed. Once we fed crushed rock slowly but steadily into that dark river, and the cold water carried it away."

Einar could imagine that life here had been very inconvenient in a great many ways. Kalavek had told him that the various races of Faerie had lived their lives according to the dictates of the nature of their magic, and the gnomes had never been content unless they were hidden underground. It must have been important to them, to endure such inconveniences.

"Vermin stealing into the passages have always been a problem, no less now than ever," the gnome said. Einar knew that he was not referring to mice. "There simply have not been enough of us to clear them from our passages in a long time."

"By what I hear, it seems that it has been somewhat the other way around for a while now," Einar observed. When the gnome said nothing, he began to think that it had been a rather injudicious remark.

"Softly!"

That one, quiet word from the dragon brought both of his companions to a sudden stop, especially when they saw that Kalavek had himself paused almost in mid-stride. They were halfway down a flight of steps and now well within sight of the bottom, even for Einar's mortal eyes, perhaps no more than two hundred feet. The shadows were deeper near the bottom; the air was icy cold, and it was heavy with a cold mist. The gnome sank back against the wall and moved cautiously back up the steps until he had retreated past Kalavek's head, giving the dragon a clear shot forward with his flames, and Einar held his musket ready. Kalavek stood with his head raised, testing the air with his long nose and listening.

"Your vermin," he said at last. "I had not thought that such things still existed in this world, but there are many people who say the same about me."

"What things?" Einar asked.

Kalavek glanced at him. "I do not suppose that I have told you that not all the races of Faerie were people. Many were as animals, without words or laws or names of their own. Some were good and gentle, such as the unicorns. Some were fierce predators ruled by a blind instinct to hunt and destroy, if only for the sake of the kill. In such a place, they must always be hungry. Fortunately, they also seem to possess a high instinctive regard for dragons. They are drawing back."

"I was wondering if I should regret if I never see such creatures," Einar remarked.

Their odd guide glanced back at him around the dragon's shoulder. "In the experience of the gnomes, such a creature is the last thing that you will ever see."

Kalavek started on down the steps, stepping slowly and carefully with his head lifted high. Now, the gnome stayed so close to his side that it was hard to say just who was leading. They had reached a depth where another series of the great square openings joined this shaft on three sides with the others, as they had already at four other elevations. Einar supposed that these massive openings, perhaps four hundred feet square, had given the gnomes quick access to the other shafts, as well as free movement of air and the venting of smoke. After only a couple more flights of stairs, the gnome paused and contemplated a narrow stone bridge that spanned the shaft directly to the floor of such an opening.

"We must cross over now into the central shaft," he announced at last.

Einar frowned. They had not always remained on the same wall of the shaft during their descent, but there were openings into other shafts to either side and directly across, so he knew that they faced east. What worried him was the bridge, which looked very narrow and had no walls or rails along its sides.

The gnome of course was unconcerned, and even the dragon was not worried by the narrowness of the way, so Einar and Torsk followed along dutifully. The bridge seemed to him a very vulnerable place to sudden attack, and he did not doubt that any magical beasties willing to give it a try would stay behind the dragon's back and make a grab at him, the weakest and least magical of the group. Torsk seemed to be thinking similar thoughts; he was staying low in the very middle of the bridge and looking around with large eyes.

They passed the bridge without incident, all the same, and pressed on into the passage between the shafts. This way proved to be the easiest walking since the entrance tunnel, for the passage was large, level and flat, without the maze of boxes and recesses, and without the shadows that threatened a sudden and deadly attack by the magical creatures that inhabited the cold, misty depths. But it was very dark all the same, and an icy air moved lightly through its wide way, and it also felt very close after the vastness of the shaft. The city of the gnomes was so open and immense that Einar had hardly felt that he was even underground, not when he had been constantly in fear of a fall from tremendous heights.

But the passage did not go on for long, not more than two hundred yards, and the great central shaft beyond was even larger than the one they had just descended. Einar had not been aware of that from his one distant and rather misty glimpse from the top, nor had he known that there were more than just the three shafts that he had first supposed. He saw now that there were four smaller shafts connected by such passages on each side of the central shaft, and four corner shafts that connected only at right angles to the side shafts.

The very next thing that Einar saw was that the great central shaft had no visible bottom. They had been within perhaps a few short flights of steps of the bottom of the side shaft, but now they stood above an expanse that disappeared into black depths. Just at the edge of his vision, he saw that the smooth, finished stone of the upper reaches turned into rough native rock.

Einar stared at the gnome. "We have to go down there?"

"That is the old city," the gnome said, which was not actually an answer, although Einar had the uncomfortable feeling that it was. The gnome peered over the edge for a long moment. "In the earliest days of our race, in dim, forgotten ages of magic, our nature required that we hide ourselves as deeply within this world as we could find or cut passages. We were beings of weak substance, and would melt away into mist if we were touched by the light of sun or moon, and even warm sunlight radiating down through the stone was a discomfort to us."

"That was so for many of the races of Faerie," Kalavek added. "Even the elves lived in the shadows of the deep forests for many a long age, coming out only beneath the moon and stars, for they could not bear the strong light of day. But in time they grew in strength until their magic was second only to that of the dragons."

"It can be so hard to be humble, when you happen to be a dragon," the gnome muttered, which Einar thought to be even more daring than it was rude.

"Even dragons are not quite what we used to be." Kalavek accepted that in good grace.

"As the gnomes grew in both substance as well as numbers and knowledge, we began to build nearer the surface," their guide continued. "We outgrew ourselves in our own industry. We needed markets for the surplus of our craft, and a reliable source of food and materials that could not be found in our mines. Too late we realized that the strength and independence we cherished was only an illusion."

"You all starved," Einar said, remembering what the dragon had told him. "Your cities had become your prisons. Why did you not abandon them? Everything you could have needed to stay alive was just outside your doors."

"Our cities had indeed become our prisons, as you say," the gnome replied. "We had become in our decline what we were in our beginning. We can no longer survive the light of day, nor bear a bright moon. We starved by the thousands knowing that a world we could not endure lay just beyond our gates."

Einar stepped closer to the dragon's head, having noticed that Kalavek had been peering into the depths since they had arrived. He leaned over as far as he dared, wondering what the dragon was looking at so intently, and he trusted that they were both thinking the same thing. How in the name of wonder were they going to get down? It did occur to him that Kalavek might be more concerned with what they would find when they got there.

"These gnomes do everything the hard way," Einar commented. "My son told me in one of his letters that in the big buildings in Chicago, they have made boxes that move up and down with people inside."

Kalavek lifted his head and turned to stare. "Why?"

"After all the steps that we have seen, I think that you should know."

"What I meant to ask is, why would you people build anything so high that the steps are too far?"

"I wonder that myself. That is an impulse that we must share with gnomes, I suppose."

"Then I should hope that you also share their love of steps," Kalavek said as he indicated the depths with his long nose. "There is our way down. Look closely at the wall of the pit, just below where the smooth stone ends, to our right. You will see endless stairs leading down."

Einar peered closely into the shadows, but he decided that he would have to take the dragon's word on this. This light was far too dim for his mortal eyes, and they were no longer young at that. The gnome led them down several more flights of stairs, until they came at last to a deep alcove, several dozen yards wide and a couple of dozen deep with wide steps leading down from one side. When Einar came closer, he saw that this was the top of the stairs that the dragon had tried to show him from above. The stairs were cut into the wall of the shaft into something like a partial tunnel, open on the outside and with no rail. At least these were the widest steps that he had seen so far, some four yards in width.

Einar stepped even closer to the edge and peered down into the depths of the shaft. He still could not see the bottom.

"I dare go no farther than this," the guide declared, refusing even to approach the top of the stairs. "The terrors of the depths respect dragons and care nothing for mortals. No gnome has descended into the old city in five thousand years."

"I ask no more than you will freely give," Kalavek said. "Indeed, I can sense the Core of Magic from here; that will be my guide now."

"Do not descend beyond the place where the shaft narrows," the gnome added quickly, as the dragon moved to turn away. "There will be no side passages above the old city, although there are many mine shafts opened below. Until the time of starvation, the ancient mines were still worked. There are many shafts as deep as three miles, and spreading out like a spider's web beneath these mountains a hundred miles or more. Not even a dragon should dare those passages now."

"How deep below is the old city?" Kalavek asked, having turned back to face him.

"It is not two hundred yards from where we stand. At the old city, you will be over eight hundred yards below the level of the main gate. You might find water in the old city, although I cannot promise that it is fit to drink. Anything you need will have to be what you have brought, and any help you need will have to be your own. I cannot even tell you if any light has endured in the old city. If not, then you will need this."

He handed Einar a small lantern made of copper or perhaps even gold, with windows of misty glass.

"If you are strong and resolved in your quest, then you could well be back in perhaps four or five hours," the gnome concluded. "I will wait here a full day at the least, to lead you back to the gate."

"We will not linger on the way," Kalavek said as he turned to the stairs leading into the depths. "At least not any more than can be helped."

The dragon seemed to be in a hurry, as if he wanted to return from the depths as quickly as possible. Perhaps even he was afraid of the darkness and the enclosed places and the unknown dangers, although Einar reflected that it was less a matter of fear than a cold and logical reason to be cautious. If such vile creatures of magic still existed in the darkness below then they might well be desperate enough to take on a dragon, or wily enough to think to attack in numbers. In all the stories that Kalavek had related in the past days, tales and histories reaching back to the earliest Age of Faerie, he had spoken little of the dark kinds, creatures of little magic, except as an often nameless and unspecified danger and terror. But Einar reasoned that, if the other races of Faerie had been dying, then surely the dark kinds had been dying as well. By their own admission, the gnomes had not been down this way to check in five thousand years.

Einar was somewhat pressed to keep this pace, except that going down was easy enough and the steps were not overly steep. But all the stairs in the city of the gnomes were steep enough, and he could well guess that going up again was going to be far more difficult and slow.

"Then you know already that the Core of Magic is still here," he observed after a minute or so.

"I do sense it, and it is strong," Kalavek said without looking back. "If no creature of Faerie could touch the thing, then there is little reason for concern that it could be stolen. My own fear has been that the gnomes would have tried to use it or destroy it, or that it might have simply faded with the long passing of the years. I still suspect some treachery from the gnomes even yet."

"Pardon?"

"Our friend has been most helpful, and yet he has also made an issue of his great fear of the depths and of the creatures that he insists must lurk there even yet," the dragon explained. "He was too afraid to accompany us any farther, but now he follows quietly."

"Is that so?" Einar glanced behind, then turned back quickly, pretending to suspect nothing in case the gnome could still see him. "Now I do wonder what he could be thinking?"

"I can sense enough of his thoughts," Kalavek said. "The danger is somewhat greater than he would have had us believe. He hopes that we will succeed and he seems to expect that we will. But something below commands him against his will, and he is afraid to cast his loyalty with us because of it. It seems that the gnomes are no longer the true masters of their own city."

Einar had been happier about the matter when he had not been certain that anything nasty actually remained in the depths of the gnome city. Now he knew that something was down there, and that it might even be waiting for them. And he was not happy about that at all. If he had to place his bets on the way things stood, he guessed that the gnome had parted company with them at the last opportunity, so that he could sneak around and warn his masters that there was a dragon in the depths. The gnome leader was in fact in a very unenviable position, caught between the hope that Kalavek offered and the vengeance of the evil that lurked below.

This was beyond any doubt the most monotonous part of the entire journey, at least as far as Einar was concerned, for there were no turns or changes, just an endless, unbroken spiral of identical steps, leading down and down into the darkness. He knew that it was not really all that far; from the pace they kept and the time it took, he guessed that they walked a straightline distance of between three and four miles. He was worried most about the dragon, who was walking the entire length of the gnome city with his head lower than his haunches, although he seemed to be bearing up perfectly. Torsk followed behind with his tongue hanging out. The dog did not understand what this business was all about and he knew for a fact that he did not like this dark, cold place. But he had never failed in his loyalty to the old man and he was not about to start now, and the dragon was always interesting. Like most dogs, Torsk was motivated in life by the fear that he might miss something.

Soon enough even Einar was able to see the bottom of the shaft, which ended suddenly in a smooth floor. A smaller shaft, barely half as wide as the one above, opened in the very center of the floor. As they came lower, he was able to see that there were openings in the wall at the very bottom of the shaft, some small and square and others large and very wide. But they were all perfectly square or rectangular; Einar saw that right away. Whatever else one might say about the odd habits and manners of gnomes, their fearfulness of others and their delight in industry, they were above all else perfectionists. They would never leave a patch stone bare and rough, not if it was somewhere that they ever had to look at it.

From all Einar could imagine, untold thousands of gnomes must have been chipping away as hard as they could go for many years to carve all of this. The true age of these mines was a matter quite beyond his comprehension; in his own mind, all the history of the world before the coming of men could not be much longer than the few thousand years since. The fact that there was an old city beneath the newer passages above meant that Behrgarad was one of the oldest settlements of the gnomes, dating from the very first Age of Faerie when the gnomes had lived deeper underground to escape the sun.

Kalavek stepped off the bottom of the stairs onto the smooth floor and turned without a pause, moving with long, slow, stealthful strides toward one of the larger passages. They all looked very much the same to Einar, and he could only assume that the dragon was guided by some magical sense. He was beginning to appreciate that their safety was largely dependent upon Kalavek's magic.

"Is there anything sneaking about down here?" he asked very, very quietly as he followed close behind the dragon.

"Nothing all that close," he replied, speaking softly, although there was no apparent concern in his voice. Not that there had ever been any.

"Do you smell anything?" he asked, remembering that dragons seemed to have very keen senses of smell. He sniffed the air for himself. There was a dry, musty scent to these lower levels. If anything did exist down here, then it must be dying of mildew.

"Nothing fresh."

Einar had guessed that already. He glanced down at Torsk, who just looked slightly bewildered and shook his head slowly. After the company that they had been keeping lately, Einar did not think to find that odd.

The passages of the old city were like the upper passages turned inside out. The tunnels were small and the ceilings low, so low for the most part that the dragon could not lift his head. As above, the stone was neatly trimmed and leveled into flat surfaces and sharp corners, although not to the glassy finish of the upper levels but rough and grainy in texture, and much of the sharp edges had been worn away. But once again the stone was grey and not brown, and although it did not glow it did seem to shed a pale light.

The passages seemed to follow the lines of original mineshafts, sometimes lifting over a rise or passing through a dip, or changing level for no reason that was apparent. They would come to sudden chambers, wide with high ceilings and odd, rectangular blocks like stone tables, as if these were ancient markets or workplaces. But there were no doorways or dark windows, only small side passages leading quickly into darkness. These were hardly the well-ordered streets of a true city, but rambling, disorganized passages that had begun as simple mineshafts.

There was a more oppressive feel to these passages, at least as far as Einar was concerned. The upper shafts had been vast and wondrous beyond imagination, confusing in their complexity of design. Here, the ceiling was low enough that Einar could always see it, and often reach up to touch it, and he sensed the entire weight of the mountain just overhead. As for the dragon, he sometimes looked like a ferret in a burrow.

Sooner than it seemed to Einar, indeed within half a mile of leaving the main shaft, they came suddenly upon what was the largest cavern in the old city. The tunnel bent around slowly toward the left, while a dim rumbling sound filled the air that had abruptly become cold and wet. Suddenly they came out into the cavern, descending at a sharp angle through a long cascade of immense stone blocks and steps. An underground river, small but swift and loud, emerged from a tunnel to their right, plunging in a long, breathless flume to the bottom. Einar guessed that it had once descended in its own series of steps that the endless passage of water had long since worn away. A stone bridge leaped across the river at the upper landing to an identical walkway on the opposite side, the dark opening of a second passage at its top.

"This whole place smells like a large, wet stone," Kalavek declared as they stood at the top landing, just before the tunnel opening. Einar had rather liked this place, but he seemed as unimpressed as ever. "Dragons belong to the sky, the forests and the mountains. It is not at all far now, and then we can be done with this place."

They descended the steps as quickly as they could, although the passage was so narrow that Kalavek had to step carefully, as if walking a tightrope. The stairs ran in an unbroken cascade all the way to the bottom, without any landings, although the main part of the descent to either side of the falls was made of massive blocks of grey stone, more than large enough—to either side of the steps—for two dragons to have stood upon side by side. And the far side of the falls was a perfect mirror image of their own way.

The bottom came quickly, although they had been able to see it clearly for some time. The descent fell away suddenly into the blackness of a pit, filled with the mist and the dull thundering echoes of the falls as it crashed into unseen depths. For the first time there was no clear path, at least not for Einar and Torsk. The wall below them was sheer and perfectly featureless, broken only by a deep groove worn through time by the waterfall, and the far wall was even more plain. Only the side walls were formed by massive blocks of smooth carved stone like giant steps, descending very sharply. But there were no stairs that Einar could see anywhere.

Kalavek had his own solution to the problem, since he was large enough to lower himself over the immense stone blocks and then lift first Einar and then Torsk down after him. Einar had to wonder how the dog would take such handling; Torsk had always maintained a cautious distance between himself and the dragon, not so much out of fear but an apparently sincere respect. But Torsk took it well.

"The gnomes used ladders here, in the ancient days," Kalavek explained, to pass the time. Their descent was long and very slow. "This is the only passage to the deepest and most secure chambers of the old city, and to the most protected of their treasures. If enemies won into the passages above, then gates would close off the tunnel of the river below, causing this pit to flood until it overflowed through drain vents at the top. You will see that the passage rises again on the other side, until it is above the level that would flood. Such a depth of water first down and then back up again forms a very effective barrier, when all others fail."

"Are you guessing all of this?" Einar asked.

"No, indeed. These things have been remembered by the dragons in our tales of the ancient times."

This was the slowest part of their journey underground, although with the dragon's help it really did not take very long. The sides of the pit closed in very tight near the bottom—very much like the drain in the bottom of a basin, Einar was now inclined to think—and filled with a cold mist from the falls. The far wall at the very bottom opened upon a dark tunnel, although he saw when he came nearer that it was in fact only a short passage, hardly more than a doorway, opening upon a large chamber with a low ceiling, and filled completely with a deep, icy pool.

At least there were narrow walkways along either wall of the oval chamber, so narrow that the dragon could hardly traverse the path. As Kalavek had said, there was another passage at the opposite side, although this side did not have a waterfall feeding into it. The water of the pool drained through a whirlpool in the center of the lake, at a measured rate that kept the level even. The water left through a passage below, where the gate must have been located.

"Do you suppose it still works?" Einar asked.

"No, I doubt that very much," Kalavek said. "The age of this place is vast, even as dragons would measure time. Almost I am amazed that these passages still stand open. The face of the world has changed a dozen times over since these ways were cut."

They looped all the way around to the far side of the pool on the narrow walkway. Here they found their way leading up again, this time through a wide circular shaft with an unbroken stairway leading up in a spiral. Once again the way was almost too narrow for the dragon, but they made the climb quickly and found themselves in a simple passage leading straight into the darkness. For some reason, the pale grey light that had guided them all this way failed completely, leaving them lost in complete blackness. Einar looked at the lamp that the gnome had given him, wondering how it worked. But Kalavek had the solution to this as in all other matters, and the dragon began to glow with a golden light of his own. His light showed only the floor beneath them and did not reach as far as the walls or even the ceiling. But the dragon was guided by other senses now.

Einar judged by the echoes that they must have passed through several long tunnels and chambers of various size, although none very large. They came in time to the first and only turn in the tunnel, and Einar suddenly saw a point of bright blue light far ahead, like a star in the distance. It did not grow in size as they came nearer, although it did become steadily brighter, shining with its cold and steady light of icy blue. Soon they left the tunnel for a chamber of some size, or so he judged by the echoes, and they saw the globe of blue light with its heart like a bright star resting still where it had been set by the dragons long ago, in a cradle of gold atop a great block of stone, and protected by a dome of clear crystal.

In the pale blue light, Einar could see great piles of gold, silver and jewels of every type, some in massive chests of wood that had long since split open and spilled their contents across the floor. There were whole mounds of precious metals, shaped in coins and in small bars. He could see very little, for the light did not reach far. There was enough here, he did not doubt, to make everyone in Norway a reasonably rich man, although it would take half the population of Norway to haul it out of this deep hole. He had come to collect only one treasure, far more precious to the dragons than all the gold in the world.

Kalavek paused for a moment, twisting his long neck to look back over his shoulder, then he turned back to the great block of stone and lifted the dome of crystal away, setting it to one side. There was nothing more that he could do. Einar took a large leather bag from his pack. Then he paused. The Core of Magic was a thing of tremendous power, and no dragon or any creature of Faerie dared to touch the thing. While he did have Kalavek's assurance that a mortal hand could touch it without fear, he suddenly realized that this promise had probably never been tested.

But he had come too far to be afraid now. He reached out and laid his hand on the Core of Magic, but found that he could not lift it as easily as that. It was a thing of no firm substance, giving only a feeling of strong resistance as he squeezed it tight. There was a limit to how firmly he could press, until it seemed that he had hold of a ball of some glowing, misty substance just small enough for him to get one hand about halfway around it. As soon as he was sure of his grip, he lifted it clear of its golden cradle and popped it quickly inside his bag.

"It is done," he said as he closed the bag, then glanced up at the dragon. "You did not need me after all, it seems. You could have just popped a bag over the top of the thing and scooped it up."

"I never expected that it could be so simple," Kalavek answered. "But for now, our time is running out. Things are beginning to stir in these lower passages. I can sense them, and I certainly do not wish to face them here, with only the one way out."

Einar slipped the strap of the closed bag over his head, and readied his old musket. Then he hurried after the dragon, who was stalking along at such a pace that the old man had to walk as fast as he could manage just to keep up. Whether or not Kalavek was actually afraid, he certainly did not wish a confrontation here in the lower tunnels. For his own part, Einar knew that he would feel better about matters once they were back to an area where there was at least some light. It was too easy to imagine evil things sneaking about in the dark, or coming unseen up behind.

They had nearly come to the end of the dark passages when Kalavek slowed and then stopped completely, and Einar knew that their time had indeed run out. The dragon was peering into the blackness ahead, as if his large eyes could pierce the darkness. Einar could sense the presence of dark purpose himself, and he knew that something deadly approached. Torsk cowered close against his legs, his soft growl almost a desperate whine of fear.

"Move away from my light, into the darkness," Kalavek said softly. "Stay completely to the left, until you find the wall, and follow that forward. I will keep it delayed, and to the right of the passage."

"It will not notice me?" Einar asked.

"You carry a magic that can be sensed by every creature of Faerie within these passages," the dragon said candidly. "All that I can do is to give you time enough to get past. Go now."

Einar moved quietly into the shadows, until his hand touched the cold, damp stone of the wall. There he paused, hiding in the dark. Kalavek stood his ground, bathed in his own golden light, his neck arched and his head low as he stood ready to spring. His wings were pulled tight against his back to protect them from attack, and his long, powerful hind legs were like coiled springs ready to thrust him forward into battle.

When the fight began, it came suddenly. Einar saw a pair of pale red eyes appear out of the darkness ahead, and without warning the dragon and the vast black shape hurtled toward each other. There was a great deal of snapping of teeth and the deep, rumbling growl of the dragons, like the purring of some immense cat, but the two adversaries moved so quickly that Einar could see little of their fight. Kalavek maintained his magical light, presenting himself as an easy target to his elusive enemy but showing Einar his position.

Einar knew what that meant, and he hurried on as quickly as he could. The dragon was indeed a creature of deep honor. He could have more easily saved himself, but he

was giving Einar the first chance to escape even at the risk
of his own life. For himself, Einar was not about to waste
the gift. There were a lot of old men in the world and not
so many dragons, but he knew that he could never argue the
point with Kalavek. He hurried on, holding his gun ready
before him, as little as he trusted its ability as a weapon
against any creature of Faerie and many that were mortal.
Very much on his mind was the thought that he might not
be running away from one enemy as much as he might be
running toward others, and this time without the protection
of his dragon.

He saw a grey light begin to grow ahead almost immediately, and he came upon the circular pit within a hundred
yards of leaving Kalavek. As he descended the spiral of
stairs as quickly as he could, he had to hope that he was
not getting too far ahead of the dragon, and that Kalavek
would be able to escape or destroy his enemy. He had not
forgotten that there were no stairs on the other side, and
that it might take him quite some time to get himself and
Torsk up the massive stone blocks of its sides without the
dragon's help. Time that they did not have.

They reached the bottom of the spiral stairs sooner than
Einar would have thought, and he was surprised to find that
he no longer felt quite so old when he had reason enough
to keep running. But once they reached the bottom, they had
to pass through the chamber of the pool, and Einar could
not pass the narrow walkway along the side as quickly
as he would have liked. They were nearly across when
a sudden noise caused Einar to pause and look back. A
moment later, Kalavek descended heavily to the bottom of
the circular shaft, his broad wings cupped to catch the air
but still falling more than flying, without the room to glide.
He immediately reared back on his hind legs, his head and
arms lifted ready for battle.

A moment later, a massive black form landed almost
on top of him, and the two combatants were immediately
locked in battle. For the first time, Einar was able to have
a look at their attacker, and he recognized it at once from
Kalavek's descriptions. It was a Shadow, in size and form

identical with the dragon but solid black in color with eyes that burned like red flame. And for all that Einar could tell, both were exactly the same size. He reckoned with reasonable certainty that they were in a whole lot of trouble.

Einar's first thought was to move as quickly and quietly as he could out of the pool chamber, without calling attention to himself. If the Shadow was to come after him, then it might make life far more difficult for both himself and Kalavek. He made his retreat both swift and silent, at least as much so as he could, but he could not help glancing back.

The struggle between Kalavek and the Shadow was fierce and violent. Locked in combat, they soon came rolling out of the passage into the larger chamber and right into the pool. It was quite deep, enough that it left the both of them swimming. They thrashed and struggled furiously, throwing up whole clouds and fountains of water, while Einar and Torsk worked their way quietly along the side of the pool. Then, just as Einar was about to slip through the passage into the pit of the waterfall, he saw that the struggles of the dragon and the Shadow had carried them near the center of the pool, and he paused to watch. Kalavek, clearly visible because of his brighter color, seemed to be forcing the Shadow across the length of the pool. The dragon suddenly dived beneath the surface and then pushed himself forward strongly, perhaps dropping down until he was able to thrust his hind legs against the bottom of the pool, driving his head against the Shadow's belly. The impact threw the black creature a short distance backward, almost into the center of the whirlpool. The Shadow struggled weakly, but he was stunned and caught off his guard, and he vanished screaming his fury into the depths.

Kalavek did not hesitate. As soon as the Shadow was gone, he began to cross to the edge of the pool in great, floundering leaps. Einar also did not wait, but hurried into the pit of the waterfall and lifted Torsk onto the top of the first of the great blocks carved into one side wall, then pulled himself up. They had a long, slow climb ahead, and that was only the first step in the long path back out of the underground city. He had just lifted Torsk up to the top of the third block when he felt large, strong hands lift him as well, up three whole levels of blocks.

"Is it gone?" Einar asked as the dragon lifted Torsk up as well.

"Not for long, I suspect," Kalavek answered, and lifted him up the next group of steps. "You cannot drown a dragon so easily, and I suspect that it is so with Shadows as well. I had stunned him, both by my ramming him and by my magic, or he would not have gone down at all. He will pull himself up again soon enough, although he must fight the whole weight of water coming down the hole atop him."

With the dragon's help, they made the climb very quickly, and Einar was very glad for that. But they were still ten feet or more from the top when Kalavek paused and lifted his head straight up, to the full limit of his long neck. He glanced down at Einar after a moment.

"I must go on alone," he said. "They are waiting, two of them, but not as strong as the one below. I will chase them into the pit. You wait here and hide in the dark, and then hurry on when the way is clear."

"I could help," Einar offered, drawing his old musket from where it had hung on his back by its strap.

"I hardly expect that to help," Kalavek said as he prepared to climb up over the edge of the pit, clinging to the blocks of the wall like some immense lizard on a sunny wall. "I recall your gun."

Suddenly he leaped with surprising speed up over the edge of the pit and straight into battle. There was a great deal of the roaring and growling that both dragons and Shadows made in a fight, while Einar and Torsk huddled close to the wall in a dark place between the blocks. Almost immediately the large black form of a Shadow hurtled back-first over the edge of the pit and fell screaming with fear and fury into the depths of the pit. Although it seemed doomed to land heavily on its back, a loud splash from far below argued that it had fallen into the smaller pool at the base of the falls.

Einar looked down into the depths, and he was very alarmed to see the dark shape of the Shadow emerge from the mists surrounding the base of the waterfall, climbing quickly up the wall of the pit directly below him. He brought his gun around and pointed its long muzzle straight down, hoping that a close shot would at least startle the creature enough to cause it to fall. This one was considerably smaller than the first, but it still looked large and fierce enough to Einar and it was swarming up the side of the pit as if climbing a ladder. It was more than halfway up when the second Shadow plummeted into the pit and right on top of the first, and they both fell into the darkness below. Einar looked up in time to see Kalavek leap into the shaft after them, his wings cupped to break his fall.

"Time to go," Einar said as he slipped his musket over his back. "That young dragon will not keep them back for long."

Torsk did not seem likely to argue. They hurried as much as possible, but it still took Einar a little time to get them both to the top of the pit. He looked up over the top cautiously, fearful as always of meeting some creature of evil while the dragon was not there, but the passage looked clear all the way to the top of the stairs that ran to either side of the underground river. He pushed Torsk over the top before climbing up himself. Then holding his musket ready, he hurried quietly up the steps.

They reached the top without seeing or hearing a thing except the rushing of the icy water in its ancient trough. But he thought that he should wait there for the dragon, hesitating between his fear of going forward and the thought that he should be covering as much ground as he could. But before he even had a chance to decide, Kalavek suddenly bounded out of the pit and raced up the steps. The larger of the two Shadows was after him only a moment later, and the smaller followed close behind.

Einar knew that he should have run, or at least hidden himself. But he could see right away that Kalavek would not be able to outrun his enemies, not pulling up the long, steep stairs. He was a large and powerful dragon, while they were small, light and swift. He had nearly reached the top when the larger of the Shadows threw himself forward in a powerful leap, coming down heavily on the dragon's hindquarters and pulling him down. The smaller Shadow was there in an instant, their combined weight keeping Kalavek pinned down while they clawed and bit at his armor. They were not able to hurt him so easily and he was at least able to keep them away from his vulnerable head and neck, but he could not throw them off and he could not fight back.

Einar did not even stop to think. He might have reasoned to himself that he could not have ever found his way out of the underground city without the dragon to guide him, much less to protect him. He might have thought that there were too few dragons in the world to leave one to die. But the simple truth was that he did what he did for the sake of loyalty and friendship. He ran down the steps to where the two Shadows held Kalavek penned to the steps. The larger of the two, sprawled across the dragon's back and holding his front legs, turned his head and looked at Einar as the old man ran up.

The Shadow arched his neck and drew a breath, a gesture Einar recognized as a dragon about to breath flame, although Kalavek had told him that these evil creatures possessed a breath of deadly cold. Knowing that his time was short, he thrust the end of his musket into the Shadow's open mouth and shot. He recalled, as Kalavek had earlier, that the weapon was not at all effective against a dragon's armor. And so he figured that this was the only place a musket was likely to do a Shadow any harm, and little enough at that. The gun made a tremendous flash and smoke, and that startled the dark creature as much as the ball stung him. He drew back in surprise and alarm, and that gave Kalavek the moment he needed to throw the Shadows off his back.

Einar did not see what happened next. He had done all he could but he was weaponless now, and he figured that he could serve both Kalavek and himself best by getting out of the way. He hurried back up the steps and then led Torsk into the dark, narrow passage beyond, at the same time doing his best to get powder and ball into the musket. They had gone perhaps a quarter of a mile when a distant, rumbling roar echoed through the passage, and Einar paused to look back. It sounded as if the tunnels behind had fallen.

"Einar Myklathun!" Kalavek's voice called from out of the darkness, still from some distance away. It was obviously a warning of his approach, so that the old man would not think it was Shadows. He was a considerate dragon.

"Standing here!" he called back.

The dragon appeared out of the misty darkness of the tunnel behind, slowing from a run to a brisk, pacing walk as he approached. He did not stop, and Einar fell in beside him.

"The Shadows leaped the river and vanished up the other tunnel," Kalavek reported. "I brought down the tunnel opening, so that they could not easily double back behind us. I do not doubt that they are hurrying to get ahead of us just now, and they likely know these tunnels. Stay close. And if they do not open their mouths, shoot their ears."

"That will hurt them?"

"That will startle them, at least," Kalavek said, his own ears twitching as he seemed to consider the thought.

Einar glanced at him. "What about the one who went down the drain?"

"I have sensed nothing of him. Perhaps the press of water carried him right through, and he will turn up in the ocean sometime tomorrow."

Einar hardly knew whether he meant that, or whether it was an example of the dragon's very subtle and unusual sense of humor. But if Kalavek could still jest about it, then perhaps their situation was far from hopeless, and Einar took heart from that. But they had gone only a few steps when the dragon stopped, bending his long neck around to stare at the mortal.

"If it comes to a fight, do not hesitate to use the Core of Magic to save yourself," Kalavek said. "I have seen it and sensed its potential. It has nothing new to teach me, and I can do just as well without its power."

"Is that the truth?" Einar asked suspiciously.

"Of course that is the truth," Kalavek insisted, confused. It would never have occurred to him to have said otherwise.

They started off again, and the dragon hurried them on at a good pace, as fast as they could manage. He would have carried them on his back, except that his sharp dorsal ridge did not allow that. It was not as far back to the main shaft as it had seemed coming in, indeed hardly more than half a mile, and they covered that in well under five minutes.

But the way was held before them. They were crossing the last of the great chambers when a massive black shape suddenly hurtled out of a dark doorway to one side, barely missing Einar and passing right over Torsk, crashing heavily into the dragon's side and sending him sprawling. Einar and the dog retreated quickly into a dark corner where nothing could come at them from behind, and the old man held his musket ready. But he realized immediately that this was the largest of the three Shadows that they had seen so far, the one that had attacked first. For the moment, his full attention was centered entirely on the dragon and Einar was forgotten, even in that first moment of surprise when the snap of a claw or tail would have been the end of him.

"Why do you fight me?" Kalavek asked as they struggled. "Give me the Core of Magic. I can bring the old magic back into the world, and we can all begin to prosper."

"I know what you intend," the Shadow hissed in fury, pausing only a moment in his attack. "Do you innocent, foolish dragons not understand the truth even yet? We are what you strive to be. We are dragons, adapted for life in this new, hard world. We do not need the old magic. When the last of your old, weak breed are gone, then we will prosper."

The Shadow leaped at him, but Kalavek caught him out of the air and tossed him heavily to one side. "I am beginning to understand matters better than you think, better even than you understand yourself. I tell you now that when the dragons die, then your own kind will die."

Einar was wondering what he could do to help matters, but he was never given the time to act. Suddenly he saw two more Shadows appear out of the darkness from the far end of the chamber, the two that Kalavek had faced beside the underground river. He saw to his surprise and horror that they were pacing slowly and intently toward him like two vast, black cats, ignoring the battle. Torsk cowered between Einar's legs, his steady growling taking on a shrill, desperate note. Einar realized immediately that they could expect no help from the dragon. He was already fully occupied with the largest of the Shadows, and they seemed to be perfectly matched.

Knowing the gun to be useless, he slipped it quickly onto his back. Then he drew out the old leather bag and opened it as swiftly as he could untie the straps, and he drew out the Core of Magic. He held it before him, directly in the fiery eyes of the two Shadows, and it began to glow brighter the nearer they came, its bluish-white light soon flooding that end of the chamber, and the Shadows blinked and turned aside their great armored heads. No creature of Faerie, good or evil, would dare touch the thing, knowing that it meant their own certain destruction. His two attackers apparently took the point quite well and kept their distance, not daring to spring at him for fear of accidentally touching the Core.

"Take it back, mortal," they said in soft, icy voices. "You are an aging descendant of a race of slaves, and you should not meddle in affairs that are beyond your right or wisdom. Take it back, and you may go."

"Ja, I mean to go, but I am taking this and my dragon with me," he said. He made a swift, threatening gesture with the Core of Magic, and they flinched. "Back away, now. I would trust none of your bargains, but I will use this to have my way."

The two Shadows hissed and snarled, flashing sharp fangs and eyes burning with rage, but they did give way reluctantly. Einar was almost surprised that they did, for he had never expected them to be so reasonable. But he never got his chance to try to stop the fight between Kalavek and the largest of the Shadows. The young dragon suddenly lowered his head and hurtled himself right into the middle of his enemy, forcing the surprised Shadow backwards across the chamber and right through into the tunnel beyond. The Shadow leaped away in desperation and ran, retreating down the narrow passage. Kalavek followed close behind.

Einar looked up in some surprise, suddenly finding himself alone with the two smaller Shadows, who looked as belligerent as ever and also just a little encouraged by this unexpected turn of events. Einar saw no hope for it, and he directed Torsk into the tunnel after the dragon, sending the dog first to watch the way against sudden attack. He backed his way as quickly as he dared through the tunnel, holding the Core of Magic between himself and the Shadows. At the same time he had to be careful not to trip on the often uneven floor with its random turns and changes of level, knowing that the Shadows would leap at him if he did happen to go down. There was not room for them in the narrow tunnel to pace side by side, but he could see the burning eyes of the larger of the pair following close behind.

At least the way was not far, opening upon the main shaft itself. There he found Kalavek and the largest of the Shadows, continuing their battle to one side. Einar stayed where he was, just before the opening and keeping the two Shadows penned within the tunnel where they could not go to the aid of their comrade. He held the Core of Magic in the very center of the opening, but his eyes were more often turned toward the battle. The dragon had been commanding the battle, if only just barely, but now he was beginning to pay the price and growing tired with the struggle. Worse yet, the Shadow was coming to realize that the advantage was beginning to shift to his side, and he was waiting patiently for Kalavek to fumble or make some mistake in his growing exhaustion.

Einar never saw what happened, his eyes momentarily turned back to the pair he kept pinned in the tunnel. He glanced back just in time to see the dragon thrown backwards against the wall of the shaft. Kalavek hit with force enough to shake the stone itself, and then he slid heavily into a weary pile on the floor. He was just beginning to pick himself up weakly when the Shadow took a deep, full breath and aimed a blast of white, icy mist at the defenseless dragon. For the moment Kalavek could only turn aside his head, his large eyes tightly closed, while a sheet of heavy icy began to spread across his neck, wings and shoulders.

Kalavek braced his legs wide against the force of the blast, then snapped his head around sharply and aimed his own fiery breath at his enemy, not a sustained tongue of flame but a brief ball of flame that hit with an explosive impact. The Shadow, taken by surprise, was knocked back onto his tail. The two adversaries leaped up at almost the same moment and rushed directly at each other. But Kalavek was crafty, diving suddenly beneath his enemy and then coming up to catch the Shadow by the tail as he passed and swinging him around. The Shadow rolled across the floor. Before he could recover, Kalavek hit him again, ramming him low in the middle and sweeping him right over the edge of the shaft into the darkness below.

At that same moment, some tremendous force struck Einar across the side and sent him sprawling; he had kept his eyes away from the pair he guarded too long. The Core of Magic was hurtled from his grasp. It did not roll, but seemed to slide across the stone floor as if on ice to the very edge of the shaft. Einar shook his head and sat up painfully, finding that he was not actually hurt. Fortunately for him, the two smaller Shadows had gone after Kalavek and had left him alone.

Einar hurried after the Core of Magic, fearful that it would disappear into the depths of the shaft. Despite Kalavek's assertion that he did not need it, it was still no doubt a very useful thing to a dragon, possessing so much magic. And with the Shadows already attacking, Einar knew that they would never find a chance to retrieve it from the unseen bottom of the older shaft. He gathered it up, its strange, vague feel again in his hands, and then picked himself up painfully. The snap of the Shadow's tail had done him no good, even if it had done him no serious injury.

Then he paused. The largest of the Shadows had returned, a vast black shape with burning eyes rising slowly straight up the shaft with long, powerful beats of his broad wings. Other Shadows, half a dozen or more, were swarming up the sides of the shaft, clinging to the rough stone as they climbed, their heads turned upward and their red eyes full of fury and deadly intent. Even as he watched, the largest of the Shadows began to drift toward him. It was staring straight at him, and he knew immediately that it meant to make an end to him and whatever small problems he represented. It settled on the very edge of the shaft, its tail and haunches disappearing below the rim, and its massive armored head was not eight feet from where Einar stood. Then it arched its neck slightly and drew a breath, preparing a blast of its deadly ice.

Einar used the only weapon he had, and when the Shadow opened its mouth he tossed the Core of Magic right inside, hoping as he did that Kalavek had been sincere about his need for the thing. The Shadow arched its powerful neck and screamed, and its entire form began to flash as if transparent to a blue-grey light within. Stricken, it lost its hold on the stone and slowly fell backwards into the depths of the pit.

But that was not the end of it. There followed a tremendous flash of brilliant bluish-white light from far below, and a great booming, echoing vibration began to shake the mountain itself, as if the very stone was trying to shake itself apart. The vast reserves of power trapped within the Core of Magic had been released, and they were tearing Behrgarad to pieces. Great runners of raw, destructive magic raced up the shaft like traces of blue and green lightning, shaking the Shadows still climbing up from below from the sheer stone walls and sending them falling into the depths.

The crack of stone echoed through the shaft, and Einar looked up to see that the bridges far above were beginning to break and crumble. Some fairly large pieces were already on their way down, and Einar decided that it was time to get under cover. Pushing Torsk before him, he hurried back to the tunnel and hid just within the entrance. When he looked back, he was alarmed to see that Kalavek was down, and the two remaining Shadows were about to make short work of him. He checked his musket quickly to be certain that it was loaded, then rushed out to help the dragon. Already smaller bits of stone broken from the bridges were beginning to crash down onto the floor or into the smaller shaft, and the mountain was shaking so violently that he had to be careful of his balance. But for the moment, all he knew was that he had to save his dragon.

He was spared the need. A large boulder suddenly struck the smaller of the two Shadows with force enough to shatter the stone, crushing its folded wings and back. The little Shadow lifted its head straight up, screaming in mortal pain, before it suddenly dissolved into a thick black mist that flowed away across the floor and into the lower shaft. Bracing his forelegs, Kalavek thrust himself up and turned on the remaining Shadow with new fury. With a swift dart of his head, he caught his smaller opponent just at the top of its neck and pinned it to the floor, holding it down for a long moment until its struggles began to diminish. Then he seized the dark creature by its neck and front leg and wrenched it around, sending it spinning helplessly across the floor and into the pit.

Einar paused a moment, seeing that even larger sections of the bridges were beginning to come down. Magic still shot like bolts of blue and green lightning up the sides of the shafts and down the tunnels, shaking apart the very stone. Then he rushed to the dragon's side. Kalavek was spent, and he looked utterly worn and exhausted.

"Come on, you foolish dragon," he declared. "We have to get under cover, at least until these bridges stop falling. Then maybe we might be able to make a rush up the stairs."

"This is not the time to die," Kalavek agreed in a weak voice, and he followed Einar back to the shelter of the tunnel.

"I am sorry about your quest," Einar said. They were huddled just within the entrance of the tunnel, while large sections of bridges crashed down into the shaft, exploding into blocks and splinters of stone with the impact.

"There is no cause for regret," Kalavek assured him. "If I had known what I know now, I would not have come here but gone on to the Fountain of the World's Heart. There was no need ever to bring you into this terrible place."

"I was glad to come for you, all the same. At least now we know." Einar ducked his head as another large section of a bridge crashed down just a short distance away. "And I will feel even better about it when we get out of this place."

Kalavek watched the falling of the stone bridges that seemed to fill the shaft with debris and dust and waited, obviously thinking very hard about how he was going to get them out. But to Einar he looked very tired, as if a faltering will was all that kept him standing, that he might almost lose the ability to care whether they lived or died any moment. And Einar had cause to worry about the harm that he might have taken in his battle with the Shadows. He had gotten the best of it, even outnumbered, but at what price? He looked thin and wasted. Suddenly he lowered himself to the floor of the tunnel, lying his full length. A great crack split the ceiling of the tunnel right over their heads, but it did not come down.

He twisted his head around to look at Einar. "This place will be coming down even sooner than I had expected. Widen the strap on that pouch and place it about my neck, so that you will have something to hold. Then place all the blankets you have, even your jacket, over the ridges of my back to protect you from the sharp edges, such as they are. The only way that I can get you out of here now is to carry you."

Einar hurried to do as he directed, pulling the two blankets from his pack. Perhaps the pale grey light was failing at last, or perhaps the air was just choked with dust, but it was getting darker. The tunnel was almost completely dark,

although the grey light beyond still sneaked a short way
inside the opening of the tunnel. Worse yet, the vibrations
were getting stronger. He trusted that Kalavek could find
his way out again even in absolute darkness, but not if the
ceiling fell on them. He felt guilty enough for letting the
dragon carry him, as tired as he seemed, but Einar was still
the older and slower of the two. He could hardly carry the
dragon.

He finished soon enough and climbed onto the dragon's
back, lying to the right side of the dragon's spinal ridge
with one leg braced over the top, and holding tight to the
strap of the pouch. Kalavek had his head bent all the way
around, watching. "Hold tight, now."

"What about Torsk?" Einar asked suddenly. The poor
dog was staring up at them with large round eyes and the
pitiable look of the sacrificial lamb.

"I have given thought even to that."

Kalavek stepped out of the tunnel and climbed quickly
to the top of a large pile of rubble. He sat back on his hind
legs, bracing himself with his tail, and reached over with
his large hands to take up the startled dog. Torsk made a
small startled sound as if he had been squeezed just a little
too hard, but he did not protest. Then the dragon thrust
himself into the air with his powerful hind legs, his broad
wings snapping out.

Bits of stone continued to fall in a fitful hail, but the
bridges were gone and the ceiling and walls were only just
beginning to collapse under the fearful shaking. Kalavek held
his wings straight and motionless like some vast soaring bird,
spiraling swiftly upward propelled by the lift generated from
all the magic he had left to command. They climbed quickly,
past endless stairs that had taken them half a day to descend,
first up the wider section of the older shaft and then into the
new levels of Behrgarad. Great cracks and gaping fissures
split the walls, crumbling the ledges and carved blocks of
ancient stone, and the debris was beginning to cascade in
great dusty curtains into the depths. If they had remained
in the tunnel even seconds longer, the way out would have
been buried.

Kalavek rose in as tight a spiral as he could manage and so avoided the worst of the falling rubble. If even a small boulder had hit him, as burdened as he was, it would have been the end of them all. But their combined luck continued to hold. Einar thought for a moment that the Shadows must by now all be dead and buried deep. They continued to rise, past the immense square openings that connected the main shaft with the others. Einar recalled the gnomes, and wondered if this would be the end of them as well. Perhaps the destruction would stop before the city collapsed completely, and they could live on in some dusty pocket. For them, remaining was more certain a chance to survive than fleeing, since they could not exist in the light of sun and moon that lay beyond their gates. Or perhaps their kind would survive in some other city, forgotten beneath remote mountains.

They reached the top soon enough, and Kalavek darted forward through one of the openings into an adjoining shaft. This was the most dangerous part so far, for now he had to bolt through the curtains of jagged rubble that lay over the openings, falling down from above, trusting his speed, his timing and his luck more than ever. Einar could only hope that he had kept his sense of direction in all this madness and ruin, especially after that long spiral up from the depths, and was leading them to the way out. The dragon hurtled out into the openness of a new shaft and spiraled again for a moment, this time to gain no height but to allow Kalavek to bend his head this way and that for a quick look about. Suddenly he turned and darted away to one side, then he slowed himself abruptly with powerful backstrokes of his wings to land on a wide ledge. He released Torsk, and the grateful dog ran straight to the inner wall before he turned to look back. Einar thought that he recognized this as the place were they had met the gnomes.

A sudden shock, the most violent so far, shook the mountain itself, and Kalavek had to brace his legs wide to avoid being thrown to the floor. Great sections of the walls and ceiling began to crumble, vanishing into clouds of grey dust as they slid away into the depths. A large section of the

ceiling just overhead fell right in front of Kalavek, so that
he leaped back in alarm. He cut around that as he bolted
for the dark entrance of the wide tunnel in the back of the
ledge, then leaped aside a second time as another massive
slab of rock nearly fell on his head.

They were inside the tunnel a moment later, with Einar
still clinging to the dragon's back while Torsk ran eagerly
ahead. Even that was not safe, for the passage was cracking
and falling even as they ran, and the way was long. The
mountain continued to shake as if trying to tear itself apart,
making it hard to run or even walk, and Einar was beginning
to think that they might not make it even yet. The dragon
began to fall often after the first mile, whether from the
violence of the tremors or his own exhaustion, sometimes
hurtling himself hard against the wall of the tunnel. But they
came to the end at last and found the doors closed. Carried
by his own momentum and unable to stop, he crashed
heavily into the door and sent all of them sprawling.

He picked himself up and peered at the edges of the door
closely, his eyes no more than inches away because of the
failing light. Einar seized the moment to stuff his blankets
inside his pack, still practical enough to think that he might
need them on the other side.

"Damned fool of a dragon," Kalavek muttered after a
moment. He sat back on his haunches and took hold of the
great metal handle bolted to the inside of the door, which of
course opened only inward. The wall had shifted somewhat
in the vibrations and the door had jammed, but it began to
yield slowly to his strength.

"You might hurry," Einar told him. He had been looking
back and saw that the mountain was splitting wide along
the line of the tunnel, now a long weakness in the stone.

The door swung easily once it was free of its frame,
and Kalavek pushed it wide. He waited until Torsk and
Einar had gone before him, then ran down the length of
the rough natural cavern beyond. The sound of tearing and
falling stone filled the darkness. They emerged beneath the
cloudy sky of a dark, damp night, just as the passage closed
forever behind them.

AUTUMN

The Season of Death

☙ ONE

IT SEEMED ALMOST that late summer had turned into a cold and dreary autumn while they were underground. They had entered the tunnel leading down to Behrgarad in the clear light of a bright, cool morning and come up again that same evening to find the mountains hidden in the clouds and a slow, icy rain. It was indeed that time of year, when the last fine days of late summer might turn suddenly into the first damp, dull days of autumn. Such was the weather of southern Norway.

At least the rains had only just started and they had not been hard, no more than a steady mist. Einar had found enough dry wood beneath the trees to get a fire started, although it was nearly the end to his patience trying to get it to burn. He had lit the fire in what little shelter he could find in the wild, beneath the wide branches of a large oak, down in the bottom of a deep dell. The light rain worked its way through the leaves and fell all about him in a slow barrage of large, heavy drops. It was not much, but it was the best that they were going to get. Both he and Torsk were covered with dust from the collapse of the city, and it was slowly turning into mud in this damp air.

It was going to be a long, lonely walk home. The dragon seemed to be in something of a mood since they had come out of Behrgarad, in fact less than half an hour earlier. He remained aloof and quiet, sitting on a hilltop above the dell, saying nothing and watching nothing, just sitting in the slow, cold rain. If he was despondent over the loss of the Core of Magic then he insisted that it was not so, and it did not seem that he was trying to lie even if he could. Perhaps he was dejected that their quest had come to nothing, and they would now be required to start again. Perhaps he was just still tired, or even injured from his fight with the Shadows.

Einar looked up, and saw the dragon sitting there on the ridge far above, forlorn in the rain and the darkness. Suddenly he knew that something was very wrong. His annoyance melted away, and he rose from the fire and quietly climbed the hill. As he came nearer, he saw how shockingly old the dragon was beginning to look. His golden and brown colors had faded to dull, dirty tans and his armor looked worn, the sharp edges blunted. He held his once proud neck wearily, his nose almost touching the ground, and his eyes were misty and tired. Einar realized that he was dying, something he knew beyond any doubt.

He walked quietly up to the dragon, touching his long neck with a hesitant hand. "Are you well, my friend?"

"I have taken no harm," Kalavek said, lifting his head only slightly. "My time to die is coming soon, all the same. I am called."

"No, do not say such things!" Einar insisted. "Do not take it so hard as that. We will go to the Fountain of the World's Heart right away. We will find the magic you need to stay alive."

Kalavek lowered his head again. "Perhaps we will see."

"Of course we will," Einar insisted, but he sounded very frightened and distressed. "What would ever make you think that you would need to die?"

"I do not want to die," the dragon said, lifting his head to look up at the sky. There were no stars, only cold rain, and he looked away. "Rest well this night. Tomorrow we go home."

"Come down to the fire at least, and eat," Einar urged him.

Kalavek rose and followed him down the hill, but he moved slowly and wearily, hardly seeming to care whether he came or not except that it seemed to please the old man. There was little enough for either of them to eat, only a haunch of venison from the previous night that Einar had left with their supplies outside the gates of Behrgarad. The dragon sat in silence while Einar warmed their simple dinner, as if too tired and despondent to speak. When Einar set his plate before him, he only stared at it for a long moment. Then he turned his head and looked out into the night and the rain.

"I wonder if there will be a rainbow when the rain ends."

"Why is that?" Einar asked.

Kalavek turned to him. "Ayesha loves rainbows above anything else in this world. I hope that she is allowed to see just one more."

"There will be time enough in the world for rainbows in the future," Einar told him sternly. "We will find that time."

Kalavek only turned his eyes back toward the night. "I recall when we were young, Ayesha would sit before the little waterfall in our hidden pool and wait for rainbows to appear. The first time I met her, she threw me into that pool. And one day, years ago, we saw a rainbow in the form of a perfect circle, such as you can only see from high in the air. We had been spying in your village, sitting hidden in a tree while a young man and a woman talked about going across the sea to a place called America."

"My son went to America, years ago," Einar remarked.

Kalavek glanced at him, and it almost seemed that he smiled. "It was your tree."

The road home was a long and dreary one, for the rain did not ever stop for very long, and the clouds hung grey and heavy low over the mountains. The dragon did not speak often, walking in a slow, weary manner with his head hung low, and Einar did not know what to say. He could not imagine why Kalavek had come to such a condition, unless his injuries were magical in nature. Except for his worn, faded appearance, he certainly did not seem to have suffered any physical harm. But Einar was busy wondering what could be done to help, and he did not doubt for a moment that the dragon could be saved. He reasoned that when a creature of magic was ill or even dying, then magic would be the cure. All he had to do was to get Kalavek to find a source of magic that would save him.

Einar regretted the destruction of the Core of Magic more and more. Even though Kalavek had promised him that it was unneeded, he still thought that it would have been very important. Perhaps, if he had not lost it, it would have given them the magic needed to keep Kalavek alive, or at least it might have given the sad, tired dragon the hope to keep searching. The search for the Fountain of the World's Heart, he thought, was not to be his quest. It was so far away, at least for walking, and there was no reason why he should have to go. But he was afraid that Kalavek would not try, if he did not go along.

At last, one dark, cold night, they came to lands that Kalavek knew well, and climbed the narrow pass in the corner of the plateau to reach the landing before the dragon caves. Then Einar stopped, standing close to Kalavek's side. Something was wrong. There were no warm, bright fires burning through the night, and no dragons taking the watch through the long hours of darkness. The whole place had a sad, deserted look. As he just stood, wondering what it could mean, a single dark form emerged out of the darkness. Kalavek hesitated only a moment before he stepped forward to meet that one lone dragon in the center of the landing. It was Ayesha, looking as old and worn as her mate.

"They are gone," Kalavek said, not really making a question of that.

"They have been going for the last three nights now," she said, her voice soft and tired. "Halahvey and Kalfeer were the last. They went to the stars last night. They wanted to wait, but the call was too strong and we did not even know if you still lived. Matters argued that you did not."

"But you waited," he observed.

"I would not leave," she told him. "I have waited to go with you."

Einar was beginning to understand something of what was happening. Laying aside his pack and his musket, he hurried over to join them. "But you cannot. We can go now to get the magic you need the stay alive. Even just the two of you are enough to bring back the race of dragons, and the Shadows are not around to bother you any more."

"Things are not that simple anymore," Kalavek said as he turned and began to walk slowly toward the caves, with Ayesha close to his side. Einar hurried after them, determined that the dragons were not going to surrender as easily as that. He glanced back, but Torsk was guarding the pack and musket and did not seem inclined to follow.

"I have come to understand things better now," Kalavek explained, turning his head to look out over the forest. The night was cold and damp, the trees heavy and brittle, all threatening of rain and autumn close behind. He looked away sadly. "When the magic began to fail, something went very wrong with the dragons. Our magic fragmented us, into the dragons as we are now, and the Shadows. Good and evil, you might say, although the Shadows are not truly evil. They are only cold and predatory. Their wisdom is very narrow and so they are fearful and superstitious."

He paused as he climbed up on the low, flat boulder where the watch dragon had always sat, and Ayesha lay close beside him. He sighed wearily, his neck bent as if he lacked the strength to lift his head high and proud as a dragon should. "But they are not a separate race, only the other half of ourselves. Each of us has a corresponding Shadow. When one half dies, the other half is drawn into death with it. Only in our Long Sleep Between the Stars do we finally become complete, in spirit as dragons were meant to be."

"Then they had it all wrong," Einar exclaimed. "When they kill you, they are really killing themselves."

Then he paused, realizing what else that meant. The last of the Shadows were dead, crushed and buried deep in the collapse of Behrgarad. And their death had made the death of the last dragons inevitable. He remembered the largest of the Shadows, the one that had attacked the most fiercely of them all. He had been the leader of the Shadows, and he had also been Kalavek's counterpart. Einar had thrown the Core of Magic at him, and he had died. And from that same moment, Kalavek had begun to die as well.

"I hardly care about that," he insisted. "You still live, and while you live it is not too late. Magic can repair the damage that has been done to you. We only have to find it."

"Not now. Not tonight, or tomorrow," Kalavek told him. "I must rest a while, before we consider such a quest. I will think upon this matter, to see if there are any answers. I cannot promise you that magic itself, no matter how much, will necessarily be enough to save us. Such a thing as that has not happened before. When the summons comes, dragons have always answered."

"Is there any harm in trying?"

"None that I can imagine, as much as the summons is not easy to ignore," Kalavek agreed. "We have fought for life since we were born. If Ayesha is willing, then we will fight even now. You have been a true and courageous friend. And that seems odd, for a man who was tired of life himself."

"Well, that is different," Einar said, although he was surprised himself that he cared so much. "It is one thing for me to be tired and disappointed with life. I am old enough, and that is the fate of mortals. You are still young, and dragons are supposed to live a very long time."

"If we can live, and if the magic can be returned to the world, then we will stay," Kalavek assured him. "Come back in two days. No longer than that, for our time is short. But you must not be sad or disappointed, if it cannot be."

Einar stood for a moment, staring down at the ground and frowning rather fiercely. Watching him, Kalavek smiled for the first time in days. "Go home, Einar Myklathun. You need rest yourself. Go home."

Einar nodded reluctantly, and turned to leave, returning to where Torsk waited and gathered up his pack and his musket. He paused to look back but the two dragons seemed not to have moved, sitting close together on the stone with their heads lifted to the sky, as if they could see stars that were hidden to him. He did not want to leave like this, uncertain of how things would turn out, but there was nothing more that he could do now. He turned to descend the narrow cut to the forest below, and started for home.

He walked all through the night, all the way down the mountain and the fjord from the dragon caves to his cabin on the edge of the village. He did not even realize what he was doing, he walked so lost in thought. The rains came again in the middle of the night, very light but somewhat colder than before, perhaps because they were closer now to the sea. Einar walked at a determined pace with his back bent to the wind and his old, worn hat hanging down over his eyes. Torsk followed dutifully behind, looking very worried in that eager manner of dogs. He had been very fond of that dragon from the start, and he had never showed much enthusiasm for anything in his life.

As he walked, Einar had come to realize that there was more implied in Kalavek's words than he had said. The dragons were doomed to die because the Shadows were all dead; indeed, most of the dragons were dead already. And the uncomfortable fact remained that Einar had killed the Shadows with the Core of Magic, and so he had himself killed the dragons at the very time that he had been trying to help them. Kalavek had told him to use the Core of Magic as a weapon, even if it meant destroying it, and he had known in his heart that he should not. Of course, Kalavek himself had not known at the time the full consequences of that act, even though he must have guessed that it was powerful enough to destroy the gnome city.

For Einar, there was nothing left but desperate guilt. It was his fault, as he saw it, that only the two dragons were left, and they were dying. And it was his responsibility to find a way to save them. He suspected that if he did not find a way, then nothing would be done. Kalavek did not want to die, but Einar doubted that he would be able to find either the strength or the will to try. And Ayesha was already resigned to die; he was fairly certain of that. He had to get the dragons to the Fountain of the World's Heart, and then make them do whatever they had to do to bring back the magic. Or else he had to think of some other means to save them.

He felt sorry for the dragons, but also somewhat annoyed. If it could be done, they had been given all the time they ever needed to bring magic back into the world and save themselves. Instead they had just waited, consoling themselves that this was what was meant to be, existing in the vague hope that things would improve, even filling themselves with the hollow encouragement of prophecies. In all the time that they had been given to find a way to save the world that they had known and needed to survive, they had done nothing. But such was the nature of dragons, hoarding their wisdom and knowledge, their time, even their very lives, wealth that they had learned to accumulate but never to use to their own advantage. That was why Einar was afraid that he would not be able to get the last two dragons to save themselves now.

Morning came. The rain had ended. In the village, people began to go about their business. Shops opened. A large part of the fleet went out for only a day's fishing, anticipating the winter storms that would soon keep them locked in port. But no one saw Einar Myklathun when he came home at last, for his house was on the very edge of the village, half-hidden under the cover of the forest, and he went straight there. He had walked all through the night, and that after a long journey and a fight in the dark places of the world. And above all else, he was in no mood to meet or speak with anyone.

Late in the day, Einar came out at last. He still would have preferred to have stayed at home alone; indeed, his intention had been to stay to himself until he returned to the dragon caves the next morning, this time cutting the journey much shorter by boat. But after he had been away for a full week, he could find nothing in the house fit to eat. There was no meat or fish to be had, the little bit of bread he could find was turning into a brick and the vegetables to rubber. Aside from that, he thought that a real, hot meal would do him good after days of travel rations, which was all that he would have gotten if he had stayed at home. The rain had stopped, as he discovered as soon as he stepped outside, and the sky was clear except for a few ragged traces of pink clouds in the sunset. The air was still damp and cooler than in summer, but hardly uncomfortable.

He almost enjoyed the quiet walk to the tavern. It was still too early for the leaves to begin to turn, with many wet days still ahead, but there was a definite feeling of autumn in the air. As he walked, Einar looked about him at the houses and the people he passed. Perhaps it was because he had spent so much time in the company of dragons, Shadows and gnomes, through ancient forests where men seldom walked and underground cities fully as large and far more intricate and fantastic as any to be seen above. Perhaps it was because it seemed to him that he had been away far longer than just the one week, but he felt surprised to see that the same old world that he had always known was just the way that he had left it, and yet somehow distant, remote and obscure as if it rejected him as something that no longer quite belonged. He certainly never thought to suspect that he had changed, while the world about him had remained the same.

Everything was so astonishingly normal, he was occasionally given to wonder if his journey with Kalavek had been real, of if there ever had been dragons living in the mountain above the fjord. He was at this time a man caught between three very different worlds. Behind him stood the world of his youth, simple and secure, a time that never would be again. Before him stood the world as it was coming to be, cold and threatening, a place that rejected him at the same time that it would not let him be. And then there was the sad world of Faerie, fading into the depths of time and yet more immediate and desirable to Einar Myklathun than anything else that he had seen in many a long year. What a strange, conflicting world this was, he thought. The last two dragons in the world were dying, alone and forgotten. And only a few short miles away, people who did not even believe in dragons went about their own ordinary lives, unaware that the greatest age of the world was collapsing about them.

But Torsk followed close behind him, looking as worried and fearful as he felt, and he knew that it had all happened. His dragons were dying, and something had to be done. He could have turned around right then and started back for the mountains. But if he was going to do them any good, he was going to have to be prepared. He might as well begin with a good dinner.

He had his dinner that night at the table outside beneath the tree, knowing that there would be few enough days for sitting outside left in that year. It was pleasant and quiet, as night fell and the sky grew dark. He was nearly finished when Mayor Thorsen and the Parson turned up suddenly and rather loudly. He should have expected it and in fact he had, but he had also hoped to be spared. They were both livid about his disappearing for a whole week without a word of warning. They had turned out half the village to look for him four days earlier, and they would have still been looking for him if it had not been for the rain. The rain itself would not have stopped them, but the danger of losing stalwart fishermen and good church ladies in the woods had been too great. Einar was surprised by so much concern, and rather touched in spite of himself.

"You are getting too old to go disappearing into the forest for so long at a time," Mayor Thorsen admonished him. "When the rains began and you still had not come back, we began to think that you had met the worst. Fallen down some wet hole, or over a cliff. You are the Forester, and should know better. What could have kept a man your age out in the wild for so long?"

"Looking in some places where I have never looked before," Einar replied shortly, which was true enough, as he filled his pipe for an after-dinner smoke along with a mug of beer. He knew that if he tried to tell them where he had actually been, they would never let him out in the forest ever again.

"What is that? You went off into places you did not even know?" the Mayor cried in dismay. "You could have gotten yourself lost, and still been wandering about out there waiting to starve. If you are not careful, you will die alone in the wild, with no one to know what has become of you. That is not a death for an old man, is it, Parson?"

"No, indeed," Parson Ondurson agreed sagely. "That would be very regrettable. I have so looked forward to conducting your funeral."

"I can certainly take care of myself," Einar insisted, with a brief glance at the Parson. "At my age, all the old places become so familiar and dull, and you feel the need to see something new. Or at least you should."

"We should never be too old for something new," the parson agreed. His mind was in some ways like a kaleidoscope, if less jumbled then certainly as quick to shift.

"Perhaps, and that is one thing. But what you did was quite another," the Mayor declared. "Explore all you want. But at least go off prepared, and tell us first that you will be away so long. Widow Haugen was beside herself, and the entire village was in an uproar."

"I am reminded of the time when Lars Hansen came in from fishing with three times the catch than he could handle," Parson Ondurson added. "He tried to put it all away as quickly as he could, thinking that he could then take a short holiday from fishing because he would then be ahead. But there were just too many fish for him. This old village had never known such a stink."

"Exactly the point," Thorsen agreed enthusiastically. Then he paused and frowned. "Or maybe not. But you must think of all the people that you have worried and inconvenienced. I hardly know how I am to maintain both peace and order in this town, if old men will go running off into the woods without a word of warning and then come sneaking back and are home a whole day that you think they must be dead. I do my best, but no one shows much consideration for my part in return. Not even my own friends."

"Oh, enough," Einar said as he rose to leave, placing his old, limp hat on his head. Mayor Thorsen would often descend to singing his largely imagined and certainly over-rated woes and nothing would bring him out of it, until Einar wanted to break a pot over his head. "I have been from here to there and back again and I walked all night in the rain, and I have a very pressing matter to consider until it seems that my head should burst. I certainly do not need to be lectured like a child before you worthies."

He thought as he walked away through the night that he should not have been so short, but he really was very worried about the two dragons. Besides, his behavior would give the Mayor and the Parson that much more to discuss while the night grew dark and the stars shone bright, and that would actually make them all the happier. He was now resolved to leave again in the morning without a single word to warn of his going, and they would see what Thorsen would make of that. If he could increase that fat Mayor's burden of cares and indignation by that much more, then he could not imagine doing the man a greater favor. Thorsen was a man who took his responsibilities very seriously indeed, and there were few enough for him in a small Norwegian fishing village for him to feel that his existence was justified.

Einar walked alone in the growing darkness, while Torsk followed quietly behind. It was now almost completely dark, a cool, clear night with many bright stars overhead and just a few dark clouds about the heads of distant heights, a clean, fresh night such as will follow when the sky has been washed clean by recent rains. As Einar walked along the lanes beneath the trees, he began to hear people calling to one another from house to house, and some were beginning to step outside and look up into the night sky. He slowed and then stopped in a place where he could see through the trees, looking up as he wondered what all this excitement could be about.

Then he saw it. The arch of a perfect rainbow in the distance, perhaps the largest and brightest rainbow that he had ever seen, rising over the mountains at the back of the fjord. There was no hint of haze or transparency as was usual with rainbows; the colors were as clear and solid as if they had been painted on the night sky. Such a rainbow was unusual in itself and would have caused enough people to stop and stare, but that was not the half of it. For this rainbow was out at night, with no trace of sunlight left in the sky, and there was not a cloud to be seen anywhere near.

Then Einar knew what it must mean. He remembered Kalavek telling him that Ayesha took great joy in rainbows. This was his last gift to her, summoned by the dregs of his fading magic. The dragons were about to die.

Einar knew, in one long moment out of time, what he had to do. He could save those dragons, if he could only get to them in time. But time was the one thing that he could not control, and he feared that the dragons would not allow him enough. How long would they linger, watching the stars through their last night in this world, and how soon could he get there? He reckoned where he stood with his plan quickly, and he realized that he was lucky. Looking down toward the harbor, he saw by the small forest of masts that most of the boats must be in, and all of the larger ones at least. And it was still early in the evening, with dinner just over. He was more likely to get people to listen to him now than in the middle of the night.

"It is beautiful, Herr Myklathun," Widow Haugen said suddenly at his side, having come up behind him in the dark. "What could it mean?"

"It means the end of the world," he said, then saw her rather surprised and worried look. "Not our world, at least. But something terrible is about to happen, if we do not hurry to stop it."

He turned then and hurried back through the streets of the village, past all the people who were coming out of their houses to see the wonder in the night sky. He did not stop running until he had come almost to the center of town and the old church that stood on the small hill near the back, up against the steep, wooded slopes where a last arm of the mountains came down almost to the harbor and nearly cut through the middle of the village. It was a church of a far older type that is sometimes seen in that area of Norway, an odd, rustic structure built of heavy rough planks and a roof with long, heavy eaves. Its tall, slender steeple rose high into the night.

Einar did not even pause as he rushed inside, a place where he had not often been in these many years of his life. He had decided long ago that this church had little enough to offer him, and there was only one thing that he wanted here this night. He stood in the very middle of that large, dark room and looked about, the only light coming from a couple of candles and from the barest glow pouring in through the windows from a clear but moonless night. Old Torsk had followed him right inside, with no hesitation on his own part, and was turning round and round as if he knew as well what his master needed. But when it was nowhere to be seen, Einar considered the shape of the building as it was from the outside, and he knew that this part was not yet under the steeple. He hurried to the far end of the room until he discovered a dark doorway leading into the rooms in the back. There, in the gloomy, dusty hall leading on back to the Parson's own rooms, he found it; four long, grey ropes leading down.

He took off his hat and tilted back his head, seeing the interior of the steeple with its heavy wooden beams and braces leading up and up into the darkness, with a single ladder along one side. Einar took a good, firm hold on the nearest rope and pulled, finding more weight and resistance than he would have expected. The rope descended only a bare hand's-width, while the one beside it lifted an equal amount. He took a firmer hold of the rope and pulled with all he had, all but hanging from the thing. The rope gave even more than the first time but still not enough, and after a long moment it began to drag back up with more force than he could resist. He waited until the rope had gone as high as it would go, then pulled down hard on it once again. The bell rang, a single peal that was loud, deep and clear, then it swung back and rang a second time. Einar pulled and pulled, as the bell began to swing faster and faster, easy enough to keep in motion now that he had it moving.

Then he reached over with his right hand and took hold of a rope from the second bell, and he pulled as hard as he could. Faster and faster it began to swing, and the second bell added its slightly higher, lighter voice to the first. Einar held a rope in each hand, pulling first one and then the other, and the unexpected ringing of the bells filled the clear, quiet night. People who had stepped out of their doors to see the remarkable rainbow, and many who had not, began to hurry to the old church, drawn by the urgency in that ringing. The sound of it filled the night and rolled across the waves of the fjord, sharp and demanding, even frantic and desperate in its rapid pealing. If Einar could have pulled those ropes fast enough, then he would have sent that sound echoing all the way up the fjord to the dragons.

"Einar, what are you doing?" Parson Ondurson asked, appearing suddenly out of the darkness. He was puffing, having run all the way from the tavern, and he was in no shape for it. He had been unable to imagine who could be ringing his bells, but it had been a safe bet that the bells were his.

"Here, you pull on these," Einar ordered sharply, handing over the ropes. He spoke with such authority that the Parson took the ropes without question and immediately began to pull, just as hard and fast as Einar had been.

"Is it important?" he asked as he pulled.

"More important than you can imagine," Einar told him. "You just keep pulling and do not stop."

How long Parson Ondurson would keep ringing those bells, Einar did not know. It would be long enough. The Parson was a trusting type; if he believed that it was necessary, whether he knew the reason why or not, then he would ring those bells all night. Mayor Thorsen would either stop him soon enough or else look for a gun, figuring that the Prussians were invading; for his own part, Einar could never imagine what the King of Sweden wanted with Norway, much less a pack of practical Prussians. He hurried through the church and out the main door, stopping on the top step. He saw that at least half the village must be gathered about, many with torches or lanterns and some with guns, at least as many as could be found in the village.

"My friends," he shouted, holding up his hands to still the nervous and excited talking. The soft chatter died slowly away as everyone looked up at him, waiting and listening. "My dear friends. The last two dragons in all the world are dying this very night. We have to go to them, to save them. We can do it, but we must hurry."

For the moment, the entire crowd stared speechless. Einar's message was surprising enough to hear in itself. But for the moment they were almost more surprised in the change in Einar himself. For quite as long as most of them could remember he had been a gruff and private man, quietly bitter with life, caring for nothing. He had certainly never given them reason to believe that he had ever thought of any of them as his friends. Now he stood before them, ringing the bells of the church and desperately anxious for their understanding and help, although not for himself. They were so astonished that they were more willing to listen to him than they might otherwise have been.

"What dragons?" someone shouted, although not suspiciously or unkindly.

"Where have you been?" another asked. "What is this about dragons? What can we do about it?"

Elnar held up his hands again. "I met a dragon in the woods. His name is Kalavek, and his kind is dying. We went on a journey to bring their magic back into the world, but we failed. Now there are only the two of them left in the world, and they will die this very night if we do not help them."

At any other time they probably would not have listened. They might have thought him mad, or only a foolish old man with a head full of things that have never really happened and did not exist. But they could see his determination and conviction and hear his sincerity, urging them to share in his need to protect these last dragons. And they could see that big, bright rainbow standing in a clear night sky, and that was a strong argument in itself that perhaps magic was real. They raised their torches and their lanterns, eager to be gone. But Einar waved his arms to get their attention, gesturing for quiet.

"The way is too far to walk, and we would never get there in time," he told them. "But a night wind is moving up the fjord. Boats could have us there in a hour, and then it is not so far up the slopes."

He descended the steps and the crowd parted before him, an old man with sharp features and bright eyes, dressed in an old jacket and a worn, sagging hat, followed by his long-legged, ugly dog. They cheered him and shouted his name as if he was a hero marching resolutely into battle and then they followed close behind, while the ringing of the bells filled the night. There was little enough magic in the world, little enough that is grand and beautiful and terrible. But for that moment, that one old man possessed all the magic and majesty of any dragon or king of elvish realms long past, and he never knew it. But he showed them how to believe, and it was wonderful.

The crowd was divided between the larger boats. A following wind filled their sails and they began to move swiftly up the fjord, as if they were being hastened on their quest. The ringing of the bells began to fade slowly behind until it became a distant echo in the night, while they set their course toward the rainbow standing before the dark silhouettes of the mountains. As long as it graced the sky, its colors bright and clear, then they knew that the dragons still lived. The little fishing boats moved through the waves and the racing rags of mist like the dragon ships of a forgotten age, each one ablaze with the golden light of torches and lanterns and wreathed in smoke from the flames.

Einar stood in the bow of the lead boat and watched impatiently as the darkness rolled slowly by. Too slowly, he was inclined to believe. Each passing minute brought the dragons that much closer to the time when they would die, a moment that Einar could in no way predict. As long as the rainbow remained before them, he knew that a chance remained. Then, as the boats neared the back of the fjord, two large, dark shapes passed just over the masts of the boats, momentarily flashing brown or green in the light of the torches. They circled around and came back again, while the villagers in the boats shouted and cheered. But Einar was tremendously relieved for his own part, and he relaxed somewhat for the first time since he had seen the rainbow over the fjord. The dragons knew that he was coming, and they would wait.

Then a strong wind stirred suddenly, coming up behind the boats and bearing them forward with tremendous speed.

Their sails lifted wide and fat, and white wakes began
to spread about their bows. The dragons were impatient,
it seemed. But they clearly welcomed this crowd rather
than rejected it, as Einar was afraid they might. His fear
had been that they would have been frightened by such a
crowd, or annoyed at the scale of this intrusion, and would
have hidden themselves or sought their death prematurely.
Perhaps they suspected what he intended, knowing that he
was coming to save them.

Now the boats nearly flew up the fjord, while the dark
walls of the mountains drew closer and closer. After a time
the dragons returned, flying over the masts of the boats
as slowly as they could. They made a magnificent sight,
even in the harsh yellow light of the torches. The night
muted colors and masked details, and so the worn, dull
appearance of the two dragons that Einar knew to exist was
not apparent. Suddenly the two dragons turned inland, and
Einar had the boats follow. In moments, they nosed firmly
in onto a beach of coarse sand and small, rounded stones,
just below a steep, wooded slope.

Then boards were laid down from the sides of the boats
and everyone climbed down onto the beach. The dragons
flew over a final time and then passed straight up the
mountainside, toward the rainbow that now seemed to rise
almost directly above them, high up the wall of blackness
that hid the wooded slope before them. Up they climbed,
finding the best path they could through the forest, around
massive boulders and up great shelves of rock, through
the bracken and ferns. But no one felt afraid, neither for
themselves nor for the success of their quest. The night
seemed full of magic, not a place of sleep nor of hiding but
a rich, full world all its own where darkness and shadows
were only deep pools. Trees moved in the cool, fresh wind
and the sound of the darkness was sharp, mysterious but
not threatening. For many, it was as if they were seeing the
world of the night for the first time, as if it was a strange
and wondrous place, a faraway land that they had locked
outside shutters and doors all their lives, missing something
that now delighted them.

At last they came to a great black wall of stone in the darkness, too steep and tumbled to be climbed. Einar led them around to one side, and one at a time they filed up the narrow pass between massive round boulders to the top. There they spread out into the farther half of the wide, flat landing that stood before a dark cliff, and their torches and lanterns filled that place with a flickering light that revealed the mouths of great caves opening like tunnels of blackness in the stone. From where they gathered, they could look up and see the base of the rainbow descending to touch the immense boulders and slabs of stone that formed the top of that low cliff, and its varied light cast a fine haze of changing colors over the leaves of the trees and the stones of the mountain. And to either side, each perched upon great stones, sat the last two dragons, one brown and burnished gold and the other green touched with shades of dull brown. And though it could now be seen that they were worn and faded, still they bore themselves with grace and dignity as they waited motionless and silent.

Then Einar stepped out before the crowd, and only Torsk dared to follow him. He stood looking up at the dragons, and called to them. "We have come."

"So I see that," Kalavek replied, for the ledge was half-filled with the people from the village and an even larger part still waited in the forest below, their lights scattered among the trees and bushes. "We had expected that you might try to come yourself, but we never expected this."

"You have left me to do the best that I can," Einar said, and it seemed by his voice that he felt both angry and betrayed. "You had promised that you would wait for me, and then we would go to find the magic that you would need to stay alive. Now you have left me to do the best that I can for you."

"Yes, I know that I promised," the dragon told him. "At that time I was called, but I did not yet feel ready to die. But since that time the call has taken a new form, and it seemed to us that the spirits of all the dragons who ever lived are calling to us, telling us that we must not be angry or afraid but to accept that this thing that seems so wrong must be right. I had believed that the last dragons must never go from this world, no matter the cost to those of us who survived. It is not a matter that we have lost the courage to live, or become too weary to refuse. I do not yet understand how, but the call to our Long Sleep Between the Stars has become a promise that is welcoming and reassuring."

"But life is the only choice," Einar protested. "You are worn and weary from what has happened to you, and you cannot trust the things that you might think you sense."

"No, my friend," Kalavek insisted as he rose to stand, and he held his long neck high and proud. "We are not confused or misled. Although we are passing beyond this world and this form, in some curious way we both feel more alive than ever before. A way is opened before us. Although we do not yet see where it leads, it beckons us with the magic of dragons."

"But there is magic in this world yet," Einar declared. "All you have to do is find it. Look at us, dragon. I have brought everyone who would come. There are hundreds of us. We all believe in magic, and we believe in you. Is that not enough?"

Then Kalavek paused and stared, for he did not at first understand what Einar was telling him. Then he was filled with amazement, and his mood softened as he was deeply moved by the meaning of this gesture. "My dear friends, all of you. But the magic did not fade because it was forgotten. The decline of the world of Faerie began even before mortal men came into this world, and it has nothing to do with you. The dragons are not dying because you have forgotten how to believe in us. Perhaps we just forgot how to believe in ourselves."

Then Ayesha rose as well, and it seemed that the dragons were making ready to depart on their final journey. But Kalavek looked down at Einar a final time. "Do not grieve, my friend. You gave me trust and understanding when I asked it of you, and then love and devotion that I did not expect. I will take the memory of it with me into my Long Sleep and dream of it often, and I go now with greater hope for the world that I will never see. Live long and live well, with all the hope and happiness that you tried to make possible for me and my own."

Then the two dragons turned their heads toward each other a final time as they spread their broad wings, and they suddenly thrust themselves into the sky from their high perches. They ascended into the night almost straight up with long, powerful strokes of their wings as they began to spiral around the wide shaft of the rainbow. Their circle grew wider as they began to climb faster, and their graceful forms began to shine as if from within with a brilliant light of pure white. That white radiance became steadily brighter as they ascended toward the bright, cold stars that awaited them. Then with a sudden flash they were gone, passing into the night without a trace, and the shaft of the rainbow drew away into the darkness.

"No," Einar said softly in protest as he took a step forward, as if he might still run after them and stop them, bringing them back into the world. But the magic faded and the night grew deep and still, as if the world was going back to sleep.

❧ TWO

THE AUTUMN RAINS began, and it rained and rained. This was the darkest and most gloomy time of year along that area of the Norwegian coast, as the days began to grow shorter and shorter and the sun was seldom to be seen behind grey clouds. It was almost as if nature herself mourned the passing of the last dragons, except that the weather was always like that.

Now perhaps it was a curious thing, but no one in the village was sad over the death of the dragons. They certainly regretted it, and no one wanted to see the dragons go away almost at the same time they had been found. But if the magic was destined to fade away and the creatures of Faerie doomed to die, then the villagers were glad for that one last, brief glimpse before it was gone. It seemed better to have seen such things only once than not at all, and far better than to never have even known that such things really had once existed. They were all very grateful to old Einar Myklathun, knowing well how close they had come to missing their chance of ever seeing a dragon if not for him, and no one blamed him that his attempt to save the dragons had failed. He had insisted that they believe in magic, and that sense of wonder and delight had not faded with the passing of the magic.

But for himself, Einar Myklathun was the saddest man whom anyone might ever think to meet, and it seemed that he too grew old and worn overnight just like his dragons. Everyone shared his grief and they thought that they understood. But his demons of guilt, bitterness and regret were more complex than they could imagine. He had not been asked to save the dragons, only to help them in their need, but he had taken upon himself the quest of saving them and he had failed. But more even than that, he had dared to care about those dragons, knowing well the consequences but foolish enough to think that this time would be different. Everything that he had ever cared about in his life had always turned to sadness and disappointment; his wife had died, his son had gone away across the sea, and the very world of his youth was slowly passing away into times that he did not entirely understand, and which seemed to have little use for him.

And so it was. Einar grieved for those ridiculous dragons and he missed them terribly, and he blamed himself for failing them, and he felt like a fool for letting himself get carried away. He did not go down to the tavern, to sit with his old friends Mayor Thorsen and the Parson. Nor did he leave his house at all. Day after grey, gloomy day he would sit by the window of his kitchen while the cold autumn rain fell almost without interruption, while Torsk would sit in the shadows and watch him with sad eyes or sleep on his back under the table with his legs in the air. If it had not been for the quiet attentions of Widow Haugen, who brought him dinners and pastries, he might have just sat there doing nothing until he starved.

He still could not believe that they were really gone. During the day he would sit and watch the grey clouds, thinking of brown and golden wings riding the winds of distant mountains. At night he would almost expect to see that young dragon sitting back on his haunches in a dark corner of the room, his long neck bent uncomfortably beneath the low ceiling, waiting to tell him stories of faerie realms that had fallen into dust centuries before either of them had been born, over slices of pie and a mug of coffee that he would not drink. But Einar was glad for the continued rain that kept him at home. He did not believe that he would have the heart to make his rounds of the woods for the feeling that Kalavek was walking beside him.

After three whole weeks and two days besides, the rain finally came to some manner of a definite end. Even though the sky remained grey and cloudy, the clouds were less low and heavy than they had been. On that day, when Widow Haugen came over with his dinner, she decided that enough was enough. By all that she could tell, about all that Einar had accomplished in that time was to keep himself and his dishes clean. He had always kept himself very busy and that in turn had helped to keep him young. Not that he looked young; everyone in the village had thought of him as a skinny, craggy-faced old man for as long as anyone could remember, until the Mayor had once declared that Einar must have been born with his musket and felt hat. But for the first time in his life he acted old, walking with slow steps and a bent back.

"Einar Myklathun, you should be ashamed!" Widow Haugen declared, taking his hat from his head and hitting him with it. "Here you sit in this cold, dark house as if you were walking about in your own coffin."

"And what else is there?" Einar asked as he took the plate that she had given him into the kitchen. "Walking around in the cold rain?"

"The rain ended this morning, if you would ever look outside your window to notice such things. Go out and look to your woods. The King expects it of you."

"The King is a busy man, and he lives a very long way from here," Einar said as he set the plate on the table. "He never expected that I should walk around in the rain, and he hardly knows whether or not it is raining here in this forgotten part of Norway."

"That is quite beside the point," Widow Haugen insisted. "You have not come down to the village, nor even left this house, since those dragons flew off and disappeared. Now everyone feels very sorry about that, and everyone understands how you feel. But life does go on, at least for those of us who are still alive, and the trouble with being dead is that you never find out that things always do get better."

"Fine words," Einar muttered. "I am not so sure that things get better as much as you get used to things being bad."

"You are talking like a fool, Einar Myklathun, and you know it," the Widow declared. "Well, it is too late, and your secret is out. Everyone knows now what a nice old man you really are. They all saw how much you can care about something that is beautiful and wonderful, and how hard you will work to save something that needs help. If you really were that gruff old man that you have always pretended to be, then you would not have given a damn whether those dragons lived or died. But three weeks later and more, and here you are still grieving."

She turned then to leave, marching across the room toward the front door. Einar glanced in her direction after a moment. "I am not grieving. I have just gotten tired of this old world and its foolishness."

"I have said enough. You talk to him, Torsk," Widow Haugen exclaimed, slamming the door behind her.

Einar and Torsk both stared after her for a long moment. Then Torsk looked up at the old man with his big, sad eyes. "Ja vel, she is right, you know."

Einar frowned, then glanced down at the dog. "What would you know? You are only talking now because that silly dragon taught you some magical trick, or else I really am getting that old and foolish."

"Nonsense," Torsk insisted. "Your trouble is that you are not more like a dog."

"And how do you figure that?" Einar asked as he returned to the kitchen. He uncovered the plate to see what they had, then took his familiar seat by the window.

"Dogs know how to live best," Torsk explained. "We never fret about the past, and we never scare ourselves with thoughts of the future. We live only for each moment, and we enjoy each moment to its fullest. We give our love and devotion without hesitation or restraint, and then we let go without a second thought. We see only the best in everyone and everything, and we never worry about what might have been. I loved that dragon. Now the dragons are gone, but the sadness of that parting changes nothing of what went before. Do you regret ever meeting those dragons for the price of their leaving, or are you just happy to have known them?"

"I do not find that so easy to decide," Einar remarked. "You dogs seem to find life very simple."

"You people want to make life so complicated," Torsk responded. "You never listen to your dogs."

"Dogs seldom have anything to say," Einar reminded him.

Whether it was some lasting magic worked by the dragons before they departed, or if it was indeed Einar's own imagination, Torsk never spoke again after that night. But Einar thought about all that was said, and he supposed that the time had indeed come for him to resume his duties. He still cared nothing for returning to his work or seeing the wild, but he did suppose that it would pass the time better than just sitting by the window. And Torsk was terribly bored and weary of worrying constantly about his master, although he never said a word about it himself.

The next morning came bright and clear, although there was a definite bite of cold in the air, just enough to argue that autumn was well and here, never again to surrender to the gentler days of summer. Torsk was well pleased to be out again and would even run on ahead from time to time, nosing into bushes and behind trees. For him that was a great show of enthusiasm, for he was most often content just to follow quietly behind his master. Einar chose not to go far, knowing that he could not dare to trust the weather in that time of year. It was no longer too early to expect snow in the mountains or even the higher forests, as unlikely as an early snow would be to last. An early snow might be pleasant enough in the village, where folk would be glad to dust off their sleds and skis. But Einar was in no mood to face a long walk home in a cold rain or an unexpected snow, and he doubted that even Torsk would be thrilled to face such an adventure, as eager as the dog was to be out. If the King thought it so important, then he could come out and count the squirrels in the trees for himself.

Einar took the path straight back from the village almost without thinking and went inland along the northern shore of the fjord. That was not the way he would have chosen if he had considered things before he started, but he would have circled around the village by remote and quiet paths and gone up into the wooded heights above the village. There were too many memories along this way, too much to remind him of all the things that he was supposed to be trying to forget. All the things that he could not stop himself from thinking about in the long, weary days since the dragons had died. All about him were the mountains where dragons had flown and the forests where dragons had walked. The fjord itself reminded him not so much of that bold and glorious quest to save the dragons, with the boats bathed in golden light from hundreds of torches and lanterns. The fjord seemed now quiet, gloomy and forsaken, and that reminded him of that long, weary, desolate journey home again.

At some time during the day, after a long moment of walking slowly for the most part with his head down, Einar came around one bend of the fjord, and through an opening in the trees he could see at last the steep, darkly wooded slopes of the mountain where the dragons had lived. He stood for a time and thought about the past, of that sheltered plateau where the dragons had once gathered beneath the stars and the rings of their watch fires, the black ashes washed away in the autumn rains. He thought of the caverns, now dark and silent. Someday soon he would like to take a boat up the fjord and return to the caves, to collect those few things the dragons had kept and used, to have something to remember them and to prove, at least to himself, that they had once lived. But not yet, probably not until the warm days of spring had come yet again.

But that was as far as he wanted to go, and he turned then and started for home. He walked even more slowly, with his head bent and his shoulders sagging as if he had been defeated by the pain and grief of memories that he had been hoping to forget. Torsk walked behind him, his own head bent nearly to the ground and his tail hanging even longer.

So it was that evening was passing and the last light was fading from a grey sky, when they came together through a small pass and into a long clearing in the woods atop a hill high above the village, where they could look down and see the roofs of the houses and the harbor beyond. A cold wind stirred suddenly, when there had been hardly any wind for all that day. Einar took no notice, but when the wind came again, strong enough to scatter the dead leaves, then Torsk stopped in his tracks and lifted his head. His ears were up and his eyes wide, as if he had heard some voice on the wind that he knew. Then he barked and began to run and jump in circles, as dogs will do in great delight.

Einar turned, amazed and confused at such unusual behavior from Torsk. The wind moved yet again, pushing through the swaying branches of the trees, and it seemed almost to Einar that he could hear distant voices or perhaps music on that wind. He no longer needed Torsk to tell him that something unexpected and unique was about to happen. There was dragon magic in that wind, something that he certainly never expected to sense again. Suddenly it was before him, the misty white form of a dragon that seemed to have condensed from the very wind in which it now hovered and drifted. Einar pulled off his old hat and took one cautious step forward and then another. But Torsk was more certain of what he sensed and he knew that he was in the presence of an old friend, and he was beside himself with delight. The shift of colors fooled the eye, the familiar golds and browns now purest white, hazy and indistinct.

"Kalavek?" Einar asked softly, unsure whether to believe the truth of what he saw, or if it was indeed only the imagination of a mind lost in the fury of desperation and grief. For after Torsk had spoken to him the previous evening, he no longer completely trusted himself.

"I have come back for this one moment to speak to you," the vision said, and the voice, although thin and distant, was that of Kalavek. "There is no point in grieving, for we both knew in the beginning that the dragons were doomed, and we did what we could to prevent that. And why above all should you blame yourself, when you tried so hard and risked yourself for us?"

Of all things that Einar might have expected from the ghost of a dragon, the last was such sincere surprise and concern, and all the pain he had felt flowed over into sudden anger. "You betrayed me, you fool of a dragon. You let me down. You asked me to be your friend and to care about you, and then you just died as if it was the most natural thing in the world."

"It was the natural thing," Kalavek said. "Death is a very enlightening experience, for there are no secrets in that life beyond and all things that were hidden or lost to us in former days are made clear. I have since come to understand many things that were once beyond my understanding, and now I know and can accept that the end of the dragons was inevitable. When Ayesha and I were born beyond our time, it was easily seen as a new hope and that the time of the dragons was returning. But it was not a prophecy, only a false hope. We were not the first but the last, for we were brought into your world by the will of all the dragons who had ever lived and died to write the final page of our long history."

Kalavek's white, misty form drifted closer, and he bent his neck forward. "Listen well, and know this as the truth. I know now the reasons why the magic left the world and all the races of Faerie were doomed to die. The history of the loss of magic and its causes were long and complex beyond my suspicions, and I see now that it is nothing that you and I could ever hope to repair. So you see, our quest was doomed to failure in the end, whether it had happened there in the depths of Behrgarad or some other day. And even though you must blame yourself for using the Core of Magic to destroy the Shadows, the last dragons thank you for that unexpected blessing. We might have lingered many years longer in that morbid, pointless existence as you found us, waiting to die. But now I am where I belong and I am whole, the two parts of my spirit joined at last in one."

"That might be very fine for you, if you like being dead so much," Einar said bitterly. "But you have left a very sad and empty world to us."

"Whether sad or not, this is your world, and so it is only what you make of it," Kalavek told him. "But I can leave you with these words of hope at least. For the magic is not gone; it has only been locked away, and it might one day return. Nor have the dragons really gone. The spirits of all the dragons who have ever lived are still a part of this world, and even in death we remain a part of the world. Perhaps your kind will never see us or hear us, but our spirits will forever remain in the wild places. And we will sing our songs of power forever to keep what small magic there will always be left in the forests and mountains and the other places that we have loved, until the day when the magic does return and we are born into a new life."

Then Einar realized for the first time that there were indeed voices in the wind, and as he listened the voices became louder and clearer until it seemed that all the world was filled with a great song. And when he looked around, he saw that the white, nebulous forms of many dragons surrounded them for as far as he could see, standing atop towering rocks in the heights and in the dark places beneath the slopes, and in the woods. He saw smaller dragons like Kalavek, lithe and compact, and others that were massive and sinuous, all with their long, graceful necks lifted in song.

"But I thought that you had gone to your Long Sleep Between the Stars," Einar said at last.

"I have gone to my Long Sleep, but I am dreaming of you," Kalavek said as his misty form rose and began to drift slowly away, becoming less distinct. "Farewell, true and devoted friend. I wish you long life and happiness, but that is for you to decide."

And then he was gone.

Einar would have kept him if he could, or gone after him if he only knew the way, for in either life or death he wished to be with his dragons. But they were a part of the lost magic, and he was a child of a mortal world. The last light faded and night settled deep and silent. Einar stood for a moment as if waiting in the vain hope that Kalavek would return. Then he bowed his head and turned for home, while Torsk followed quietly.

The next day remained clear, cool and bright and the day after that as well, and for that time of year such kind weather was something of a blessing. Einar spent those two days pondering the words and the good will of the shade of Kalavek, and also the question of whether he had spoken with Kalavek himself or only some spirit of his own imagination. Early in the evening of the second day, under the last gentle light of day, he sat alone at his favorite table beneath the trees outside the tavern with a mug of good beer before him, and he contemplated such matters. Torsk sat at his side and watched him very closely, not with his previous anxiety and grief but with a new interest, in hope that his master might return at last from the darkness to his old self. And also with some exasperation, for even a dog's patience must eventually wear thin.

"Was he really there?" Einar asked after a time, looking down at Torsk, but he did not expect an answer. "I wonder if he will ever come again. Perhaps so, if I continue to disappoint him."

It was finally beginning to occur to him that there was an important difference between grieving and holding dear a cherished memory, and that letting go was by no means the same as forgetting. That might have seemed like such a simple, obvious thing, but the fear of grief and disappointment had caused him to forget such things long ago. He had avoided any closeness or concern to escape the possibility of sadness and loss, and he expected disappointment in all things so that disappointment would not catch him by surprise. Now he was surprised at himself.

"Those dragons, they were afraid of nothing," he told Torsk. "Not love or devotion. No quest. No danger. They were not afraid even of death."

"Or life," Torsk added.

"Or life," Einar agreed. Then he glanced down at the dog, but Torsk only rolled his eyes and tried very hard to look innocent.

Einar looked up then and saw that Mayor Thorsen and the Parson were walking along the road toward the inn and talking together, which was to say that the Mayor was holding forth on some subject like Marc Antony at Caesar's funeral while the Parson listened intently with a dour face and nodded from time to time. Einar was in no better mood for their ways than he had been, and for the first time he was beginning to understand why. Such consistent griping was enough to get on anyone's nerves, but he was beginning to find their relentless pessimism and complaints especially distasteful from two such men, the Mayor and the Parson, who were supposed to be the wisest and most responsible heads in the village.

Perhaps his impatience was because he knew that he had been as guilty of such unswerving pessimism in his own time.

"Einar Myklathun, there you sit like Zeus on his throne," Mayor Thorsen exclaimed as they came up. "We were beginning to think that you had died and gone away like your dragons. It was peaceful enough without you, but we were beginning to miss that ugly dog of yours."

"I had not missed your company at all," Einar answered caustically. "Torsk may be an ugly dog, but he talks less and his advice is generally better."

"Well, I for one am surprised at you even yet," the Mayor continued as he took a seat at the table and took out his pipe. "I would have never guessed you for the one to carry on so, wandering off into the woods and ringing the bells, all for the sake of dragons. You will never live this down, you know, even if you should live to be older than the mountains."

Einar said nothing, being in no mood to argue. But that was one matter very sensitive to him. After making such a spectacle of himself, he certainly was in no hurry to face the whole village.

"Better that the dragons should all die anyway," Thorsen continued as he puffed his pipe with satisfaction. "This is our world now, and they had outlived their time. There is no need for magic any more. This is a whole new world, a time of steam engines, electric lights and metal ships. And you were a fool to trust those dragons as it was. They wanted something from you and were on their best behavior, no doubt. But they would have done with you as well as look at you when they were finished with your usefulness, you should doubt that not. Dragons were evil by all accounts, but cunning and subtle. Is that not so, Parson?"

"Eh?" Parson Ondurson glanced up. "Faerie tales, all of it."

"But they were real enough," the Mayor protested. "You saw them yourself, surely."

The Parson shook his head, more concerned with his pipe. "I never did."

"Then you did not go up the fjord in the boats with the rest?"

"No. I stayed and rang the bells, as I was told."

Mayor Thorsen made a face and puffed on his pipe for a moment. "The point is there, all the same. Dragons are evil, and they are not wanted. You were wrong to try to help them, but it was easy to be misled by them, I will allow. It is certainly wrong for you to carry on so over them. There are dangers enough in the world without you going off to look for them. You always have to be careful of what you do, because you can never really know what the results might be. Even when you mean well and do your best, you can still be surprised by the unexpected turn of things. It is better that you never take it upon yourself to do anything except your own appointed task in life, and leave the unexpected for better and wiser heads to figure out."

"Excuse me," Einar said as he rose from his chair and walked over to the door of the inn, where Knutson the innkeeper was waiting and listening. "One large pitcher of cold water, if you please."

Thorsen took no notice. "You should place yourself in my position for a moment. Do you have any idea how hard it is for me to keep peace in this village, with several hundred people all trying to go their own way? Even their daily chores are dangerous enough, with fishermen going out to sea, and the threat of fire from stoves and lamps and such. And what would I ever do if there was an exceptionally hard winter, or an avalanche or fire coming down the slopes to the village?"

Knutson returned to the door of the inn. Einar took the large, white ceramic pitcher of cold water and carried it back to the table.

"And into the middle of all of this, you want to bring dragons!" the Mayor declared in dismay. "Of all notions!"

Einar brought the pitcher down hard, right over the top of his head. The thin ceramic of the pitcher shattered without fuss, and its full contents of icy water poured down over the Mayor's unsuspecting head. That shut him up in a hurry, as few things could, and he sat blinking in surprise with water in his hair and running off his nose and pieces of pottery on his round head, while Einar stood over him looking very grim and satisfied. The Parson stared for a long moment in profound confusion before he opened his mouth to make some comment. But Einar stared at him so hard that he shut his mouth again and sat puffing on his pipe and looking about at the afternoon light in the trees, as if nothing had happened.

Now by that time Einar was beginning to attract quite a crowd, a talent he seemed to be cultivating lately whether he wanted or not. Men are known for their qualities and failings, and Einar would have been as surprised as anyone that he was suddenly found to be as entertaining as he was unpredictable, and quite a change for a man who had hoarded his privacy. On this day, he was to surprise himself and them all even more, for he was not finished yet. Satisfied with his part so far, he turned then and walked right through the middle of the loose crowd and down the road, as bold and self-delighted as any hero marching off to battle, certain of victory.

Right through the village he went, with Torsk hurrying close behind and a fair section of the village following as well, wondering what he could be about now. But Einar took no heed of this procession, marching forth with determination and purpose. He walked right up to the door of one house and knocked loudly, then waited with his hands in his pockets. The villagers all stared in anticipation; they could hardly imagine what he would do next, after breaking a pitcher of water over the Mayor's head, but they expected to be amazed. The door opened after a long moment, and Widow Haugen looked out at him in surprise and curiosity.

Einar actually took off his hat and bowed to her like a true gentleman. "Frau Haugen. Eh, Lisa, I should say. It has come to my mind how often you have prepared my dinner. I hope you would not be offended if I were to invite myself to dinner this time?"

"I would never be offended," the Widow said. "I just wonder why."

"Because you are as kindly as you are patient," he told her.

Then Widow Haugen drew back and held the door and Einar stepped inside. Torsk paused a moment on the doorstep and looked back over his shoulder at the villagers gathered about, with his tongue hanging out and a great expression of idiotic delight on his homely face. Then he stepped inside, and the door closed quietly.

WINTER

The Season of Waiting

THE COLD, WET, rainy days of early autumn passed in time to those last bright, cool days just before the coming of winter. The sky was the deepest blue, and the leaves of the trees were brown, red and golden as they stirred in the brisk fall breeze. On just such an autumn afternoon, the bells of the church rang with that same brilliant pealing as they had on the night the dragons had died, except that this time they rang not in urgency or demand but in boundless joy. For on that day, Einar Myklathun wed the former Widow Haugen, and all the village came to wish them well.

Too long had Einar denied love, faith and friendship in the fear that anything cherished might become a curse when taken away. The dragons had taught him nothing that he did not already know, for their nobility, their patience and their devotion had earned them nothing they sought and in the end they died, perhaps all the sooner because of their efforts. But they had at least tried, and they had met their deaths with greater ease and peace for knowing that they had tried. They had lived and loved without hesitation, completely and selflessly, and the fullness of their lives had robbed their deaths of its tragedy. And if Einar had learned any lesson of them, it was that one, simple thing, that trying was better than failing, and fullness lost was still preferable to the emptiness that had never been filled.

And so it was that afternoon, in the bright but gentle light that leaped down through the trees and golden leaves that danced in the cool breeze, that all the people of the village lined up to either side of an aisle they formed before the steps of the old church and cheered as Einar and Lisa, who was now Frau Myklathun, marched boldly and happily through their midst. The bells rang loud and furious, their bright notes echoing across the forests and the fjords in a song of boundless delight. There was a long, merry party beneath the golden light of lamps long into the deep hours of the night, with many a toast with mugs of good brown beer and slices of cherry pie in honor of the dragons, who had made this all possible. For Kalavek was named best man, which was a remarkable title for a dragon, and Ayesha was a maid of honor, but they were important guests who were not present, except perhaps in spirit.

And it was a joyous time indeed, for Lisa's own four children, with their husbands and wives and many grandchildren, had come to the wedding, all the way from Bergen and Stavager and even Christiania where they now lived. And the greatest surprise of all was that Einar's own son Carl had come all the way from America, and his wife Anna, who was also from their village, and even their three young children, whom Einar now saw for the very first time. So it happened that Einar was more surprised than anyone, for he had never expected it and had sent no such word to his son. It was indeed the doing of Mayor Thorsen and Parson Ondurson, and it was both their present to Einar and their amends for the years of dour company that they had been. Carl and Anna had grown into a handsome couple indeed, richly dressed and refined in manner but also gracious and friendly to all in the village, very different indeed from the gawky children they had been on that day long ago when they had sat on the bench beneath the tree and made their plans, while the two half-grown dragons had listened in the branches above. And Einar was very pleased indeed, to say the least.

So it seemed to Einar as if he was awakening from dark dreams into a new life of brightness and joy. If he had any regret, then it was for the years that he had wasted on hollow beliefs and foolish fears. From that time on he was the merriest man in the village. People would smile fondly as he walked past with his old felt hat and his musket on his shoulder, and from that time on Torsk would run and bounce ahead rather than follow him quietly behind, and he would cock his head to any song and took his delight in playing with children. But they never saw nor spoke with the spirit of Kalavek ever again, and if the dragon ever dreamed of him, as he had said, then Kalavek was satisfied that Einar had found his own full share of happiness and peace. But if an Age of Magic ever returned to this world and the dragons were restored to life, then Einar did not live to see it. Nor has it happened even yet.

A couple of days later, Einar and his son Carl walked alone in the woods, taking their time and enjoying themselves while Torsk ran and played in the leaves. Then Einar was obliged to tell Carl the full story of the quest of the last dragons, in greater detail than he had yet told the story to anyone in the village except the Mayor and the Parson, and of course to Lisa. Carl would not have been inclined to believe the story, whether his father believed it or not, if he had not heard so many people in the village speak of seeing the dragons for themselves. Something truly amazing had happened here, but no one seemed in any hurry to say anything to the outside world. They would rather keep their secret than face scorn and disbelief, and they seemed to look upon their one brief vision of the last dragons as some private magical gift.

"If you had come to live with us in America, you would have never seen those dragons," Carl remarked, and he seemed uncomfortable. "On that matter I feel almost as if I should apologize. We would have been pleased to have had you . . ."

"And of all those letters, asking me to go to America?" Einar asked, and he looked amused.

Carl shrugged helplessly. "I never knew what I should do. I would have felt lacking if I had not asked you to come, but I knew that Chicago is no place for you. I am a man of business, and that is my place. You are a man of a different age, of an older world, and there is nothing wrong with that. What would you do there, except to sit beside the window? There are no woods for you to go for a walk, just streets. What would you shoot, but pigeons and trolleys? And I will tell you one thing more. The winters are just as long in Chicago, and it snows just as much. But the snow is dirty with the smoke from the fires."

Then Einar smiled as they walked along. "It was an uncomfortable matter for us both. Your offer was obviously well meant and it was very difficult to know how to refuse, but I knew that I should not leave this place. The trick in life is always knowing what is best."

The first days of winter came soon enough, ordinarily a cold and dreary time in the west of Norway. But as the days grew short toward the end of the year it seemed almost as if the weather was determined to be kind, and if winter could not be avoided or delayed then it should come ever-changing with sudden, deep snows followed by bright days and deep nights. And if the nights of the lands so far north must be long through the winter, then at least they should not seem endless and oppressive but possessing a deep, mysterious life all their own. Night had always been the dragon's time, and the nights of that winter seemed determined to prove that they had not forgotten the dragons. It was easy enough to think that Kalavek was still out there in the wild, perched atop some rocky peak or ridge while he watched the frosty stars.

The final days of the year drew near, and soon Yule was at hand. And that was a happy time in the village, even when the weather was bad. The snow was a thick blanket to cover the ground, and it hung heavy in the branches of the trees and cascaded over the deep eaves of the houses like frozen waterfalls. At such a time in years past, Mayor Thorsen would have been likely to wander nervously about the village looking for damage and other problems. But this year he stayed home enjoying his pipe and the fire, or sitting and talking with his friends in the tavern, trusting that the world knew how to take care of itself without his intervention. And Parson Ondurson spent more time outside of his church than within, and he played with the children in the snow or would simply stroll along looking at the trees and the snow, or he would stop and listen for whole minutes if a bird sang. His own habits and manner had changed lately, and he was far less likely to preach on Sundays but more likely to reflect upon all the small things in life that are good and of the quiet wonders of the world. Such matters were still a part of his own profession, for all the world seemed at peace and the Devil was far away.

Then Yule came at last. Warm, bright lights escaped from the windows of every home as folk and family gathered for the Yule feast, and the log was set on the fire and mugs of beer and cups of wine and fresh pastries were passed about. And as night fell, it seemed that every house became a pocket of warmth and brightness in the deep peace and stillness of the winter snow.

And so it was that what began with the high and ancient ends with what is small and simple and very mundane, and yet as important as all the world. Old Einar Myklathun lived happy and content to the end of his days, and those were very long indeed. Yule was a very merry time after that, for now there were new children to visit on the holiday, and many grandchildren. Old Einar would bounce them on his knee while they laughed with delight and Torsk would bark with the excitement. Then he would tell them stories of the forgotten ages. Stories of strange faerie creatures in distant lands, and of the empires beneath the sea, and of the golden cities of the gnomes beneath the mountains of their own Norway. Last of all, he would tell them the story of the last dragons, and he told that story best of all, for he had been a part of it. They might have believed him, and perhaps they did not . . . . Well, what did it matter? It was still a good story.